NO ONE ELSE CAN HAVE YOU

Kathleen Hale

HARPER TEEN

For my mom

HarperTeen is an imprint of HarperCollins Publishers.

No One Else Can Have You
Copyright © 2014 by Full Fathom Five, LLC

Library of Congress Cataloging-in-Publication Data
Hale, Kathleen, 1986-
No one else can have you / by Kathleen Hale. — First edition.
    pages cm
Summary: As sixteen-year-old Kippy of Friendship, Wisconsin, reads
her best friend Ruth's diary, she is shocked at what she learns and
spurred to solve Ruth's murder, certain that the boy who was arrested
is innocent.
ISBN 978-0-06-221119-4 (hardcover bdg.)
[1. Murder—Fiction. 2. Criminal investigation—Fiction. 3. Secrets—
Fiction. 4. Conduct of life—Fiction. 5. Best friends—Fiction. 6.
Friendship—Fiction. 7. Diaries—Fiction. 8. Mystery and detective
stories.] I. Title.
PZ7.H1352No 2014   2013008055
[Fic]—dc23   CIP
                                                AC
Typography by Alicia Mikles
13 14 15 16 17   LP/RRDH   10 9 8 7 6 5 4 3 2 1
❖
First Edition

PROLOGUE

A police officer comforts a woman on the shoulder of a rural highway. Behind them is a cornfield. The corn is shoulder high, not yet ready to be harvested. The officer has on a Green Bay Packers hat, and the woman is wearing a sweatshirt decorated in teddy bear appliqués. She is clutching a cell phone and crying hysterically. She and her husband own the cornfield. She's just found something terrible in there.

"Deep breaths, don'tcha know," the officer tells her. Trees line the opposite side of the road and starlings dive-bomb in hordes from one tree to another. The branches bend under the birds' collective weight and fling leaves across the road with every ricochet.

"Now, Barbie Schultz, I sure know you're upset," he

says. "You betcha—how many times do we have to deal with some hubbub in your cornfield? It's disrespectful and deplorable, these delinquents and pranksters." He raises his eyebrows. "But I can't help you till I understand what's happened in specifics—no ma'am—so I need to comprehend what all you're saying." He takes a step toward her. The scattered foliage makes Velcro noises underneath his feet. "So, let's try this one more time, okay?"

"In the middle," she says, gasping.

"Well, there we go, Barbie." The cop nods encouragingly. "Okay then." He gestures for her to continue.

"There's a tree in the middle," she sputters. "See, Frank and me set up scarecrows around it." She presses her fingers to her lips. The nails have been lacquered pink to match the teddy bears' noses. "But whoever did this they . . . they did something to the scarecrows, and even worse to the—"

"Another vandalism, eh?" The officer brings out a small pad of paper and a pen. "The nerve of these kids."

"No." Barbie shakes her head. "Not this time—no, she's hanging from that big tree like a Christmas ornament—blinking!"

"She who?" The officer clicks his pen. "Talk at me."

Barbie takes a deep breath. "Well, she's hanging by her neck but believe you me, it was not a suicide." Her hands flutter at the field. "The poor thing's mouth is sewn shut."

The cop looks directly at her for the first time. He starts to tell her that she called in a disturbance, not a body, but she keeps on going.

"Fancy red thread all through her lips." Her eyes are wide. "Straw coming out through some of the stitches. They tore apart our scarecrows and that's what they did with the filling. From the looks of her cheeks, her whole mouth's been stuffed full."

The officer drops his pen.

THE DAILY FRIENDSHIP
Local Girl Found Murdered

Tragedy struck Friendship, WI, on Saturday, when the body of a local teenager was found in the cornfield off Route 51. Ruth Fried, 18, supposed missing since Friday night, was pronounced dead upon discovery. Police were unwilling to comment on the condition of the body.

"Suffice it to say that a lot of the guys cried," said Sheriff Bob Staake. "I told them to stop the waterworks, but with something that gruesome, it's to be expected. That's what happens when you spend most of your time cleaning up after pranksters and luring lost pets into your squad cars with ham. Small towns make you soft.

"We've prematurely harvested the corn for evidence," he added.

When notified of Staake's plans to raze the corn, Mr. and Mrs. Frank Schultz, owners of said cornfield, expressed willingness to cooperate.

"The corn will be hard this year, I guess," said Frank. "Overly firm, I mean. But I'm sure people in this great town will be more than ready to buy it and rally for a good cause."

Sources around town confirmed this willingness to purchase the prematurely harvested corn. Profits will go to a Ruth Fried fund, the purpose of which is still being decided.

According to police, who are in contact with the victim's parents, Fried was on her way to see her friend Kippy Bushman, 16. "I guess I'd rather not talk about it," said Bushman. Fried's boyfriend, tri-sport athlete Colt Widdacombe, could not be reached for comment.

Police are still investigating potential leads.

"At first we thought it was a foreigner, maybe a terrorist," said Staake. "But now we're focusing on someone local. I promise right here, right now, that justice will get served."

When asked if he had any suspects, Staake answered, "Sure do."

Fried was a junior at Friendship High School. This month, Fried was voted homecoming queen, an honor usually reserved for seniors. She was also vice president of the school yearbook.

"Oh, we'll miss her," said Ed Hannycack, principal of the high school. "Ruth was a solid B student and a true delight." Hannycack added that all schools have been closed until safety is restored.

HUNTING SEASON

My name is Kippy Bushman, and I am bereaved. Right now I'm bereaved on the toilet. Well, not like going to the bathroom or anything, more like using it as a chair. For some reason the motel put a television in here, so I've got the seat down and my pajamas on with my knees pulled up toward my face. When you're sharing a motel room with your dad, the bathroom's pretty much the only place you can have privacy. And the shower is pretty much the only place you can cry, if you want to avoid getting hugged. So I've been hanging out in here, watching a lot of Diane Sawyer, and occasionally taking off my clothes to cry my guts out.

Dom and I have been staying at the Great Moose Motel since last Saturday night. He says there's no way he's letting his Pickle run around when there's a homicidal maniac on the loose. I'm getting a little claustrophobic, to tell you the truth, but I guess I can see where he's coming from, hiding us here. I mean, they found Ruth in the corn behind our house.

Every so often while I'm sitting here thinking about her, my brain is bombarded by seminormal thoughts brought on by too much daytime television. "Should I start taking vitamin D supplements?" "Do I need a paraffin-wax-treatment tub thing for my foot calluses?" It doesn't seem fair, in a way, because maybe I should be sad constantly for the rest of my life if I'm the one who gets to be alive. But the weirdest part is when this other feeling creeps in: a sort of vague annoyance, like Ruth has gone somewhere and not invited me.

The thing is, we were supposed to have a sleepover that night. She was on her way over and the next day they discovered her less than two hundred yards away from our back door. She almost made it. And the thing on top of that is I have a car and she doesn't—didn't—so I could have gone and gotten her. But I didn't.

That's the part that makes me keep climbing in the shower to cry. I should have picked her up. I should have gone and grabbed her.

.   .   .

Ruth Fried—pronounced *Freed*, like free, or freer—was my best friend. Around here, it's first and last name every time you run into a person, at least to their face, no matter how well you know them. And if you can't remember first and last, it's ma'am or sir. No exceptions. Who knows who came up with our pleasantries, or how they did it, but that's the way it is in Friendship.

Anyway, people were always getting Ruth's name wrong, calling her Ruth Fried, like a fried egg. "Do you think it would help if I put some of those pronunciation symbols next to my name in the yearbook?" she asked me once. "I'm yearbook vice president, so I could probably totally do that—Wait, sorry, does it sound like I'm bragging?"

"I think you're very conservative with your power," I told her honestly.

I thought pronunciation symbols were an awesome idea. But none of the other people on the yearbook knew what pronunciation symbols were, and didn't think anyone else would, either, so they wouldn't vote yes on it.

Certain memories of her like that keep playing on repeat in my head, but others I can't even find. Unless I sit down and look through the yearbook, I can only recall her face at certain angles, like her profile in the passenger seat of my car. There's one other recollection that won't quit popping up, though, who knows why: how when we were little—maybe eight or nine—we saw this thing on TV about street performance, and afterward we decided to make some money by dancing at the end of Ruth's driveway. We didn't realize that it was different in a city, and that no one would slow down on a rural highway to put change in our hat. We must have stood there twirling crazily for an hour before Mr. Fried came out and asked what we were doing.

Ruth was the only person I ever knew who wanted to be somewhere else as much as I did. The only one who got what I meant when I said, "Friendship as in you and me is great, but Friendship, Wisconsin, sometimes feels like a bad dream that's too boring to be called a nightmare."

In a place where no one else seemed to understand anything except how to gut a buck and go to church and be over-the-top nice without ever really bonding, Ruth and I made each other feel less lonely.

But that's not the sort of thing I should write in my eulogy. Especially when everyone I'm talking to will be from the town I'm badmouthing.

I can hear Dom rustling around on the other side of the door. "Honey, Mrs. Fried's on her way over," he shouts pleasantly. "Finish up in there and let's skedaddle."

"Finish up what?" I call, wiping back tears. I want to

hear Dom, who's a trained psychologist, try to describe what exactly I'm doing in here. The way he talks, you'd think I was constipated or something.

"Sweetie, she'll be here any minute, she's imminent," he pleads, and his voice is muffled in that way where I know his ear is probably pressed against the door. "It's time to pull yourself together in bits and bobs and change out of those pajamas, okay?"

I roll my eyes. "Fine, but you have to promise you won't make her do a trust fall or something." Dom works as a counselor at the middle school, and is prone to some pretty touchy-feely suggestions in times of crisis.

"All right, Pickle. I promise. Can I get you anything?"

I want Ruth. As soon as I think of her, it's like there's a bird trapped in my chest—a vulture clawing my lungs and reaching its beak into my throat.

I can't remember if it was like this the last time someone died on me. For some reason I didn't expect it to physically hurt. But the pain is enough to make me want to call 911 and be like, "Listen, I have an emergency: Is this a broken heart or a heart attack?"

"I'm fine," I say.

Ruth already got buried because of Jewish tradition. But the memorial service is tonight, and Mrs. Fried is stopping by beforehand for some reason. I have no idea what she wants.

She and Dom must have spoken because she never called me. I haven't heard from her since she texted me asking if I'd write Ruth's eulogy. I wrote back right away saying that of course I'd do it—not thinking about how hard it might be to actually start. Now I'm supposed to address an entire crowd in just a few hours, and I haven't written down a single thing. I keep trying and none of it is good enough.

I mean, Ruth was beautiful in a way that made you want to touch her face—she had dark, thick, curly hair, and nice skin, and big brown eyes—but that wasn't who she was. Ruth Fried was easily annoyed by fakeness and she wasn't afraid of feelings. She was the only person I've ever met who could make me feel better about losing control—encouraged it, even.

"That's it, Kippy Bushman, get riled!" she'd say.

Or if I was all frazzled, about to cry because I wanted so badly to do well and not everything was perfect, she'd elbow me gently and say, "Listen, I think you just feel things more deeply than most people." She could make me feel okay about basically anything.

I read in one of Dom's psychobabble books that they can't diagnose anyone under the age of eighteen with a mood disorder, because apparently teenagers are so selfish that no matter what it will seem like they've got one. And I understand that now because no matter how hard I try to write a eulogy for Ruth, I can't come up with anything that is just about her, and not about how much I miss her.

Mrs. Fried walks in wearing all black and carrying a shoe box, and I'm so shocked at the sight of her that I start looking around the room to distract myself. Stressing about what Dom has done to our motel room is somehow easier than taking in Mrs. Fried's unwashed hair and shaking hands.

Basically Dom covered the bedroom mirror with a bunch of towels and put a T-shirt over the one in the bathroom "just in case." He'd read somewhere that Jewish people do that when someone dies. I didn't know much about it, but I figured he was bastardizing some tradition, and tried to coax him out of it by telling him he was being totally weird and embarrassing, which, per usual, did nothing to stop him.

"It's called sitting shiva," he told me. "That's what Mrs. Fried is doing at her house and I feel like it's only respectful that we recognize her family's customs."

"Just because she's sitting shiva doesn't mean she has to take shiva with her everywhere," I begged.

"Oh, Chompers—just simmer, okay?" Dom smiled sadly at me and went back to futzing with the mirror. Dom has lots of names for me: Pickle, Chompers, Cactus. Sometimes if he's trying to be funny he'll call me Pimple or Chocolate Butt, which is only okay because I'm acne-free and thin. Not to brag. I mean, things aren't so great that I've ever gotten asked to a dance or anything.

"Well, at least don't use my bra to cover up the corner like that," I mumbled.

"Maybe don't leave your bras all over the floor," he said, and used a sock instead.

Anyway, it doesn't matter, because Mrs. Fried doesn't notice any of it. She shows up clutching a shoebox, her gaze peeled on her hands. But even though she won't look at me, I can see her eyes are so bruised and burnt from crying it looks like she's been hit in the face with a baseball bat.

"Dominic Bushman," she says softly, glancing at Dom. Ruth used to tell me her parents thought it was strange how when we were little everyone else was calling their parents Mommy and Daddy, and I had Dommy. I guess people think it's weird how I call him by his first name, but it's not like we're progressive or anything; like everyone else in Friendship, Dom's a true conservative. He says it'd be stupid to be from Wisconsin, needing oil the way we do in winter, and not vote Republican. When it gets below zero around Christmas, Dom will go out and start my car a half hour before I actually leave for school, just so that it's warm when I get in it. According to Dom, Republicans are just trying to stay warm.

"Hiya, Nita Fried," Dom says, sounding way too cheerful in my opinion. "Welcome, welcome."

Mrs. Fried grimaces. "On the way over here I probably saw a dozen bleeding bucks strapped to the roofs of cars," she says. "I hate hunting season." She makes a spitting sound and puts the shoe box down on one of the double beds. Seeing her without anything in her hands makes me want to crawl between her arms, fill up the empty space—not just because I feel bad for her, but because other than the bloodshot eyes and matted hair, she looks exactly the same as she did when Ruth was alive, and that makes me want to hold on to something.

I take a step toward her. "I hate hunting season, too."

"Please don't touch me," she says in a crackly, flat voice, like she can read my mind. She plops down on the bed beside the shoe box. "I'm so tired of hugging people, I could self-immolate." She looks straight at me. "That means set myself on fire. All day the neighbors have been bringing meat loaves. I hate meat loaf."

"Okay," Dom and I say in unison.

"I'm so sorry." She covers her face with her fingers.

"I'm not myself." She takes a long, shaky breath. "Dominic, could you get me a candy bar or something from the vending machine?" She sighs, drops her hands into her lap, and looks at Dom with tears in her eyes.

"Of course." Dom pats his pockets for his wallet. "Whatever you need." He shoots me a reassuring smile and hustles out of the room.

As the door latches behind him, she turns to me. Her face looks like it weighs a hundred pounds. I can feel mine getting hot.

"Hi," I say.

She gestures to the shoe box. "I brought this for you. Take it." I walk over and pluck it from the bed. Inside are some pictures that Ruth and I were going to use to make a collage: us at eight years old, wearing boxers on our heads and crawling through her backyard on our elbows like soldiers. The two of us at the third-grade Halloween parade: Ruth as a princess and me as an "animal on TV," wearing cat ears and a cardboard television on my head with a square cut out for the face.

"I can't have them," Mrs. Fried says blankly. She seems mad at me. Does she wish it had been me on my way to her house Friday night, instead of the other way around? Should I apologize for being alive?

Everyone grieves differently, I remind myself. Dom's only

told me that about a bazillion times.

I pick up a photo of Ruth and me with our arms around each other, smiling so big that you can see the matching rubber bands on our braces—green and gold, Green Bay Packers colors. We didn't even follow football. We were just trying to fit in with the boys at school.

I catch myself accidentally bending the photo. When Mom died, Dom and I hid all the pictures of her for almost a year, not because we couldn't stand to look at them but because we were afraid to destroy them. The urge was to hold on too tightly—accidentally crumple every photo in our fists because we wanted to absorb the image. I put the pictures back into the shoe box and replace the lid.

"How is the eulogy coming?" Mrs. Fried asks quietly, reaching into her gigantic purse.

"Oh, you know. Fine." I squat down next to my suitcase and dig through the underwear and socks, tucking the shoe box securely into one of the corners.

She exhales. "There's something else." I hear her rustling in her bag and turn to see her tugging out a notebook. "It's Ruth's journal. I thought—I don't know—I thought there might be something sweet in there you could quote at the service." She bends over and slides it across the carpet. "I can't handle it right now."

"Okay." I pull it toward me. "Thank you." Quoting

from it is a good idea. It's all I have to go with, at the very least. I turn the notebook over in my hands. "I didn't know Ruth kept a diary."

She stands and clears her throat, smoothing her shirt against her belly. "I'd like to read it eventually, her journal, I'm just not ready right now. Not to mention her handwriting." She takes a step toward me. "Kippy, it's not just about the eulogy. I need you to do me a favor."

"Anything." My heart is pounding. I get up off the floor.

"I need you to censor it for me." She licks her lips, which are so dry I can hear her tongue slide across them, and takes another step toward me. "I thought maybe you could make it so that when I'm ready, none of it will . . . offend me." She grabs me by the elbows so that my arms are stuck at my sides.

"Mrs. Fried?" I can feel her cold, bony fingers through the fabric of my T-shirt. Her breath smells like fish.

She stares at me with those bloodshot eyes, glancing around nervously like Dom might walk in—and then leans into my hair and whispers, "I need you to redact the sex parts."

I open the cover of the journal—just some regular composition notebook—and feel the closest thing to a thrill since Ruth said yes to sleeping over last Friday. It's kind of exciting to read your best friend's secrets. I mean, hopefully you know all of them already, but it's still kind of cool to think, "Ooh, what sort of nice things did she think about me that maybe felt too romantic to say out loud?"

Except then I remember Ruth's handwriting, which is indescribably terrible. There are no spaces, for starters, and the penmanship looks like letters written on top of other letters—like graffiti that's been scrawled over existing graffiti, so you can't tell what either thing said.

I flip through, looking for my name, and am able to recognize a few Ks. It takes me about ten minutes a sentence—just to recognize each letter and then retranscribe it onto a separate sheet of paper, so I can read it—and this is what I end up with.

Ruth here. Kippy is so pathetic it makes me nauseous. She just told me that sometimes she gets lonely before bed and talks out loud to me like I'm there, like a fucking prayer, like I'm some god or something!!!
If we lived anywhere else, like any place remotely interesting, I'd have way more options, and she and I wouldn't even know each other.

A door slams. "Hello?" Dom calls. "Honey, are you back in the bathroom again? Where's Mrs. Fried? I've got that candy bar—did she leave already? I didn't know which kind she wanted so I got a bunch."

"Just a second!" I call.

Today I told Kippy to get a hobby so it's not so obvious she's crushing on me. I flat-out said, "You've got too much time on your hands. It's like the corners of your mouth get wet whenever I'm around." I can't fucking take care of her anymore.

I don't remember her saying that.

Personally I don't even know who she's more jealous of—me for having a boyfriend, or Colt for having me. Like, whenever we try to include her in things all she does is stare at us while we make out. We'll be bowling and I'll be on his lap not even doing anything, and all of a sudden Kippy will be all, "Hey, I thought we were having a sleepover?" Seriously, girl, what a buzz kill.

I get off the toilet seat and stretch out on the bathroom floor, pressing my cheek against the cool tiles, waiting for something to happen. But for some reason there isn't any urge to cry, just a silent weight behind my stomach, near my spine, and a hardness in my jaw. Everything feels okay, empty even, and I suddenly can't remember anything about Ruth except for that cocky look in her eyes every time she told me to grow up.

"Chicken?" Dom says. From the sound of it, he's pressed up against the door again. "I've got a Mars Bar, Snickers, a thing of M&M'S—"

"I'm not hungry!"

I'm going to transcribe one more sentence and if it isn't something nice I'm setting the whole thing on fire.

Ruth here . . . made out with Jim Steele today. Officially cheating on Colt ☺

Okay, seriously, what the heck. For the record, Jim Steele is, like, one hundred years old. Well, fifty, but still, ew. Rumor is he used to be some badass New York lawyer who came back to the Midwest to remind himself what life's about, but that doesn't change the fact that he's practically a grandpa. He's got a bunch of sisters in Friendship—he grew up here, I guess—so he's got tons of nieces and nephews. People call him Uncle Jimmy, which, given the fact that he was making out with Ruth, is probably just as perverted as it sounds. Mostly I can't believe she never told me.

There's a knock on the door. "Chompers?"

"Go away," I snap, and roll onto my back. The memorial service is in three hours and I'm all out of ideas. I mean, Ruth was my best friend, but what are you supposed to say about someone who lies and sometimes secretly hates you and also hooks up with old men? Someone who you've already been trying not to be mad at for being dead in the first place?

STUFFED

Friendship, Wisconsin, has a population of 689 people—well, technically it's 688 now, I guess. Anyway it feels like pretty much everyone is at the memorial service. The fact that Ruth's family is Jewish—the only Jewish family in town, actually—means they're having the memorial at Cutter Funeral Home instead of at a church. There's a line out the door that wraps all the way around the sidewalk. About fifty people are milling about on the front lawn, occasionally standing on their tiptoes, trying to see what's going on inside. I'm just sort of standing there, watching them—my arms wrapped around the food we brought and the wind whipping through my tights. I'd pretty much rather be anywhere else.

"You can do it, Chocolate Butt," Dom calls from the car. He's running his engine in the parking lot. He was planning to come with me but then I asked him if I could please do this one thing by myself, since we've sort of been up each other's butts the past week. The truth is I'm hoping it'll be easier for me to improvise a eulogy without him staring at me. I didn't end up writing anything.

"Honey, that's one hundred percent reasonable to want to go it alone," Dom said. "But just so you know I'll keep an eye out from the Subaru." Dom's all about keeping an eye out these days. "I'll meet you at the reception."

Robert Cutter is outside, playing bouncer, instructing everyone who's just arrived to stay on the grass.

"The service room and hallways are filled to capacity," he shouts. "I'll open the windows so you guys can hear the rites, but that's all I got, okeydokey?"

He takes one look at my face and nods, waving me through. Rob's dad and grandpa cremated my mom, so he knows me, and everyone who knows me knows that I was Ruth's best friend. I mean, apparently. Who knows anymore if she even liked me, and it's not like I can confront her about it.

"I'm sorry for your loss, Kippy Bushman," Rob says as I walk by.

"Okay," I grumble. I wish I could go back to being demented with grief. Feeling angry at a time like this is enough to make you hate yourself.

Inside everybody's smashed together in a buzzing ruckus. They're playing Ruth's iPod over the speakers. I recognize the playlist, but it's the wrong sort, and someone really needs to change the track. Whatever's on is, like, sexy dance music or something.

All of a sudden, a bunch of girls run up to me and attack me with stiff hugs, the kind where you're pulling away just as much as embracing, the kind Olympic gymnasts give that say, "Great job on the high bars! Now I'm going to put poison in your face glitter!" It's Libby Quinn and those girls. Ruth was kind of a loner, but she was dating the most popular boy at school, so the popular girls sort of took an interest in her.

They're all bawling. "We're so sorry for you," they keep saying. "You're so sad. Bless you, honey."

Something about all the popular girls at my school is that they're really Christian, or at least they pretend to be. Libby's the worst of them though. She's always screaming, "Oh my Gah," because she refuses to say, "Oh my God." And if she hears you saying, "Oh my God," she'll correct you ("Gah, say Gah!"). Ruth always said it was annoying how both her and Libby got held back a grade because

Libby gave it a bad name, being so mean and legitimately slow and all. With Ruth it wasn't about a learning disability. She got held back because she couldn't name ten animals in two minutes, which they had us do back in kindergarten. Or at least that's what she told me. Who knows now whether it was true.

"Oh my Gah, Kippy," the girls are saying. I hold the cookies I've brought protectively above my head while each one drapes her arms around my shoulders. Before driving over here, Dom and I went back to the house and he stood watch so I could bake. He was reluctant at first to return to "the scene of the crime," but Dom knows firsthand how important it is to bring homemade food to a thing like this. He's always reminding me how when Mom died, he and I existed on funeral food for like a month. The two of us were comatose—hardly able to move, much less pick up the phone and order pizza. If it hadn't been for all those sweets and casseroles, we probably would have starved.

Libby Quinn walks up last, like some kind of queen about to knight me. She presses at the corners of her eyes, trying to push away the tears without messing up her mascara. One of her girls plucks the tray of cookies from my hands.

"Oh, Katie!" Libby coos. She's about a head taller than me in her heels, and when she pulls me toward her I land face-first against her gigantic boobs. "How are you, honey?"

"It's Kippy," I say, and hear the words vibrate dully against her sternum.

"We're all so worried about you," she says, shoving me off her. One of the girls hands me my cookies back and the whole group smiles in unison. Before I know it, they're all skittering off in their high heels, looking around to see who else is coming inside.

"Thank you?" I call after them.

Friendship is small enough that you can all sort of recognize one another. But so far I don't think most of these people knew Ruth. Not really, anyway. It was the same at my mom's funeral. Lots more people came than we actually knew. Dom called them Grief Gawkers. Still, it wasn't this crowded. I mean, Ruth was popular by association, but nobody has this many fake friends.

So far, I don't even see Colt, but he's probably around somewhere, unless he was too sad to come. Sheriff Staake (pronounced *Steak-y*) usually makes a point of coming to important town events, but he must be out prowling for the killer, or standing watch like Dom, because there aren't any cop cars in the parking lot. Friendship police vehicles are pretty conspicuous. They have big yellow smiley faces on the sides. The sheriff's car is different because the smiley face has sunglasses on it.

I wiggle and weave through the hordes, still holding the tray of cookies above my head. "Sorry," I'm saying. "Excuse me, I'm doing the eulogy, sorry." After a while the crowd becomes a single-file line. I stand on my tip-toes and see Ruth's family, all lined up and letting people grab on to them and kiss their heads. Davey's with them, Ruth's big brother. I haven't seen him since freshman year of high school. He never came back to Friendship after he was deployed. I guess the army gave him leave or some-thing for the tragedy. He was special ops. My neighbor Ralph said that means he's trained to kill.

Davey sees me squeezing past these strangers and breaks away from greeting people to walk toward me. When he graduated high school he was all skinny, but now he looks like he could lift a truck. I notice he's got a pretty heavy-duty bandage on his right hand.

"Kippy Bushman," he says, taking the cookies from me. A buzz cut looks good on him. "How are you?"

I feel like I should know the answer to this by now, but I shrug. Davey's face is wet, either from crying or people's sloppy kisses. I look again at his hand. This morning I watched a Diane Sawyer interview where there wasn't one awkward pause. The trick is to pose good questions.

"So how was being in the war?" I ask.

I'm always saying the wrong thing.

"Is this thing on?" I hold the podium with one hand and tap the microphone with the other. Someone has finally turned off the dance club music, and Rob is going around the room, cranking open all the windows. Davey brings his thumb and index finger together and signals "okay" from his lap. According to the pamphlet they gave me at the door, he's next up on the eulogy schedule.

"Hi," I say slowly. My voice echoes in the small room. I glance at my backpack, which is still on my seat and has Ruth's diary in it. I don't know why I even brought the journal. Staring at it across the room is not helping me think of what to say.

"Or as they say in France, *bonjour*," I add.

I'm not very good at these things. Last semester I gave an improvised speech in debate class and threw up in my mouth. I look out at the audience and swallow, reaching instinctively for my necklace. It's half a heart, and touching it used to calm me down because Ruth was supposed to have the other half. She said it was the gayest thing we'd ever done, but I always thought she wore it. Only, when Dom said it was okay to ask Mrs. Fried for Ruth's necklace, Mrs. Fried said they didn't have it, so apparently Ruth wasn't wearing it when she died. Maybe she lost it and just never told me because she didn't care. Or Jim

Steele told her it was stupid and the two of them smashed it with a hammer or something while laughing about how pathetic I was.

I crumple the hem of my cardigan in my fist and chew on the edge of my tongue. My face is hot and probably bright red. I suddenly remember the feeling of climbing back down the ladder of a diving board in front of a long line of other kids. I have to at least try.

I take a deep breath and jump in. "What can one say about friendship? That is the question." I spread my arms like some kind of preacher and look out at the Frieds, who are saving my seat in the front row. They stare back at me. Maybe if I hold this pose long enough, and let the question sit, someone in the crowd will actually answer it—for a moment I even see myself leading a call-and-response thing like on the evangelical channel. But the room stays quiet, and within a few seconds there's a sour taste in my mouth. I lower my hands, drum my fingers on the podium. Someone in the audience coughs.

"Well, Friendship is our town, for one thing," I blurt. "And everyone knows what our town motto is: 'Do Unto,' plain and simple—'Interpret that as you will,' Principal Hannycack once said. Um." Mrs. Fried forces a smile at me from the front row, and I feel sick.

"But friendship is also another thing," I go on. "It's

a thing between friends, and you have it when you're a friend to someone, and they're friends to you, and the equation makes it so that you're friends together, amen." My face twitches. Did I just say "Amen"?

"Ruth was super-duper," I announce. Super-duper? I swallow a few more times, fighting off the urge to barf. "In conclusion, friendship, the thing I'm describing, it was, well—Ruth and I had that until she was murdered—I mean. Holy geez." Wide eyes blink against black outfits. "Thank you and please make sure to try the sugar cookies I baked for this occasion." I wave good-bye.

Ruth's mom won't look at me, and Mr. Fried's face is twisted like he might scream. The microphone rings as I scuttle away from the podium. Libby Quinn and her posse whisper at each other in the doorway. "*That* was the best friend?" I hear someone say.

"A big thank-you to Kippy Bushman," Davey says when it's his turn, "for, um, trying her best." He spreads his paper on the podium and goes into the stuff you'd expect, introducing himself, talking about his relationship with Ruth. The stuff normal people say.

"She had spunk," he says. "Even as a kid, she could be crazy. One time she set up this elaborate system of trip wires around the house, and I fell on one and broke my teeth." He laughs. "Dad made her point out the rest of them to us, but there were so many she couldn't remember where she'd put them. Our whole family was falling down everywhere for about a week before we found every one." His smile fades. "I think she felt bad about it." There's something weird about his voice, and all of a sudden I realize it's that he doesn't sound like his dad—that he's lost all trace of a Wisconsin accent. Or maybe he never had one to begin with. Around here, the accents usually kick in toward the end of senior year, when people decide what they're doing next, and whether or not they're going to stay. Talking like you're from here is a way of digging your heels in.

"You know what," Davey shouts. "I'm with Kippy, I can't handle this." He wads up the piece of paper he's reading from and throws it at the crowd. "What the fuck is this? What are you even supposed to say?" He bangs the podium. "Do you people know how Ruth died? No, you wouldn't, would you, because everyone around here's too damn nice and what happened is too unsuitable to talk about, am I right?"

The crowd is silent. Even Mr. and Mrs. Fried are sitting stock-still in their seats. He's right. We're too polite to shout at him to stop. It goes against everything in our town to share the nitty-gritty details of anything even vaguely private or graphic. All they would say on TV or in the papers was that Ruth's death was "bad" and "totally sicko" and "you don't want to know."

"They should call her killer the scarecrow murderer," he says dully. "Because whoever did it tore apart the Schultzes' scarecrows. They crammed the straw into my sister's mouth before sewing it closed."

"Young man!" Across the aisle from me, an angry-looking grandpa type stands up, points a quivering finger at Davey, and starts to say something. But Davey pins him with a look, gripping the edges of the podium so hard that you can see his muscles through his dress shirt. The man sits down.

"Red thread," Davey says, still staring down the man. "Her mouth was decorated like a baseball, do you hear me? Someone broke her teeth stuffing straw down her throat. Her neck was bulging from it. They even found pieces of straw in her stomach."

I can hear the sound of fingernails on fabric beside me and turn to see Mrs. Fried gathering her husband's coat sleeve in her fist.

"She was alive when it happened," Davey says. "She probably had to watch her killer take out that needle and thread. They only dropped her from that tree branch after the fact—after she'd already suffocated on her own teeth and bile and straw. Then they did her like a buck from a basketball hoop."

In Friendship, people go hunting, then tie up the kills by the hind legs and disembowel them so they can bleed out on the pavement. On the way over, I leaned against Dom's passenger window and counted the number of dead bucks tied to people's basketball hoops. I got to seven before we pulled into Cutter Funeral Home. My stomach lurches.

I grab Ruth's diary, flipping through to the back. I can feel Mr. Fried giving me a warning look, but I ignore him. I can't believe I didn't think to check the entry for the day Ruth died. Maybe there's something there that I can decipher without going letter by letter.

I turn to Friday and there's nothing. The last entry is a Venn diagram. I can't really read it, but I'm pretty sure it's comparing Colt's and Jim Steele's penises, which are both apparently huge (the overlapping part says "=huge," with penis drawings). I shove the diary back into my bag.

"But the thing that really gets me," Davey is saying, "is how my sister was a solid, surly girl—the kind of kid I could punk around, you know? But they could tell by the lack of marks on her body that she didn't fight back. When it came down to it, she let herself be dragged. Just went limp and let herself be pulled out to that big old tree."

Davey starts to cry so he can hardly get the words out. It's a crappy, violent sight. "She must have been so scared. . . . It must have been so bad that she just gave up."

I try to imagine Ruth looking up at the stars, getting hauled through the corn. What could she have been thinking at the end except "I want to go home, I want to go home"? I feel too sick to cry because it's all my fault—the thought comes floating back to me like the shadow of a plane about to drop a bomb. I was so mad at her for those first few hours when she didn't show up at my door. She was supposed to come at 8 p.m. Friday night for our sleepover. By nine, I thought she'd ditched me for Colt again. By eleven, I thought she was a dick. The next morning, I finally buckled and called Mrs. Fried, who called the police. But at that point, Mrs. Schultz had already stopped by the field to check her crops. Pretty soon, cop cars and an ambulance were clogging up our street. And after a while, the ambulance turned off its lights.

"Anyway, somebody had better watch out," Davey yells, wiping his eyes. He shakes his head. "I don't even know you people—not really—it could be any of you— and if you're in here"—his eyes blaze—"if you had the guts to stuff my sister and show up today . . . just know that I am more than willing to go to prison for the things I would do to you—"

"Jesus, Davey!" Mrs. Fried shrieks. She stumbles into the aisle, and Mr. Fried shakes his head and struggles after her. Davey just stands up at the microphone, staring out at us, looking confused. I try to start a slow clap, but nobody joins in. I'm thinking about how maybe I should slink out, too—jump into the Subaru with Dom and ditch. But it would be even ruder to not go to the reception. And I figure I should stick around and grab our baking tray from underneath the cookies. For some reason, that's what I am focusing on.

Davey was right about one thing: everyone's a stranger now. Feeling safe is a hard habit to break in Friendship, but now that it's broken, I don't think people will trust each other for a while. Our neighborhood is the kind of place where lots of people have one another's keys. Most of the time, no one around here locks anything, except maybe their gun cabinets. But after the murder and the hubbub and the roped-off cornfield, you could hear doors clicking shut down our street like dominoes. When Dom and I went home to bake the cookies, I saw some neighbors taking out their trash, and they were all sort of eyeing one another across their fences—looking antsy and going about their business in a quiet kind of hustle, like something was chasing them.

The reception is being held down the block at the community center, which is usually used for school dances. I am standing in the corner, by the window, where during homecoming I waited for Ruth and Colt to be done slow dancing so I could do "the awkward turtle," which is what Ruth called my only ever dance move. Now I'm watching my cookies disappear one by one off Dom's tray. The room is filled with the sound of soft condolences and chewing. People mill around, carrying tiny plates full of casserole, meat loaf, or cookies—occasionally stuffing their faces, occasionally ducking down to talk to Mr. and Mrs. Fried, who are smushed together on a sofa in the opposite corner. Everyone's eyes are red. Dom is by the bubbler, refilling Mrs. Fried's glass. I feel like I'm underwater.

"So," I say quietly, and then look around for someone I can pretend I've said it to.

Davey is a few feet away from me, nibbling on the rim of a Styrofoam cup. He keeps glancing nervously at his parents. I stare closely at his bandage for the first time, and realize with a twitch that one of his fingers is missing. The dressing there is reinforced and tinted pink.

"What the heck happened?" I blurt, stepping toward him.

Davey startles. "What?" He follows my gaze. "I don't know, Kippy, things happen." His voice is garbled. He spits a piece of Styrofoam into his cup. "In this case, the military happened."

"Sorry."

"It's not your fault," he says.

But it is, I think. Not his hand, but what if I'd called earlier and Ruth was still alive? And then something even more terrifying hits: What if I keep asking myself that question for the rest of my life?

I notice that people are starting to hold my cookies up in front of their faces, looking all perplexed, and that some of them are actually hawking chewed-up cookie back into their hands. I realize that maybe I accidentally used salt instead of sugar. I was barely paying attention because I was too busy watching this Diane Sawyer report on dog weddings. I push past Davey and start tearing cookies out of people's hands.

"Cut it out," I am saying, filling my arms with cookies, dropping some onto the carpet. My heart is hopscotching in my chest. "Give me that." I stumble to the trash can and chuck the armful into the bin. The conversation stops and people hold their meat loaf slices more protectively. Mr. and Mrs. Fried peer at me from the couch. I grab Dom's tray and tip the remaining cookies into the garbage. I am covered in crumbs. I scan the room and people look afraid of me, except for Dom, who quickly puts down Mrs.

Fried's drink and hurries toward me, his face all loving and concerned. My eyes burn because I don't want him to be nice, and suddenly the funeral guests turn to liquid. The air around me vibrates. "I'm really sorry about everything," I say to the shapes of Mr. and Mrs. Fried. "Like about Ruth, and how I messed up everything I needed to do today."

Dom's arms are already around me, but I shrug him off and run out of the room, out of the building, into the cool, autumn air and toward the parking lot, the metal cookie tray popping in the wind.

Ruth and I thought it was weird our parents were Republicans. Our plan was to save the world by saving gas, so we decided to walk as much as possible until it got too cold. Our neighborhoods were only ten minutes apart.

But then Mrs. Fried said we could only walk the stretch of Route 51 at night if we wore special reflective gear, so that the occasional car or truck could tell us from shadows and we wouldn't get hit—which meant that every time Ruth came over, she had on this ultra-intense crossing-guard regalia: a neon-yellow vest that took batteries and flashed orange and red when you walked. She and I called the vests Grab Me Garb, because they made us look like bait.

Ruth was always the brave one. The squirrels in my

yard would hang out like they owned the place, squatting on their fat butts, eating acorns, or whatever, like they were corn on the cob. I always told her they probably had rabies, but Ruth would hiss at them—like, get really close and hiss right in their faces. Once, she snuck up and grabbed one, and while it arched its back and flailed around trying to bite her, she went into one of those shot put spins and sent it sailing into the trees.

Before Davey gave his speech, I had this really distinct picture in my head. That she kicked, fought, swore. That whoever did it left the cornfield beaten and bruised from the fight. And now all I can think about is how it wasn't like that at all. How maybe she even tried to run away, her heart suddenly chicken, forgetting entirely that she was lit up like a Christmas tree.

I hear Dom chasing after me, but I just speed up, making a beeline across the parking lot, heading for the car.

"The cookies were bad," I shout over my shoulder, throwing open the back door and shoving the pan inside. I am hiccupping. I am ugly with tears.

Dom trots up behind me. I struggle under his hug, but he holds me tight. "Hey . . . *hey,*" he says softly. "Let's stop a sec, okay?"

"But the cookies . . ." I dissolve into involuntary groans and hiccups. Tears and snot are like glue across my face.

"It doesn't have to be about the cookies," he says. "It's okay to be upset about what you're upset about." He leans back and looks at me, still holding on. "As someone who also appreciated Ruth as a person, I can only imagine how hard this is for you."

"Yeah, but that's not the point," I plead. I'm thinking about how I will have no one to stand with in the hallways. How part of me wishes she would come back and the other half doesn't even know if she liked me.

"I'm a bad friend," I finally say. "The cookies were bad and I was bad. I was really, really bad." I stare at the ground, brushing Dom's hand away as he tries to wipe my cheeks with the sleeve of his sweater.

"My little porcupine," Dom says softly. "There are different kinds of bad."

"Oh, just quit it with the psychobabble," I snap and shove him off me. I barrel into the car and slam the door.

I watch Dom sigh and go around to the driver's side. The minute he gets in, I yell at him again. "I'm not going to revel in this with you, okay?"

Yet as we drive back, I am relieved by this sadness creeping in. Fall used to be my favorite season. All that happy red, bright and scattered everywhere. Now I look around and all I see is death, moving across the leaves like a fire.

GUT SHOT

Dom's scheduled to give a talk at some PTA meeting the day after the memorial service. It's for parents of high schoolers, and he wants me to go with him. Apparently, most people are bringing their kids. I guess they don't want to risk leaving them home to be murdered.

"Come on, Cactus, time to skedaddle."

I groan and tell Dom I'd rather stay at the Great Moose Motel and shove pencils in my eyeballs than listen to him embarrass me in front of the entire town. Then I crawl into my double bed and pull the covers over my face, hoping he'll leave without me.

"I love you, Huggersmith," he says.

"My stomach hurts," I grumble.

For one thing I don't really feel like running into any more tear-stained faces, especially when I can't seem to wipe this angry look off my own face. Plus, Dom let it slip he'll be giving a speech today titled "Hugging Your Teenager." He was always doing stuff like that when I was in middle school. Once for an assembly, he got onstage in front of the whole sixth grade and gave a presentation called "Love Your Body While It Changes!" There were illustrated diagrams and a mannequin, and Dom kept winking at me the entire time. It was terrible.

"Everything you're feeling is valid, Kipster," Dom says, putting on his counselor voice. I hear his knees crack as he crouches beside my bed. "Go on, talk at me, honey, it doesn't have to be all pretty."

I peek out at him from underneath the blankets. "I guess I wish you'd fart outside," I say. "I mean, that's where I'd start, if I started expressing myself."

"Okay, so you're deflecting, I get that, you betcha." He plucks his phone out of its belt holster. "And you can stay here while I'm out, but not by yourself—no way, no how."

So now Ralph is coming over.

Ralph Johnston has been keeping an eye on me since Mom died—which basically means he's been my babysitter since he was two years younger than I am now. So it doesn't really make sense that I'm not old enough to look after myself, and there's definitely grounds for raising my voice about how unfair Dom is being. But I don't feel like arguing.

Plus, it's Ralph. He's lived across the street from me my whole life, and if it weren't for the age difference I'd probably just call him my second best friend . . . or promote him to hypothetical first best friend, since Ruth could give a crap. Basically I have no friends.

Ralph actually called last night to say sorry for not coming to Ruth's memorial service. He obviously knew her pretty well—or at least, he'd exchanged basic pleasantries with her for the nine years she and I were inseparable— and so he'd barely known her for a long time. Anyway, on the phone last night he said he was sorry, but that when it came down to it he just wasn't ready to go back to Cutter Funeral Home.

"I dragged my heels," he said. "I wasn't brave enough to leave the house."

And I couldn't argue with that. Ralph's parents were like family to me—but when it was time for their funeral last winter, I locked myself in the bathroom and pretended to be throwing up until Dom relented and let me stay home unchaperoned. At that point it had been eight years, nine months, and four days since Mom had died. So I can't even imagine how Ralph must have felt about returning to Cutter less than a year after both his parents were displayed there.

"No worries," I told him. "You didn't miss much except me mucking up."

The last time Ralph and I were at Cutter Funeral Home together was when he and his parents went with Dom and me to pick up Mom's ashes. For moral support, or whatever. I remember being downstairs while everyone else went up to help Dom fill out the paperwork. People had been holding me on their laps for weeks, and I hadn't gotten to see her yet all by myself. Standing there with her ashes was the first time I fully realized how different it would be without her. I had been momentarily forgotten, left alone with a bag of ground-up bones. And Mom would never have allowed that. Even if the bones were hers.

Anyway, I couldn't stop touching them. The ashes, I mean. I opened the bag and grabbed handfuls. And by the time Ralph trotted down looking for me, I was elbow deep in remains. I caught his eye and froze. I was so afraid that Ralph, who was older, would tell on me, or make a face like I was gross—I mean, who tries to hug their mom after she's been pulverized? But instead he just said, "Yeah, it's like construction rubble, huh?" It was. Like gravel or a bag of broken shells.

And that's the thing about Ralph: he's not judgmental. He never has been. I can't really put my finger on it, but I think it has to do with the fact that he's really good with computers. Like, it makes him look at the world differently, because he can break a problem into pieces—and when you're zooming in on yourself, he can zoom you back out.

The point is, we get along, and I've never felt self-conscious around him, and I can't say that about most people. I can wear what I want and say what I will, and ask dumb questions and mess up. But he never thinks I'm weird or what some might call a loser.

"Jesus, Kippy Bushman," Ralph whines when I open the door. He's got on a matching Windbreaker set and those wrap-around sunglasses that ESPN poker players wear. He used to wear the same thing every day: baggy jeans and funny, screen-printed T-shirts—with real zingers on them like *Eat Sleep Code* or *I can explain it to you but I can't understand it for you.* But ever since he took a break from computers, this is his new uniform.

I smile. "Hi, Ralph Johnston." First things first, I try to figure out which of his eyes is pointed at me, and then I stare at it. I think most people just don't make eye contact with Ralph because it's easier, but I always want him to know that his lazy eye is cool with me. "Nice purple

Windbreaker. You look like a mafia wife."

"That's fine. Listen, I really need to get started on some things, is that okay?" His arms are full of electronics—some Xbox controllers and a bunch of games, still in the wrappings. Before Ralph got so into video games, engineering programs and tech schools all over Wisconsin and even outside the state were sending him postcards to apply. But Ralph dragged his feet, and then Mr. and Mrs. Johnston died, and Ralph inherited the house, and suddenly he wouldn't code at all anymore. He started buying collectibles and weird figurines. And then he bought all these Windbreaker sets and started with the video games. The only reason he goes on the computer anymore is to buy more stuff.

Sometimes I worry about him, but then I remind myself that what he's going through is all part of the process. After Mom died I got obsessed with all sorts of weird things—from good-luck troll dolls to step-by-step strategies on how to wrestle an alligator or a great white shark, if one should get you. Survival, basically. It goes in cycles. After becoming well versed in different sorts of animal attacks I started getting into people I could emulate. Batman. Harriet Tubman. Harriet the Spy. All Dom's books concur that your mind goes through phases like that to distract itself. You've just got to be patient, really, and allow for ample rehabilitation time.

"Kippy, sorry, but you're literally blocking the door."

I move aside, mumbling apologies.

"Thank you." Ralph shifts under the weight of his electronics, and one of his controllers falls onto the carpet. "Jesus. Could you show me where to plug in, is that all right?" Ralph has this frantic, apologetic way of talking—always on full volume. Ruth once called him an obnoxiously polite emergency siren. "*Danger! Tornado!* Is that all right?" I think part of her wanted to be my only friend, because sometimes she'd ask me what I even needed Ralph for. It always felt too pathetic to say, "Because he never ditches me like you do."

"There's one right here, but I don't know how to set it up," I say, directing Ralph to the bedroom TV. "There's another one in the bathroom for some reason, but it's mounted on the wall."

He grins. "I call this one."

"Is that Ralph?" Dom calls from inside the bathroom. A toilet flushes.

"Dominic Bushman," Ralph shouts, struggling out of his sneakers. "I would give you a high five, except you're in the bathroom and I have all these electronics to deal with. I'm actually very busy, is that all right?" He falls onto his knees in front of the television and carefully removes and folds his sunglasses, then begins untangling the cords. His Windbreaker crinkles and gasps.

Dom opens the bathroom door, wiping his hands on his pants. "I can see that, Ralph." He looks nervously around the room. "Keys, keys, keys."

"They're in your coat," I tell him.

He claps once, grabbing up his coat, and winks at me. "Call my cell if you need me, Pimple," he says, and touches my head as he swoops past me out the door. "I'll be home around three." The door slams behind him and I lock it like I've been told to.

"Listen, Kippy." Ralph changes the input on the television. "I think you should use the bathroom television to watch the local channel, is that all right?" He uses a controller to outfit a medieval, gnomish character on the screen with facial hair, ammunition, and armor. "Sheriff Staake is supposed to make an announcement today."

I can feel my pulse in my neck. "About what?" If they've got the killer, then it's over and we get to go home. "Did they find someone?"

"Jesus, Kippy, I don't know—that's why one of us needs to keep an eye on Channel Five." Ralph gapes at me and one of his eyes rolls slightly to the left. "But you betcha that's what I think, and I'm certainly relieved about it, too—ten more seconds with this town's new fright and

I'd be sleeping on a cot in here with you and Dom. It's jittery at home." He shivers, then switches the controller to one hand and roots around in his pocket, pulling out a small doll. "Also I brought this for you."

"Ah cripes, Ralph," I say, seeing it's one of his cherished Norse collectibles. "I can't take that one, it's your favorite."

"Kippy!" Ralph scolds, throwing down his controller. "Thor is associated with thunder, lightning, storms, oak trees, strength, destruction, healing, and the protection of mankind." He holds up the Thor doll, shaking its beard in my direction. "I want you to feel better."

I take the gift and try to handle it in a way that reflects its supposed worth. Kind of like I'm accepting a sword. I usually don't love Ralph giving me presents because I worry he's going to run out of his parents' inheritance. I know it takes time to get loss out of your system—or at least to build up enough emotional scar tissue so you can go through the motions and be who you were before everything went wrong. But when Ralph snaps out of it I want him to have enough money left to go to college like he'd planned. Back when he first graduated high school he told everyone that the applications were too much pressure—that he'd get to them later. Then a few years passed and all of this stuff happened. But he might still go.

"Okay," I say, rubbing Thor's beard with my thumb. I glance at Ralph, who seems uncomfortable—we've been through four deaths at this point, but we don't really talk about feelings, and that's how we both like it. So I try to think of a question that will make him feel important and distract us both. One great thing about Ralph is that he's spent so much time on the internet that he's kind of like a human Wikipedia, so I tend to go to him whenever I need facts. Like for school papers, or because I haven't talked to him for a while, or something. "Um hey, what's with all these ladybugs?" I point to the reddish dots lounging on our walls. Tons of them get indoors every fall, but I've never asked about it. The whole time we've been at the Great Moose, they've made it feel like camping.

"Hmph." Ralph snaps to attention, scanning the room. "Well, Kippy, autumn is a funny time for insects, it turns out. Not only is the environment getting cold, but also their lifespan is coming to an end. They fly inside seeking warmth, not knowing what's happening." He shrugs. "They come in here to die."

"Huh," I say. "Thanks." I start toward the bathroom to turn on the other television, but Ralph calls after me, and I spin around in the doorway.

"I want to tell you that I'm sorry for your loss," he says, looking at his knees. "I know that's a thing people say, and you're probably sick of hearing it. I mean, it gets exhausting—heck, I know it. So I'm not going to say anything else about it except for 'I know it hurts, and I'm right across the street.'" He clears his throat. "Also, 'Anything you want to be, you can come be that with me. Rain or shine, no problem.'"

My eyes burn and I taste metal. *Anything you want to be, you can come be that with us. Rain or shine, no problem.* It's what Mr. and Mrs. Johnston used to say to me after Mom died. And it was a big deal, too, because in Friendship, people just want to ignore the bad stuff and keep on bringing food until it all goes away and we can return to our pleasantries—our "How's by you?" and "What about this weather?" Around here, it's a big deal to acknowledge someone's sadness with your words.

I gesture slightly with the Thor doll. "Thanks," I say, and shut the bathroom door so I can cry.

After Mom's funeral, there was a period I barely remember when Dom didn't want to get out of bed or even talk to me, and Ralph's parents would come by and drag him outside with them, and force him to go for a walk. After a few seconds of trying to shake them off, he'd just go blank—turn pale and dead faced—and let himself be led around by the elbows.

I was never alone during those walks. Ralph was already really good at gadgets then, and usually while his parents were taking care of Dom, he'd wave me over into his garage and let me sit on one of the folding chairs while he took apart old calculators and put them back together. Sometimes we'd go inside and I'd watch him play Lemmings, which was this old computer game where you had to guide little green guys through a sort of maze so they wouldn't kill themselves, which is what lemmings do. After a while I started to look forward to our hangouts so much that I'd go and sit on my front lawn whenever I saw that he was home. I'd pretend to be doing something until he saw me and took the hint and waved. I don't remember how long it took for him to switch from calculators to computers, just that one day I came over and there was a giant PC splayed out in pieces on the dusty concrete. And he wasn't taking it apart, either. He was building it from scratch.

In retrospect, I'm sure Mr. and Mrs. Johnston were behind Ralph's hollered invitations, at least at first. They were behind everything back then. They came over to make sure I was awake in time for school, then brushed my hair and waited with me at the bus stop. They mowed our lawn and shoveled our driveway, brought us baked French toast in the morning and casserole at night. For a long time I'd look out at their porch light just before bed and our house would feel a lot less empty.

They did that for a whole school year. After that it went back to normal, and they didn't cook for us, and they didn't come over so often. They retreated back into their own lives out of politeness, because anything else would have said we couldn't look after ourselves, and we grew apart again except for pleasantries. But Ralph would still wave me over when I was out on the lawn, or I'd come around looking for him. And every so often Dom would work late and Ralph would stop by and make me popcorn.

Now that I think of it, I'm not sure if we ever told Mr. and Mrs. Johnston thank you, but after they died, we did give Ralph our full attention, which Dom assured me was the same thing if not better than a Hallmark card with gratitude scribbled all over it. Ralph stayed at our place a lot, because he said his smelled too much like home. He'd wander around our living room, tottering like a baby, clutching photos of his folks. We understood. But eventually Dom confiscated all Ralph's family albums because he didn't want him to ruin the pictures through too much accidental crumpling.

"You'll thank me later, buddy," Dom told him.

The whole thing was really tragic. I mean, Mr. and Mrs. Johnston were older, as far as parents go, but they

didn't die of natural causes. They hit a deer on the highway. A ten-point buck. Apparently it didn't die right away
and kept twisting its neck around. It broke their windshield and gored them with its antlers before they could
grab their shotgun from the backseat. A few months later,
I was driving with Ralph and we hit a deer, too—we were
fine, but the deer wasn't. It was up on the hood of the
truck, bleeding more than you'd expect—even from an
animal that big. Its head was lolling and it was screaming.
The thing about animals is that they shriek when they're
hurt. I've only heard the sound a couple times but I'm
pretty sure the terribleness of it has something to do with
the fact that every kid in Friendship except me (I wanted
nothing to do with it) gets taught how to shoot an animal
through the neck or the head. Anything else is called a gut
shot and creates an awful noise. Not to mention it ruins
the meat.

Anyway, if I'd have been Ralph, I would have freaked
seeing a half-dead deer two months after the same type
of animal had basically murdered my parents. But he was
strong about it—really courageous—probably for my
sake, actually, knowing him. He just got out of the car,
grabbed the shotgun from the backseat, told me to cover
my eyes, and shot the thing right through the face.

Later, he sold his truck for parts instead of waiting for

repairs, which I thought made sense. Better to start fresh, in my opinion. He drives a minivan now.

Anyway that's why hunting is like Mardi Gras around here—not just because people think it's fun, but because otherwise the deer die of starvation or we hit them with our cars. It's more humane for everyone involved if we simply murder them. Most of the cars in the high school parking lot are dented and have bumper stickers that read *Hunting Is Heroic*.

I've got the remote between my feet, my eyes peeled on Channel 5. Usually the local TV channel is reserved for high school football scores or bake sale announcements blared in text across a bright-green screen, but Sheriff Staake said to stay tuned.

"We've learned a bundle in the past few days," he said a little while ago, his friendly pink face scrunching up left and right. "School should be back in session soon, that's all I'm gonna say. But hear you me, pretty soon we're all gonna give a big sigh of relief." He smiled, his face lit up like a jack-o'-lantern. "We'll be releasing all the details in about a half hour. Keep us in your crosshairs."

The idea that local police are trying to figure this out is pretty crazy. I mean, you'd think they'd get the FBI. I'm not saying Friendship cops are stupid, just that they're not used to something this serious. It feels like most of the time they're either staking out the dam for radical Islamic terrorists or perpetuating false rumors about razor blades in apples. The only time I ever really saw them hustle was when I got my hand stuck in the tampon dispenser. The whole squad turned up, Jaws of Life and everything.

I glance at my watch—ten minutes until Staake's announcement—and flip open my laptop to watch clips of Diane Sawyer. For whatever reason she calms me down.

"In other news, a black widow spider was found in an elementary school in Kansas today," she says, frowning slightly. "Luckily, a janitor found the deadly arachnid before any innocent children did."

I wish Diane were covering the case. She's a true professional and way easier on the eyes than Sheriff Staake.

"A giant, rabbit-shaped cloud was spotted over Rochester, New York, this morning"—Diane stares deeply into the camera—"spurring many residents to whip out their cameras."

It's really incredible. No matter what she's saying, the way she makes eye contact is enough to make you feel heard even though you're only listening. Not to mention she looks great. I mean, she's what, eighty now? And she's got the face of a baby angel. Bloggers say she's had a lot of plastic surgery, but even if that's true, I think it's noble that she rearranged her face in the name of journalism.

On the other side of the bathroom door, I can hear the sounds of Ralph's video games. "Punch you in the face, you like that don't you—*I'm a wild card!*" he hollers. He's playing Total Escape 3: Druid Mountain. It's his new favorite.

I glance at my watch and shut my laptop. Sheriff Staake should be on TV any minute, but for now it's just cancellations. The bright-green screen bleeps scrolling red messages: *Glass-blown pumpkin sale CANCELLED until further announcement. . . . Free cider CANCELLED due to unforeseen circumstances. . . . High school yearbook meeting CANCELLED.* Ruth's murder has shut down the whole town.

I'm starting to feel crazy looking at the racing text. Radioactive green and true red. Whoever chose complementary colors is an asslord. The combination is like putting your brain in a microwave. That's another thing I appreciate about Diane Sawyer: she keeps things simple. Vanilla stories, manageable haircut, beige suit.

Elk club cakewalk CANCELLED.

I tear a piece of toilet paper off the roll and hold it in my lap—something to do with my hands. I'm about to swap channels again when suddenly the bright-green background dissolves into static, and Sheriff Staake's face pops up, waving in horizontal stripes across the screen.

"Bart, there's something wrong here with this here picture, don'tcha know," he gripes. The screen straightens out and Sheriff Staake smiles. It's all very low budget compared to Diane Sawyer. Staake's not even wearing makeup, for cripe's sake. You can see every pore. His nose looks like a strawberry.

"Okay, citizens," he says. "The hunt is over." I tuck my knees under my chin and feel my toes curl against the lid of the toilet. "The alleged killer was found with a shotgun. There were also traces of the victim's DNA in his car." Sheriff Staake puts his hand over the microphone, but I can still hear him say to someone off camera: "Anyone found out yet if we're allowed to say his name?" I open my mouth to yell for Ralph but nothing comes out.

"He's over eighteen," someone says.

Staake licks his lips. "I'm sorry to say that Colt Widdacombe is being charged with murder in the first degree." He squints at the camera. "There's really no question, his DNA was everywhere—including some places we can't mention on TV." He smiles apologetically. "The good news is that our town is safe again, but our thoughts continue to go out to the victim and her family. Let's take a moment of silence for Ruth Fried." Staake folds his hands under his chin and closes his eyes. I look down and realize I've been tearing up toilet paper this whole time. My lap is covered with it.

Sheriff Staake resumes talking and I've got this feeling like horrible indigestion, until I realize it's just my stomach muscles coming unclenched. Have I been this scrunched the whole time? Is this the collective sigh of relief Staake promised us? I hear myself cry out like a wounded animal and realize I am sobbing.

CROSSHAIRS

Colt Widdacombe is not a nice guy, but it never occurred to me to tell Ruth he was evil. He called her Honeybuns and Sweet Tits. How do you kill someone you have nicknames for? I thought love meant wanting all the time for somebody to be alive—I mean it's not like if you don't love someone, you want them to be dead, or anything. But if you've chosen somebody, like really picked them out, then death is kind of where you draw the line, right?

So I guess he didn't love her, maybe? Or maybe you can feel both things at the same time? Like you can't really hate someone enough to kill them unless you like them tons, too?

I remember there was this one time I picked her up

from his place after another fight they'd had, and she had a fresh bruise on her chin, and a bright red cheek like she'd been slapped. When I asked her what was what she rolled her eyes and told me, "Sex, Kippy, grow up." She said it was some totally consensual erotic thing. But now who knows.

The point is Colt was bad—definitely bad. The evidence is all there. On top of possibly beating Ruth, I feel like he also probably cheated on her—I mean, before they started dating, he certainly got around. He had this weird habit of pranking all the girls he hooked up with, as a way to embarrass them for not going far enough, or just to break up with them, I guess. Sometimes he'd even use pranks to ask them out; the way he and Ruth started dating was he toilet papered the trees in her yard over and over again, until finally she called him and was like, "What the heck?" and he left roses on her lawn.

He kind of tortured everyone, come to think of it. The police were always cleaning up after him, and he never really got in trouble—probably because he won all of our football games for us. He'd spray-paint pornographic stuff on the water tower or splatter Principal Hannycack's house with cow pies. One time he managed to send a warning on hospital stationery to every family in Friendship saying there'd been a botulism outbreak, and everyone in town needed to bring his or her poop to the police station to be tested. It was pretty convincing and the police ended up with a lot of poop. Even Dom and I brought our poop.

But his favorite thing to do was this thing he called Batting Practice, where he'd lean out of his car with a baseball bat while driving down the wrong side of the road and try to knock over a mailbox. Apparently he was pretty good at it. Ruth said he had this technique where he'd steer with one knee. He got our house twice. I'm not sure if Ruth was with him. Based on her diary, and the way she felt about me sometimes, she might have suggested it.

"It's cool if you fantasize about him sometimes," she used to say. "I mean, who doesn't, am I right?"

The truth is, there was something about the way Colt ran around vandalizing things that made him look epic and talented, like Jason Bourne from all those spy movies. And the annoying thing is that Ruth was right about him being sort of irresistible. His nickname was the Honeycomb, because everyone said he attracted girls like bees to honey. I mean, the guy does look like a Ken doll and Superman had a baby—and I know that's biologically impossible, but still.

Anyway, at first it was defacing the homes of girls who wouldn't give him blow jobs, and now it's murder. I guess that's just what happens when you're not paying close attention because you're too busy thinking somebody's a hunky sex muffin, or what have you.

"Jesus, Kippy!" Ralph is knocking on the bathroom door. I can hear beeping on the other television screen, and I realize he's dragged the controller cord to full capacity, and is still playing with one hand. "Has something happened? Jesus, Kippy, it's not fair, come out and talk to me, please!" He knocks more softly. "Is it women's things?"

I go over to the door and lean my forehead against it. I keep thinking about all those red flags, Colt's delinquent behavior. I never liked Colt and should have been louder about it.

"Kippy?"

I sniff in boogers. I'm embarrassed about how I probably look, but I remind myself that it's just Ralph, and I know how bad he wants to hear the news.

I open the door and Ralph immediately pauses his game without taking his eyes off me. He hasn't seen me cry since I was seven.

"Kippy." He drops the controller and starts patting my head and shoulders at the same time, like bongo drums, trying to comfort me, I guess. "Shhh. Stop right now, what's going on, is it all right?"

"The TV—it's Colt," I blurt. All I can think about is that time Ruth confessed to me that sometimes she and

Colt used fuzzy handcuffs. How I said it sounded creepy, but then she just got this look on her face, that "maybe you'll get it one day when you're not such a virgin" face that always made me want to scream. I should have tried to break them up right then.

"Colt did it," I say, but somehow it sounds funny. Maybe because my mouth is screwing up in all directions. I try again: "Colt murdered Ruth."

"Oh, that rotten boy," Ralph says, pulling me in for a proper hug. "Of course he did."

The more I think about it, destroying my mailbox wasn't the first time Colt targeted my house. He did something even worse back in middle school.

Middle school is not something I'm thrilled to think about. Ruth once called it my most awkward of awkward phases—which, as she pointed out, is saying something. Back then I wore silver eye shadow caked on so thick that by the end of the day my eyelashes were full of gray dust. Middle school was also when I got my hand stuck in the tampon machine in the girls' bathroom. Dom's guidance counselor office was right down the hall, so of course he came in and rubbed my back in front of all the firefighters.

"Oh, Pickle, you should have told me you were

menstruating," he said. "I could have gotten you the proper equipment."

Ugh.

Anyway, middle school was before Batting Practice, back when Colt was still going through his graffiti phase, and one night he swung by our house after bedtime and decorated our garage door with a rattle and the words *MA-MA!* We might not have known it was him, except he also spray-painted his full name in cursive on the second garage door. The church rushed over and repainted before the cops could make Colt clean it up himself. I guess they wanted to erase it before it sank in—and the strategy worked. I didn't even understand that it was about my mom until Dom explained it.

"Only a psycho makes fun of someone for not having a mom," I remember telling Ruth. At the time, part of me was hoping maybe Colt liked me. But based on Dom's reaction, I'd caught on pretty quickly that I was meant to be upset. "It's so rude."

Ruth must have told Davey about it, because a few days later, he cut class to come by the middle school and throw Colt against some lockers. "You better watch out you don't make too much of a name for yourself," Davey apparently warned, holding Colt by the collar. "I'll be waiting for you after practice."

Davey got suspended for a week for physical intimidation, and everyone was so focused on "what a hooligan that Davey Fried is turning into" that they didn't even stop to think about what Colt had done to our house or the potential darkness brewing in Colt's heart. In retrospect he was obviously crazy the whole time—all that pent-up rage—and if all of us had only known then what to look for, this whole thing might not be happening.

I wonder if I'm the only one who sees it that way.

Colt invited himself over to watch a movie once. I was pretty psyched because, let's face it, he looks like a god. We made out but I wouldn't go any further because I had church the next day. Anyway my dad keeps our garage stocked with Premium White Tail Urine from the local Buck Fleet—you know, you put it all over your gear and bucks come out of the foliage thinking you're a doe and *bam.* So Colt must have stolen some of our bottles and messed with the vents in my car, because the next day I turned on the heat in my truck and the whole world smelled like pee, and for, like, weeks bucks were coming around and humping my fenders. When I confronted Colt about it, all he said was "Next time don't be such a prude." So no offense but in my opinion it's been obvious this whole time that he killed her.

—Mara Hale (Age 17, junior at Friendship High)

Colt was cheating on Ruth with me, if that tells you anything. He said I had a better rack. He was going to break up with her for me, too, you know. He probably just lost his nerve and tried to get out of things the easy way, if you want my opinion.

—Libby Quinn (Age 18, junior at Friendship High)

Colt was an okay guy. I played sports with him for two years, four teams. He could be a regular dick now and then, but he wasn't the violent sort. I'd know.

—David Fried (Age 21, recently returned from Afghanistan—could we argue PTSD?)

That boy was 100 percent rotten. Do you know he put a dead skunk in our mailbox? Right after our son dropped a pass from him and we almost lost that one game. Boy oh boy, I've talked to people around town, and everyone says the exact same thing: Colt Widdacombe always added insult to injury. He's not right in the head. The boy needs to get what's coming.

—Ed Storm (Age 53, grocer)

Colt and I dated for like a week, and he was always trying to get me to give him BJ's at school. Like, by the cars or in the basement, or if we ran into each other by the vending machine he'd try to drag me into the boys' bathroom. I didn't want a reputation so one time I didn't do it and he told everyone I looked like a walrus from the waist down. I don't, you know.

—Amy Heberle (Age 15, sophomore at Friendship High)

We hooked up freshman year and instead of just breaking up with me like a normal person (like with a text, or whatever) Colt forked my whole lawn the night before a cold frost. Do you know how hard it is to get a plastic fork out of frozen ground? It's impossible. They break off in your hand.

—Julia Wayne (Age 18, senior at Friendship High)

I always knew that Colt Widdacombe was a bad egg. Did you know that when my husband broke his hip, that boy came round our house and trenched the yard with his car? Drove it in circles all over our grass. Back then, you told me there was nothing you could do about it because the boy had a game the next day. Well, now look what's happened. You should be ashamed of yourself.

—Rita Alverson (Age 79, retired)

I mean, the dude is, like, pretty evil. He hooked up with Sarah McKetta—that paraplegic girl—and then dumped her three days later, saying her legs were too skinny.

—Justin Becker (Age 18, senior at Friendship High)

I hope he gets the electric chair.

—Sarah McKetta (Age 17, junior at Friendship High)

Ruth here. Feeling protective of the big bro, who's started writing me letters like I can help him or something. It's like, dude, I'm just trying to make it through each boring day out here, at least you're doing something real. He's a big guy now (physically), but when you interact with him it's like being with a kid— like maybe he's not growing up right because his job is to kill people. I mean, you can practically see the tear stains on the page. The 'rents keep getting the same updates as always: everything fine, no one dying, lots of love. And I don't want to tell them about my letters because I know they're already freaked out thinking he's going to die all the time. For now I just keep writing back telling him to shoot everyone, get the whole war over with already, ha ha. If I were being honest I'd tell him to come home, sit on the couch a while, fuck the special ops—I'd say, "Listen, Dave-o, nothing's worth losing your mind over." But the words won't come out because I'm not used to him and me being serious. Basically I'm hoping the tough love will work better. Remind him of himself.

FRESH MEAT

Dom's modified "autumn display" is still up in our front yard. He gets pretty festive during the holidays. Usually around Halloween he puts two scarecrows on plastic chairs and positions them to look like they're talking. But he must have stopped home after his "Hugging Your Teenager" meeting and taken them down out of respect for the Frieds (I told him about the scarecrow murderer stuff Davey spewed at the memorial; Dom was all, "I don't know what to say, Pickle. Let me hug you."). So now it's just an autumn-themed wreath on the ground, with some gourds around it in a circle. It looks pretty creepy, actually. Like a crop circle. I lean my head against the passenger window and tell him everybody's going to think we're in a cult.

"Ha!" he says. "Keep your hands off my art." He thinks I'm joking, because usually we have this thing where he'll put out his display, and then I'll heckle him for it, and re-arrange it, or straight up hide the decorations. Like when he puts out the big plastic igloo at Christmas I'll drag it around back or haul it on top of his car. It's a seasonal game we play. But he's totally missing the point because I'm not in the mood for pranks. I legitimately think the gourds are creepy. Our whole house seems creepy for some reason.

I glance back at Dom, and he's staring at me. "What?"

"You look so much like your mom today." He smiles. Dom is kind of short and stocky, with dark hair and olive skin, whereas I'm lanky and pale and blonde, like Mom was.

"Oof," I scoff. Around here we say "oof" when we're really peeved or disgusted or overwhelmed. It's a super polite-sounding, pointed noise. I mean usually I don't mind Dom's comments, but I guess I just don't really want to be compared to a dead person right now.

I unbuckle my seat belt and stare out the window. There's three deer in the next yard over, frozen at the sight of our car—thinking we can't see them, I guess, if they only hold still. It's crazy how certain creatures can be so timid and destructive at the same time. Dom clicks the garage opener and they all sprint off at the noise.

"Ready, honey?"

"No." I glance back at our house. I guess there're certain views from inside our house that I'm not ready for yet. Like the cornfield, for starters.

"What's on your mind, Sugar Brains?" Dom asks. It's the tone of voice that would usually drive me crazy.

"He never seemed nuts," I mutter. "Just arrogant and annoying and nasty. But also maybe I should have known."

"Don't beat yourself up, Cactus—heck, I'm a trained professional and even I didn't think he was anything other than obnoxious and a little untamed." Dom does some verbal nodding. "But see, that's the thing about mental illness—not to sound offensive or anything, but it can be very annoying, like you said. Very hard to watch, hard to empathize with. It comes across as pure selfishness—the only difference is it's not self-serving."

"Which is why Colt was always getting into trouble," I say. "He wasn't channeling his selfishness in productive ways. He was being self-defeating."

"Exactamundo." Dom reaches over and unlatches my door, pushing it open. "You're my smart girl. Now go ahead, Chompers—home sweet home. Meet you in there."

·   ·   ·

As soon as I bang through the front door I hear Ralph shouting at his video game in the other room. I've never been gladder that Ralph has a key to our place. Dom's just pulling the car into the garage—he'll be in any moment—but I can't stand an empty house. Not even for a second. Especially not right now.

"Ralph, how goes it in there?" I call.

"I'm winning for now," he shouts, and even though he's bragging there's a tinge of caution in his voice, like I shouldn't bother him.

The garage door rumbles shut and Dom saunters into the kitchen. "What will it be for dinner, Chocolate Butt? Hot Italian sausage on a kaiser roll, or Chicago deep dish from The Pizza Place?" There's only one pizza place in Friendship and it's literally called The Pizza Place. Hot Italians are usually my favorite but tonight I just want to feel lettuce in my mouth.

"Something lighter," I say. "A salad." After the news came in about Colt and I finished crying on Ralph, I immersed myself in Diane Sawyer clips. In one of them she did this whole thing about the health benefits of substituting salads for our "usual go-to's." She said vegetables help with everything from basic lethargy and depression to digestion and ensuring a longer life span. Then she did a segment on the year's best rainbows.

"Eat lasers!" Ralph shouts. We can hear him clicking frantically on his controller.

"A salad." Dom looks at me like I'm speaking Chinese. He furrows his brow. "You mean like a potato salad?" In Wisconsin, nobody knows about real salads. We grow fresh vegetables for the rest of the country, sure—and when you're a kid, the Friendship lunch ladies give you a side of frozen peas with your bologna, or whatever. I guess we also grow corn, but mostly that goes to feed the cows.

Anyway, when it comes down to it, we're a hunting town, and all anybody keeps around is meat. Rabbit and wild turkey, or burgers and bratwurst if you want to be casual. Venison, too, obviously—and lots of sausage: venison sausage, cheddar-cheese-infused chorizo sausage, Italian sausage, summer sausage. I remember when Ruth was thirteen, she told everyone she wanted to be a vegetarian, and her parents kept offering her chicken, saying it was the lighter option—"Hardly even a meat," they kept saying. She had to revert back to being a carnivore just so she wouldn't starve.

I stare back at Dom defiantly. "I want a salad." He sighs and opens the freezer with a smack, still looking very confused.

It occurs to me that we probably don't have a single vegetable in the whole house, except for frozen stuff. "Never mind," I say, but he waves at me like, *No, no, I'm doing it, see?* and starts throwing various things into a bowl. First bacon bits, which we usually use on our baked potatoes, then cheese—lots of shredded cheese. He rips open a bag of frozen peas with his teeth, then goes to the pantry and gets canned tomatoes, and dumps those in, too. Before you can say "Gross," he puts the whole thing in the micro-wave, beeps in five minutes, then turns around with his arms crossed, looking proud.

"Kippy and Dominic Bushman," Ralph calls. "Are we getting a pizza or what? I have cash, I'll chip in."

"We're eating salad!" Dom shouts.

"Oof." I feel like I'm going to cry again. I put my head down on my crossed arms and peer out over my wrist, so Dom won't see how annoyed I am. "Don't we at least have carrots or something?"

"Carrots?" Dom crosses the kitchen to put his elbows on the counter across from me. "Pickle, talk to me," he whispers. "Is this a female body-image thing?"

I moan into my forearm. I can still see the perfect sal-ads that Diane Sawyer laid out on the news anchors' desk. "I saw it on YouTube."

"Tell me about it," Dom says, misunderstanding. "Those buxom models in the underpants ads are enough to give anyone a complex—heck, even I feel fat looking at some of the ads online." He pats my arm. "I wish you'd talk to me more about the real stuff, Cactus, the Colt stuff," he adds gently. "You're not alone if you're upset, don'tcha know—you should have seen the PTA." He raises his eyebrows. "There was an uproar of I-told-you-so's, you betcha."

The truth is I don't want to talk about it—at least not with Dom, who might grab my knees at any second and start singing "I'll Stand by You." The microwave is whirring with our garbage salad and if we have to chat I'd like it to be about something that has nothing to do with anything.

"Hey, check out this clip of that journalist I told you about," I blurt, reaching across the counter for my laptop. I watch the screen turn from black to blue as it boots up. "It's even cooler than the one I showed you before—What?" Dom's giving me a funny look.

"For one thing I'm familiar with this Diane Sawyer, and it's just she's been a lot on your mind lately, that's all." He licks his lips. "You think maybe this is"—he shrugs, trying to be nonchalant—"I don't know, one of your new obsessions?"

My face gets hot. Ralph's in the other room and even though he's got the TV on too loud to hear us, I still wish Dom would lower his voice. "I don't know, Dom,"

I whisper. "Maybe I'm dissociative, maybe I'm a psychopath. How's that?"

He tries to reach for my hand, but I pull away. "Hey, remember after Mom?" he asks. "How you wrote a whole little book on surviving animal attacks? I'm only suggesting that beneath these fascinations might lie something articulable."

"Oof. Listen." I close the laptop and take a deep breath. "For once could it just not mean anything?"

Dom smiles. Behind him the microwave beeps, finished. "Sure," he says softly, getting up.

My phone buzzes and I jump. Who could be calling me right now? Ralph and Dom are the only people who call me anymore and they're both right here.

Ruth cell calling . . .

I leap off my stool and run into the living room—bounding over Ralph and ducking into the hallway, clutching the cell phone in front of my face. What a huge mistake—a total mix-up. Where did she go? How did she fight him off? Whose body did they actually find? My chest is tight with relief and excitement—but also there's that heart-dropping-into-stomach thing, like when you're in your driveway after dark, searching your car for a textbook you probably left at school, and all of a sudden you feel like someone's watching you.

I press Talk. "Hello?" My voice sounds strange. Shaky and scared and hopeful.

"Kippy, it's Davey."

I exhale, deflated—"Oh"—and walk back to my stool in the kitchen, trying to look like, "whatever." Across the room, Dom is pulling a steaming bowl of melted tomatoes out of the microwave with bare hands and cursing under his breath. He puts it back and reaches for a pair of oven mitts. "Right, duh. Hi, Davey."

"They gave us her phone back today and I really needed to get in touch with you."

"I mean, it makes total sense and also I knew it was you, so." I roll my eyes like, *obviously—definitely didn't think it was your sister or anything*, even though Davey can't see me. Dom puts the steaming bowl down on the counter with a triumphant flourish and I wave him away.

Davey clears his throat. "So here's the thing: some girl named Libby is on her way over here, and at first I was like, 'Yeah, okay, fine,' because that's what I've been saying all day—but it's almost dark, and I'm beat, and I literally can't take another visitor. Could you do me a big favor, and call her cell or something, and tell her not to come, please?"

"Libby Quinn?"

"Yeah, make any excuse you need to, just—"

"No, it's just that I don't have her number."

"What? She said you guys were friends."

Dom hands me a soda and a fork, and uncaps a beer for himself.

I sigh. "The last time I talked to Libby Quinn, she put my face in her boobs and called me Katie." Dom gives me a look. I poke at the contents of the bowl, and one of the tomatoes dissolves with a hiss. "Which is not my name."

Davey makes an exasperated noise. "Listen, could you at least come over and run interference? I seriously can't talk to another repressed, fake . . . neighbor type . . . I'm hanging by a thread here." He sounds accusatory, like I've done something wrong. I remind myself that grief does weird things.

"Sure, let me——" My mind spins, wondering how I'll explain this to Dom, who once joked that he'd be fine with me hanging out with boys once he was dead. Plus, on the car ride home, Dom kept emphasizing how much he loved me, and how much perspective Ruth's death had given him and every single parent in the PTA—and how he wanted to spend as much time as possible with me these next few days. At one point it seemed like he might cry. "Give me ten minutes."

"I appreciate it," Davey says.

I hang up and peek at Dom, who's staring at the

steaming bowl, looking suspicious and a bit disgusted. "Ralph, you want any of this?" he yells.

"What?" Ralph shouts. "One sec, I'm playing."

I give Dom a small wave to get his attention. "I'm really sorry, Dommy, but I've gotta go."

He looks aghast. "Wait, what? Pimple, if it's about this terrible salad, I can get us a new thing." He reaches for me. "How about we call The Pizza Place and get a full sausage pepperoni, and have them put a vegetable on it?" He smiles at me. "I'm sure they've got a vegetable, honey."

I give him a pleading look. "Davey's having an emotional crisis and I need to go sit with him." I reach for my bag. "Come on, Dom, you know how much you condone emotional check-ins. Please . . ."

"No." His tone has completely changed.

"Dom!"

"What's going on in there?" Ralph calls.

"Nothing!" I shout back.

Dom takes a deep breath. "Kippy, could you just stay here, please—the poor Frieds, I think about what they've lost and I just—"

"Get off my nuts," I snap, slipping on my backpack. I look away, feeling guilty. It's something Ruth used to say to me. "I want to hang out with someone my own age."

Dom purses his lips. "I wouldn't say he's your own age—"

"Quit it!" He's always acting like every boy likes me, and it's humiliating.

He sighs. "You know that I trust you—and that I'm not averse to compromise. As long as there's adult supervision—you know how I feel about that, Kippy—"

"I said quit it! I mean, it's just like, for cripe's sake, you know? I could use some frigging breathing room is all."

Dom clears his throat and crosses his arms. "All right, that's okay. A bit irrational but—you know what . . . you can be upset, you're a teenager, it's your job to be upset." He reaches primly into the cutlery drawer for The Pizza Place take-out menu. "I, on the other hand, am a grown-up. So I will not be getting upset. I will be eating a delicious, meat-covered, deep dish pizza. With Ralph." He looks up at me, stern. "You be home by 8."

The fact that I had my own car was always a big gripe with Ruth. It's just a used Astro van, not some baller deal or anything—only slightly cooler than Dom's worn-out Subaru. It's got the weird captain's chairs in the middle row, and the thick fabric curtains on the side windows. But Ruth got jealous. It didn't even help that I let her name it Rhonda. She said she'd put it to better use than I did. Take boys out. Roll around in back. It adds almost ten minutes to my trip, but I take the long way to the Frieds' so that I don't have to pass the cornfield.

There isn't any wind to rustle the pine trees lining Davey's driveway; they're just standing there, like watchmen. The lights inside the house and the lamppost by the mailbox are off. The only way I even know anybody's there is that Libby's white SUV is parked in the driveway—I guess she beat me. Plus, Pasta Batman is sitting by one of the pine trees, like he usually is, wagging his tail. The Frieds have these two enormous dogs, Pasta Batman and Marco Baseball. They're both some kind of Great Dane/Saint Bernard/werewolf hybrid. I remember the first time I came over, we pulled up in Mrs. Fried's truck, and my first thought upon seeing them was "We might not be able to kill those things with the car." I envisioned them bouncing off the fender, getting up, cracking their knuckles, and then diving through the windshield to eat our necks. Each one looked like some sort of sasquatch/gorilla, or a dinosaur with fur. The sort of animal that brings emergencies to mind, like "It will get me."

"Davey and I named them when we were so young we were still a little bit retarded," Ruth explained quietly, introducing me to the dogs later that day.

"Mrs. Konik says we're not supposed to say that word," I reminded her. "It's a real bad one." But I knew exactly what she meant because at the time I had a cat named Mother Peanut Butter.

Anyway, Pasta's too ancient to be scary now. I slam my car door and he hobbles over, and out of habit I whisper, "Hi, funny doggie!" Before I can give him a hug he tips onto his arthritic spine, panting, waiting for me to rub his belly. The driveway pebbles crunch underneath his squirming back. I hear muffled shouting through the pine trees, give him a few quick pats, and then speed walk across the driveway, ducking through the branches.

On the other side, Libby is cowering behind a clipboard, fingering the cross around her neck. "Davey Fried, I'm just asking you to be a team player!" she snaps.

"How many times do I have to tell you, I won't sign it?" Davey shouts at her. He's leaning against the side of the porch, sucking down a beer. Behind him there's a twenty-four pack of Milwaukee's Best, which everyone here calls Beast, and a pile of food—platters, casserole tins, Jell-O molds. Overflow from well-wishers, I guess. It's swarming with flies.

Davey tosses his now-empty can at my feet. "You're late."

Libby clears her throat and glances at me, twirling

her necklace around one finger. "I was just telling Davey how, like, everyone in my family went to UW–Madison, including my parents and both my big sisters. But well, my grades aren't supergood"—she tumbles on—"so, like, I decided to do this Ruth Fried fund for the corn, which my parents said was a really good idea because it showed I'm well-rounded, but, like, I just need Davey Fried to be the first one on the petition, otherwise—"

"Hold up," I say, smiling wide—because if she says "like" one more time I'm going to run away with my arms flailing. Mostly I'd like to ask her how she can admit all her ulterior motives about college and stuff and not feel mortified. It just doesn't seem fair that Libby gets to go around happy and healthy saying all sorts of weird stuff, and meanwhile here I am with my acid reflux—my muscles tightening up after every stupid thing I say. Ruth once said that the whole reason I'm so thin, probably, is because I'm tense all the time.

"Please just sign it," Libby whines.

"Fuck your mother, Libby, how's that?" Davey takes another big sip of Beast. "Sex her right in the butt."

"Whoa, Davey, come on." I force a laugh. "That's . . . it's unhygienic."

"It's gross," Libby snaps. "It's disgusting and it goes against the Bible."

Davey rolls his eyes and barges inside, slamming the door behind him.

"Katie, I just don't get it." Libby bats her eyes at me. "The fund is, like, for his *sister*."

It's Kippy, I want to say. But instead I stare at her feet. She's got on this pair of high-heeled boots and dark jeans, and per usual her whole getup is making me feel embarrassed of my moose-print turtleneck. "Hey, where did you even get that outfit? There's only one store in town."

She rolls her eyes. "It's called the internet."

"Well, anyway, you've got to go."

"*What?*" Libby gapes at me. "That's ridiculous— signing my petition only takes two seconds. I don't know if you understand this, Katie, but it's my project and it's an original idea—and it shows initiative—my parents said so."

There's a sour taste in my mouth. It's so weird how people who've never lost somebody think they deserve a medal or something for bothering people who have. "You've got to go, Libby Quinn. As Ruth's friend I'm asking you." My voice is shaky. I look up and she's glaring at me. "Listen, maybe I can talk to Davey about the petition thing, okay? As far as petitions for dead people go I think it sounds very . . . Well, it's fine."

"You can't just, like, take all of her," Libby snaps. "You're hogging her memory—and you know she didn't even like you. She told me once."

My heart beats in my ears. "Seriously?" Just then Davey comes barreling out of the doorway with a whole recycling bin full of empty Beast cans.

"Libby Queen, please leave," he says, halting next to me.

"It's Quinn." Libby gives her hair a sassy shake. "And no way because my parents say it's good to stand your ground, and also I brought you that whole Jell-O mold." Pasta Batman trots up and starts sniffing her crotch and she swats him away. "And also then I had to watch you, like, throw it on the ground, which was totally rude, and also—"

There's a blur beside me. Davey is dumping the entire contents of the recycling bin on Libby's head.

"Oh bajeezus," I hear myself saying.

"Oh my Gah." Libby blinks at Davey, her mascara running down her cheeks from the dregs of stale Beast, but you can tell she's trying to hold it together and look like this is no big deal. "All right then. I'm going," she says, licking a droplet of beer off the corner of her mouth. "But only because I've got plans." She turns and teeters across the gravel on her heels. "I'll pray for you," she calls over her shoulder, sounding pissed.

"Why did you do that?" I mumble as we watch her drive away. But Davey doesn't say anything, and the two of us stand there like that, all silent for a while, which is not what I want. I want to throw garbage on well-wishers, too, and it'd be nice to talk about that with someone who gets it. Who doesn't think that kind of uproar is weird, even though I guess I'm pretending it is.

"Davey?" Basically all I want to do is talk about feelings, because finally here is someone who probably has a lot of the same ones I do. Only Davey and I have never had a conversation like that before and I'm not sure how to start.

I glance at the flies circling the leaning tower of Jell-O molds and casseroles, and wonder how much other food is piling up inside. "Hey, Davey?"

"You can go now," he says, plopping down on the stoop. He reaches for another beer. "Seriously, just leave."

My heart drops, embarrassed. But then I remember that Davey was the one who invited me here and he's probably having some kind of total breakdown. "I can listen," I say. "I mean, if you're having some kind of emotional debacle, or whatever, I actually know a lot of ways we can deal with those." I start counting on my fingers. "One, my father is a trained psychologist, and two, I have read a lot of important books." My hands are sweating.

Davey stares at the road. "You're not safe out and about. You should be at home."

"But I am safe." I force a smile. "Because they've got Colt, and everything's back to normal now—wait, you know that, right?"

"Yeah, see, that's the thing." Davey takes a deep breath, like he's about to tell me something terrible. "I just don't think Colt did it."

BEAST

"Have you completely forgotten what kind of guy he was?" I ask Davey, stretching the hem of my turtleneck over my knees for warmth. It's getting cold, but I'd rather make out with Pasta Batman than go into the Frieds' house. All those family photos and familiar smells. I'm pretty sure our homecoming photos are still up on the fridge: Colt and Ruth with their arms around each other, and me standing next to them, looking put upon. Marco Baseball noses open the front door and slobbers on my ear, then tries to pet himself with my arm.

"I mean, what about that thing Colt did to my garage door—the graffiti about my mom?" I add, trying to rile up Davey's protective streak. I push on Marco's butt, forcing him to sit. "That was pretty dang sick, am I right?"

"Oh, let it go," Davey grumbles.

"But I thought you hated Colt."

"Oof, Kippy, come on—you're smarter than this."

I squint at him, trying to look for signs of insanity. It doesn't make sense that he would be on Colt's side all of a sudden. He and Colt were on the same basketball team and football team before Davey graduated. They weren't close or anything, but Davey knew enough to hate Colt when he started dating Ruth. I read some of his letters home about it. *Are you seriously letting that pissant follow you around? Sis, the boy is bad news. Take it from someone who heard him talk about girls in the locker room. . . .*

Anyway, it's sort of hypocritical that Davey would all of a sudden change his mind. This is all probably just part of some kind of postwar flip-out.

"I'm telling you," Davey says. "It isn't safe."

I nod, pretending this makes sense. When Ralph heard Davey was home, he told me about PTSD and how it's mainly about soldiers not being able to let go of the drama of war. Like, they've been trained to sit around listening for explosions or footsteps, but now that's no longer necessary and they're not supposed to kill anybody, either. Their survival instinct's on full blast and all the controls are stuck.

Davey raises his eyebrows at me. "I mean, I know

everybody wants this to be over, but it's not exactly over if they've got the wrong guy, is it?"

"Hm." I should probably change the subject. "So, when do you go back to battle?" I shouldn't have said that.

Davey gestures with his bandaged hand. "You don't go back once a body part is missing, Kippy. They don't let you."

I let out this weird squawking laugh, then lower my voice, trying to sound conspiratorial. "How'd that happen anyway?" I tap the bandage where his finger should be and he recoils in pain. "Sorry!" I reach for his beer can. "Here—oh, it's empty—but maybe it's sort of like an ice pack still." I press the can to his nonfinger and he howls.

"Just." He hisses through his teeth. "I appreciate it, just sit there, okay." He cracks another beer and offers it to me. I shake my head—Dom would have a meltdown. Plus, there's always the chance he might swing by unexpectedly to make sure I'm chaperoned. He's been showing up at the Frieds' out of nowhere like that ever since I turned thirteen. "Where are your parents, anyway?" I ask, trying not to sound nervous.

Davey grimaces. "They bailed this morning. Staake came by early to tell them. Dad was basically comatose and Mom kept stressing about running into the Widdacombes at the grocery store."

"So, zero parental supervision?" I bite my lip. Dom would lose it if he knew.

Davey gives me a look.

"I'm just kidding," I stammer. "It's not like I'm some baby who needs grown-ups or something. It was a joke." I force a laugh. "They are gone though, right? Like officially?"

He shrugs. "They're off on some Canadian retreat thing to save their marriage. They signed up as soon as the cops found Ruth but decided to go early once they found out about Colt. Real problem solvers, those two." Davey motions for me to take the beer again but I shake my head more firmly this time. "The truth is I think they hated being around me." He starts drinking the beer he offered me. "I think when one of your kids dies, you hate the other one for a while. I kind of get that." I notice he's sort of started to slur his words.

"Listen, stop it." I pluck the beer from Davey's hand and put it by my feet. "This is an official intervention. I've read lots of books about grieving, and pretty much all of them say drunken despair is not the way to cope because it keeps you stuck. No more Beast."

Davey looks at me like I'm crazy. "You know, I can just open another one."

"No, because I want to know about Colt. And I need you to make sense. How come he didn't do it?" If Davey's going to have his own version of a postgrief obsession, then I'm going to sit here and encourage him to get on with it—sober. "I'm listening, okay?" Ruth might have been a bad friend, but that doesn't mean I have to be. "Now start from the beginning. Tell me everything."

Sometimes at school Ruth would see Colt in the hallway and leap straight into his arms. "Yo girl, stop broadcasting our business," he'd say. But usually he'd catch her. She used to say she "loked" him. That she was on the verge— "the precipice," she said—between like and love.

"It's scary how much I loke him," she told me. "Because I'm like, 'Ugggh, Colt, maybe I'll kill you so no one else can have you.' It's like I can't get close enough or something."

I always knew exactly what she meant—how sometimes there's this slamming need for proximity, and you want to show someone the full weight of your attention by laying it on them, head to toe. After Mom died, I'd lie in wait, then pounce on Dom, yelling *banzai!* while I got a foothold on his neck or shoulder blade. I'd wrestle Ruth's dogs until they yelped, or squeeze Mother Peanut Butter so hard she could barely hiss. This thought would pulse through my brain: "I have so much love to give and nowhere to put it!" and then Dom would have to pry

Mother Peanut Butter from my fingers.

"All right, Miss Huggersmith, calm down," he'd say.

Eventually I had to go to a support group about it. But even after I learned to control myself better, I still felt that way, especially around Ruth. I loved to hug her, which she always seemed fine with—at least to a certain point. I just always felt so grateful to her for wanting to be around me. When we were kids, I would sometimes cling to her like a koala. "Personal space, Kipster," she'd remind me. And I'd reluctantly retract my claws.

So I get it in a way—I mean, I still think that love is mostly about wanting someone to be alive forever, even though that's impossible—and I'm not saying that Ruth brought it on herself for being huggable, or anything, just that the whole Colt thing makes sense to me now on more than one level. I mean there's real evidence, for starters—all that DNA. But also if you really like someone, and want to really lay it on them, well, you could turn into a monster, probably. Especially if you had something really dark already lurking deep inside of you.

Colt is guilty. Davey will understand that, eventually. He just needs somebody to talk him through it—to take up the opposing argument—and I can do that. I mean, I might be really good at saying the wrong thing, but I also took debate class last semester.

In response to my request, Davey huffs. "Okay, for starters, Colt hooked up with Staake's daughter. If I were Staake, I'd still be pretty pissed about that. I'd have a fucking vendetta."

"So what," I explain. "Everyone's hooked up with Lisa Staake." It's true. She's like some kind of blonde rabbit in heat.

"And in terms of the evidence—of course Ruth's hair was all over Colt's car," Davey continues. "They were dating, for God's sake. They probably saw each other that day at school. Of course she had his DNA on her hands or whatever."

I raise my eyebrows meaningfully. "Yeah, but Sheriff Staake says it was other places, too." I don't want to bring up sex, specifically, but Davey saves me the trouble.

"Maybe they did it at school that day, or something." He shrugs. "That was sort of Colt's style."

"Ew." I wrinkle my nose.

"Oh come on, Kippy, think about it: Staake needed a fall guy because the whole town was about to have a stroke." He rolls his eyes. "You know how Friendship is. No one wanted to think about it anymore—when was the last time people around here decided to dwell on anything?—and Staake wanted to make himself popular by easing the tension. And the thing is, Staake's not that bright. My parents went to high school with him and were telling me he barely graduated. The guy was a numbskull. They were both livid that he was even handling the case. And you know what? When I was in high school, Staake planted weed on some of the potheads in my grade—not something I can prove, obviously, but I knew those guys okay, and they weren't the kind of dumb where they'd keep marijuana in their lockers." He reaches down by my feet and retrieves the beer I confiscated. "I told my dad about it and he said there'd always been rumors that Staake liked to cut corners."

"Still," I say, grabbing the beer from Davey and pretending to take a sip of it so he won't. "It's not fair to call Staake dumb when he's been doing this for, like, twenty years. I mean he's the sheriff, right? He had to earn that somehow."

"You don't understand it, okay?" Davey shuts his eyes. "The thing that really haunts me—the thing that I can't get out of my head—is how in Afghanistan, I mean . . . you know what I did over there. I killed people. But I knew dudes who *liked* to kill people. There were certain guys none of us wanted to be around because they took this thrill from it. I know those guys. I know how they talk. I know how they think." He looks longingly at the beer in my hands. "I know them."

I pretend to take another sip, nodding, as if I hear war stories all the time. "Go on," I say, and brace myself for the real underlying emotion to come out—the memories of battle, dead children, men screaming. Davey obviously needs to talk about Afghanistan, not Colt.

"Colt wasn't like that," Davey says, shaking his head. "Yeah, he was a douche bag, but he was also a huge pansy. Softhearted. It was part of what made him so annoying." He turns and pats the twenty-four pack of Beast behind him, as if to remind himself it's still there. "I mean, I remember this time that Colt and I had to stay later than the rest of the football team so we could finish this math test. Yeah, I was in the sophomore math class as a senior, so sue me."

I shrug like *pfft, math, who can even do that stuff?* even though I'm very competent at mathematics.

"Anyhow, the rest of the team had already taken the bus to Marquette, but Colt and I had to drive separate. We hit a moose on the way."

"A moose?" I balk. "Are you sure it wasn't, like, a superhuge buck?" I've never seen a moose in Friendship.

"I know. It was crazy—moose are monsters."

"They stand up to six and a half feet at the shoulder, can run up to thirty-five miles per hour, and are double-jointed so they kick in all directions," I blurt. I remember certain facts from my days of being obsessed with animal attacks. "I'm actually surprised it wasn't in the papers." Around here moose are about as rare as murder.

"Right. Anyway, I know you know how gruesome something like that can be because of what happened to your neighbors. Colt and I were fine, but the car was fucked, obviously, and there was a ton of blood." Davey shrugs. "The kid was shaken up. At first I thought it was because of the collision—those things leave you scrambled. But in our case the carcass was too big—we couldn't haul it off ourselves—so we had to put the car in reverse and try to sort of slide out from under it."

"Was it still alive?"

"A little bit. But you know . . . it was on its way. And I had our family's gun in the car."

"I can't believe Ruth didn't tell me about it."

Davey shrugs. "It wasn't her problem." He picks at his cuticles. "So one of us had to drive off it, and one of us had to brace against this dead moose, to keep it from just staying there on top of the car—I mean it was a wonder we didn't die, really—and it was my car, so just automatically I got behind the wheel. I gave the other part of the job to Colt." He raises his eyebrows. "Anyway, Colt gets blood on his hands and just starts puking and sobbing—I'm not even joking. Afterward, he begs me not to tell anyone, says it'll ruin his image. Someone who reacts that way, they don't do what someone did to Ruth." He makes a face like he's tasted something foul. "It takes a sicko to . . ." He glances again at the beer in my hand and this time I hand it to him.

"Maybe Colt is schizophrenic," I say softly. "Maybe after you graduated the killer instinct sprang out of him—I mean, certain types of psychosis don't kick in until after the age of eighteen."

Davey stares at me. "You're always doing that."

"What?"

"Thinking you know everything about everyone's brain just because of your dad."

I bite my tongue, trying not to look humiliated. "Sorry."

He stares at his feet, turning the beer in his hands. "Don't you think Ruth would have told you something like that? Like if Colt were straight-up crazy, or whatever?" He peers at me skeptically. His blue eyes stand out bright against his red-and-orange plaid shirt.

I think of Jim Steele and Ruth making out. Of the journal in my backpack. "You'd be surprised."

He laughs. "Fine, shoot down everything I say."

"Check her phone or something if you're so paranoid—I mean, you called me from it tonight, didn't you? Maybe there's something on there. A creepy text from Colt—"

"I already did," he says. "The texts were all deleted. *Somebody* deleted them."

"See?" I shrug apologetically. "You've got no evidence."

"Fuck—you know what? I'm sick of you playing devil's advocate." He looks away. "Suffice it to say that you are not the only one who thinks I'm crazy for saying this—do you know I went in and gave testimony about Colt's character? Staake came at me afterward like I'd bit him, telling me how I was a disgrace to the country and everyone knows I got kicked out of the military."

"Is that true? Did you get kicked out?"

"It doesn't fucking matter! It's like mass hysteria here. All these girls are going in and out of the police station, offering their insights on the Honeycomb. It's all high school drama—all exes—dredging up old hurts and rooting against the poor little shit because they've got a vendetta—just like Staake. Probably Staake's own daughter's been weighing in on however she thinks Colt slighted her." He drains his beer and tosses it on the grass. "You should go in there and tell Staake what you know—tell the truth about Colt and don't exaggerate." He points a finger right in my face. "You'll regret it later if you don't—when you've grown up and matured enough to wonder whether you did the right thing while everyone else got caught up in a mob mentality."

"Geez, Davey, just because you're—" I was going to say "troubled" but stop myself just in time. Instead I reach over and untie his shoelaces like I was only teasing—then realize it probably took him a while to tie a bow, having only nine fingers and everything. Our knees are almost touching, and I can feel the warmth of his leg through his pants, and all of a sudden butterflies explode in my stomach—which is embarrassing and happens all the time, usually on the bleachers during assembly, no matter what the person next to me looks like.

"Stop it." Davey jerks his foot away and scoots over. "What I'm saying is, if you know anything, or think of anything, and you just sit on it, you're being a bad friend. You're fucking over Ruth."

Whatever butterflies I had all crackle and dissolve. "Everyone knows you've got PTSD," I hiss. He gives me a look that makes my stomach hurt, and I try to seem self-confident as I stand up and skedaddle toward Rhonda.

"Welcome home," Dom mumbles as I come in the door. He's standing at the kitchen counter in his bathrobe, putting leftover pizza into Tupperware containers, not looking at me. "You're half an hour late."

"I know."

He pushes down the Tupperware cover with a loud click. "This is your one get-out-of-jail-free card."

"Okay." I take a few steps toward him, unsure whether giving him a hug might fix things.

"Ralph and I sure had a fun night, you know." He smells like fabric softener. "Also, your laundry's folded on your bed, and I had them put a couple broccolis on the corner of my pizza, so you can have those slices for breakfast or something if you want—oh, and here's some chamomile tea." He reaches behind him and hands me a mug.

It's embarrassing how hard he tries sometimes even though he's obviously sort of annoyed. What does he think? That someone other than me is watching and there will be a medal or something? "Thanks, Dom."

"So"—he carries the container to the fridge—"what did Davey want?"

"Nothing."

"And how are Frank and Nita?" He means Mr. and Mrs. Fried.

"Fine."

"Fine?"

"As fine as they can be, I guess." I shrug, blow on my tea. "They say hi."

Dom tightens his bathrobe. "I taped a show I'd like us to watch. It's Oprah Winfrey Network—top-quality broadcasting—and it's about grieving as a team." He glances at me sideways. "Are you in?"

I sort of can't believe I got away with being at someone's house without the parents there. It might be superstitious, but I figure I should do something to make it even. "Sure."

"Good." He claps a hand on my shoulder and the two of us walk into the living room. Mother Peanut Butter is situated on our big corduroy couch. She died years ago but we got her taxidermied in what I used to think was a funny pose (saluting). One of the windows is open and letting in that familiar cornfield smell, which is somewhere between wet dog and fresh-mown grass. I feel claustrophobic.

Dom squeezes my shoulder and I jump. "Kippy?"

"What? I'm fine." As soon as the sun comes up you'll be able to see the cornfield from pretty much any of our windows. It's not something you notice at first, like a haircut; the corn was there and now it's not. I looked at it this afternoon when we got home and it took a few seconds to kick in: how there are just a few stalks sticking up here and there within the stubble. How the whole thing has been reduced to some kind of buzz cut topped with reddish leaves from nearby trees. It should be reassuring, I guess, because it's all gone and now there's nowhere to hide, or something. But upstairs from my window you can also see the willow tree where Ruth was hanged. When we came home yesterday to bake the cookies I went up there and sat on my bed for a while. I kept seeing clusters of shriveled-up brown leaves in the branches and thinking it was her hair. "I'm fine," I repeat. I plop down on the couch and start absentmindedly petting Mother Peanut Butter.

"Honeybuns." Dom eases in beside me. "It was tough seeing Davey, wasn't it? You're a sweet girl but I don't want your listening skills to get taken advantage of. God bless him for what he gave our country but it's the last thing you need at this point—honestly I'm not sure he's equipped to be in the world quite yet, don'tcha know." He pats my knee. "And you know I'm also not fully certain why exactly he's reaching out to a teenage girl in his sup-posed time of crisis—it doesn't help that you're so pretty, no sir—"

"Dom!"

"It's a fact." He reaches for the remote. "What are kids saying? It's sketchy. And second of all I don't like it."

"You didn't give a first of all." I scootch away from him. "And for your information, Davey's fine. He just doesn't really like anybody in this town, which makes him pretty sane, in my opinion." Dom grunts, presses play, and some cheesy voice-over starts, narrating a shot of the ocean: "In times of crisis, the urge may be to roll up like an armadillo. But if we are to survive, our task is to unfold like a butterfly and flock together."

"They're getting all their animals confused," I complain. I bring my feet up underneath me and poke Dom in the ribs. "I want attention."

He pauses the show and makes intense eye contact with me. "I'm here."

There's this urge to sit on his lap but I'm too old for that. I sigh. "It's just that not everyone's as crazy as you think they are." I cross my arms and lift my chin, indicating that he should turn the stupid show back on. "That's all I was going to say."

Ugh, Ruth here. Bad cold today and I'm pretty sure Kippy gave it to me. She's been walking around like a drippy hose with snot on her face since Wednesday. But knowing her that might just be her style.

Anyway, I told her to get over here and drop me at the drugstore so I can cut this thing off at the knees and feel halfway normal again. She wanted to make it some kind of hangout but I clarified I'd walk home. The truth is, Big Daddy said that if I want to head over to his house after I'm done picking up some cough syrup, he'll show me exactly how unafraid he is of catching what I've got. He made it pretty clear that after we were done fucking I'd have to go into his awful basement again, and check out his new taxidermy project, which is admittedly creepy. Sometimes he says I'm so gorgeous he'd like to mount and stuff me, and I'm like, so mount me, then, Daddy. He's got a huge dick.

AMBUSH

After Dom went to bed last night I decided to read a little more of Ruth's diary. It took forever, obviously, because her handwriting is so messy it looks like she wrote everything while jumping up and down on a trampoline. But I was feeling sort of bad about what I'd said to Davey—basically telling him he was crazy, or whatever—and I thought if I slogged through another entry, well, maybe I could find something.

Clearly I scrolled for the next K, looking for my name, and clearly what I found was not uplifting. For starters, I immediately ran into some very mean insinuations about my hygiene—which, even though I sometimes have chocolate around my mouth, is actually just fine, thank you. There was also some more unsettling sex garbage about Jim Steele, so. Ew.

Anyway, the more I think about it, the more I feel like maybe someone should go and talk to Jim Steele. Not me, obviously, but a real officer of the law, which is why I'm bringing Ruth's diary to the police station. At the very least, getting it off my hands means I won't read any more of it. Having it around is giving me a stomachache—not to mention a bad self-image. And according to the ten billion or so books that Dom has given me about my body, self-image is very important at this stage in my life.

The police station is on the second floor of the courthouse, right by the railroad tracks. On the way there, Rhonda and I pass the Buck Fleet, Circus Video, and this place called Italian Restaurant—which, like The Pizza Place, is exactly what it says it is. I take a left and drive west toward school, which starts again tomorrow. I can already tell it's going to be a shit show. Mostly because of what people have started posting on Facebook.

Libby Quinn

COLT WIDDACOMBE IS A MURDERER

Like • Comment • Share • 15 hours ago

Mara Hale, Carly Schulz, and 37 others like this.

Jessica Easto I knew it was him all along, what else is a tri-sport athlete good for except violence?

Michael Schulz LOL but seriously I hope he rots
in hell
Hannah Hughes <3 <3 <3 in Ruth's memory amen
Andy Harnish PUT HIM IN THE ELECTRIC CHAIR
Dan Paul honeycomb sux

I went and disabled Ruth's profile late last night. People who'd never even talked to her were posting all sorts of weird stuff on it like, "RIP babe, gonna miss you in science." I didn't have her password but I emailed Facebook pretending to be her mom, and included a link to an article about her murder, and they shut it down pretty quickly.

I turn up the radio and roll down the windows, letting in a blast of cool air, which reeks of dead leaves and an impending chill. The flag outside the high school is at half-mast, and someone's put a giant wreath around the neck of the great white shark sculpture, which stands in the middle of the front lawn. Our mascot is the shark. The Friendship Sharks. Also, I guess there was some kind of candlelit-vigil thing I wasn't invited to because there're flowers and banners and things tied to the fence along the sidewalk. Teddy bears stapled to poster board—right through the paws, like stigmata—with messages like *WE LOVED YOU R.F.* and *THE ANGELS CARRIED HER HOME*

TO ISRAEL, which actually seems kind of offensive. I mean, Ruth was Jewish, not Israeli. She was born here. Her parents grew up in Milwaukee. It's not like her family was playing *Schindler's List* all the time or planning to be buried in the hallowed homeland. Geez.

Anyway I've never really understood the whole candlelit-vigil thing. Some of the seniors put a few together after the school shootings down south, and from what I can gather it's usually just a bunch of girls crying with all their might on purpose. The whole idea of people, like, weeping while holding fire seems irresponsible to me. Whenever I imagine vigils, I think of a hundred ponytails bursting into flames.

I take a right, planning to pull over a block from the station, but there are cars parked all down Main Street. As I drive up to the courthouse lot I hear shouting; the whole place is jam-packed full of protesters. Everyone's holding signs like the ones tied to the fence—*RUTH FRIED: HOMECOMING QUEEN! RIP!*—but most read like the Facebook posts: *CITIZENS AGAINST COLT WIDDACOMBE* and *GET HIM OUTTA OUR TOWN!* I scan the crowd and spot Libby Quinn leading some kind of chant. Everyone's screaming in unison, red-faced and sweaty despite the cold weather. A few of the sign holders are lunch ladies from my high school.

Even Ralph is with them—which is nuts, given his general aversion to leaving the house. He's holding a sign that says *JUSTICE*. It's a pretty big deal for him to be here. He probably thought it was a thing all my friends are doing—because no matter how many times I explained it to him, he never really got it through his head that my only friend was Ruth. "But you must be popular, Kippy," he always said. "You're the coolest girl I know." He probably thought he had to make up for not being at the memorial service, and that this was the next best way to be supportive. I'm kind of flattered, in a way.

I roll down my window and call out to him, but he can't hear me above the chanting: *"We! Want! Justice!"* Libby spots me and hands off her megaphone to someone else.

"Katie Bushman!" she cries, trotting over. My heart does this embarrassing flip that she got half my name right. "This is so exciting." She smiles. "I mean, do you see how far I've come with the Ruth Fried Foundation Brigade? Wait till I tell everyone you're here. Did you bring Davey?" She peers into the backseat. "Oh . . . well, that's okay. Did you bring your own sign? Never mind, don't worry, you can share one of mine." She shuffles through her stack of poster boards and offers me one that says *IF NOT US, WHO? IF NOT NOW, WHEN?*

I squint at it. "What does that even mean, though?"

Libby flips the sign around so she can read it. "I don't know, actually, I got it online from a union website." She shrugs, holding it out to me. "You can totally borrow it." She bats her eyelashes. "Also, I wanted you to know that I've forgiven you for standing idly by while I was attacked with a recycling bin. Water under Gah's bridge." She shakes the sign at me.

"Thanks, Libby"—I push the sign back toward her—"but the thing is I'm actually here to talk to the sheriff, no offense."

She frowns. "Ugh. You could at least join us for a second and send your message to the killer. He's right up there." She points to a barred window on the second floor of the courthouse. It didn't occur to me that Colt would be inside, but I guess that makes sense. I stupidly imagined him being carted somewhere überofficial, like Alcatraz or Guantánamo Bay. If they do the trial here, Jim Steele will represent the state—I know because we did a unit at school called The Law, and he came to talk to us about it. And if the trial is here then all these people in the parking lot might be the jurors. Oof.

"Also, I met your neighbor," Libby says. "What's with his eyes going different directions"—she lowers her voice—"is he special needs? Also—"

I roll up the window while she's still talking because I sort of can't deal with it. "Sorry!" I mouth. I wave good-bye and gently honk my way through the crowd, browsing for a parking spot.

Sheriff Staake's got on shiny black riding boots, a wide brimmed hat, and these pants that sort of poof out at the hips. It's not the usual uniform, and part of me wonders whether he's dressed up hoping the crowd will see him, or that camera crews will suddenly roll in. He's even got a riding crop.

"Bushman!" he says, smacking the crop in his hand. "You're late." He gestures for me to sit down. "You want a Sprecher root beer, or some water from the bubbler?"

"I'm okay, thanks." Aside from his TV appearances, the last time I saw Sheriff Staake was when he came to my third-grade class to speak against the use of inhalants. I remember that on the way out he confiscated all the scented markers from the art nook. "That's really nice of you, though."

"Of course. Now, you're the Fried girl's closest buddy, isn't that right?" He smiles big, his eyes crinkling into nothing. "Bet that means you've got a lot of dirt on Widdacombe." Outside, they've started singing the national anthem.

"Actually"—I pull off my backpack and rustle around inside for the diary—"it's about Jim Steele. Basically Ruth was doing it with him—you know, Uncle Jimmy? I dog-eared the pages I could find with his name. Sometimes she calls him Big Daddy—it's a gross code name. Anyway I thought maybe—"

"Whoa there, kiddo." Staake collapses into his swivel chair. "Slow down. Take it from the top."

I take a deep breath. "Jim Steele is a true weirdo, sir. Here are some reasons: One. He was having a sex rela-tionship with my former best friend—and by that I mean Ruth. Two. He said things to her like 'I want to taxidermy you,' and then she got viciously murdered. Three. He col-lects dead animals." I slide the diary across his desk. "Here, that's yours now. I know a lot of people around here collect taxidermied animals—dead pets or mounted deer heads or whatever—Dom and I got Mother Peanut Butter mounted after she passed away. And when she's not situated on her favorite spot on the couch, we even make her the center-piece at our kitchen table. But Jim Steele does it himself, like a hobby. He'll pick up dead animals off the road or go out and shoot things just to put them in funny positions. Colt had to go see him to get out of a drinking ticket once and said there were squirrels in can-can dance lines, foxes with their arms around each other, and seagulls slapping each other high fives with their wings. That takes a pretty sick sense of humor if you ask me."

"I thought I told you to slow down," Staake grumbles, snatching the diary away. "And what exactly do you mean by sex relationship?"

"You know, sex things. Mrs. Fried gave me the diary in the first place because she wanted me to redact the sexual details—that means cross them out with a Sharpie marker, in case you're wondering—but there're so many of them it's nearly impossible, and also I thought some of them might count as evidence, or whatever, which is why I'm here."

Staake peers at the diary. "Is this even handwriting? It looks like a dog wrote this." He sighs and snaps it shut, sliding it back to me. "Anyhow we got enough evidence as it is, we're chock-full. It's an open and shut case, not to boast; this boy Widdacombe did your friend, no question." He lifts both feet onto the desk, crossing his legs at the ankle. "I'm sympathetic—you betcha. It must be hard—yes ma'am. I heard Davey Fried got up at the memorial and spilled the beans on the whole shebang— every gritty detail of the corpse and so forth—including those bloody bald patches on Ruth Fried's skull from where Colt dragged her by her hair." He shakes his head. "I bet the whole thing is giving you nightmares, no doubt."

He tosses me a Sharpie marker. My hands are so sweaty that it slips out of my fingers like a bar of soap and clatters on the floor.

"I actually didn't know about the bloody bald patches," I say.

"Well, if you've got any more questions about it you just let me know—sometimes the particulars bring closure. I get that, yessir." He crosses his arms. "For instance, did you know her bra was all askew? She'd obviously been fondled."

"Please stop." I'd rather not think about my former best friend's dead boobs.

Staake smiles. "Anyhow, all that there diary book says to me is that you've got a lot of crossing out to do—that's your job, isn't it? If I were a parent and could read that penmanship, well, I sure wouldn't want to know my daughter'd had an affair with Uncle Jimmy, no ma'am. Not at all. Any more hullabaloo about Ruth Fried's shenanigans is just going to hurt her family. My mission's the exact opposite. I'm ready to put this thing to rest." He raises his eyebrows and nods at me. "Go ahead, Bushman, use that marker."

I look down at the Sharpie near my foot and can almost hear Mrs. Fried's dry lips cracking in my ear as she begged me to redact the sex parts. "Okay," I mumble, leaning off my chair to snatch it. I open the diary to one of the dog-eared pages. It's the one I read last night—the one where Ruth describes how Uncle Jimmy said he wanted to mount and stuff her. I uncap the Sharpie but hesitate. "Don't you want to talk to him, though?" I bite my lip. "At the very least—"

"Listen, I understand you might be after the age difference with this one, but your friend was eighteen, she could make her own decisions, wanton or not." Staake clasps his hands against his belly, reclining deeper into his swivel chair. "There's nothing we can do."

Wanton? Also, how hard is it to at least go talk to Uncle Jimmy? Maybe Davey was right. I mean, even if Staake isn't exactly officially mentally handicapped, he's simply not putting all the pieces together. "But you should check all the facts." I recap the marker and place it on his desk. "Diane Sawyer's just a journalist, and she has to fact-check, and meanwhile you're a sheriff running a murder investigation."

"Now I don't like your tone—and who the heck is Diane?" Staake scowls. "You come in here and I offer you root beer like a reasonable person, and you try to poop on my parade."

"Sorry," I blurt. It just slips out. You're not supposed to fight with anyone in Friendship, least of all a police officer.

"Also I think the phrase is 'rain on your parade,' not—"

"Listen here, Bushman—"

"No, you listen—wait, sorry—" There's no sense in getting on his bad side. I found this thing online where Diane Sawyer said you should never alienate your sources. "It's just . . . can I ask you one more question?" She also said that you can never really know the whole story, but facts will paint a pretty good picture, and your sources point you toward those facts.

"Well, unfortunately I have nothing better to do." Staake looks at his watch. "Shoot."

"Um." I didn't actually have a question ready. But now that I know Sheriff Staake is kind of stubborn and simple, I feel like I can't go home until I ask enough stuff to find out if he's maybe truly cutting corners like Davey said he was.

"Spit it out, Bushman."

"Um." I think of the view from my window, all that razed corn, the whole field empty except for the willow tree where Ruth was hanged like a buck from a basket-ball hoop. "Sheriff Staake, why did you cut down all the corn? I mean, I know it said in the paper that it was for evidence—but where is it? I mean, did you dust it or . . ." I'm hoping it's all in a warehouse somewhere, with scientists going through it stalk by stalk, looking for bits of hair or clothing. I'd like to be able to go home and feel like our house is safe even though it hasn't got a moat around it—or even an alarm system, come to think about it. "I was just wondering."

"For chrissake, Bushman"—Staake gives me an exasperated look—"you can't get a fingerprint off a cornstalk. We cut it down so we could see better."

"You mean you just threw it all away?" My mouth feels dry.

"No." He shakes his head and rolls his eyes like I'm stupid. "We *sold* it."

They don't want the diary and they sell the corn without even looking at it first? How much other evidence are they sneering at? "But that's totally illogical."

Staake laughs through his nose, sliding his feet off his desk. "You know, I'm sick and tired of people telling me that." He walks over to me and turns my chair around so I'm facing the window. "Bushman, I want you to take a good look." He gestures to the cars parked on Main Street. "This is my town. It might be a boring place, but it's my game and my rules, and I plan to keep it nice and boring. Nice and safe." He pats my back. "Now are we about done here?"

I can't think of any more questions except maybe asking if he ever graduated from high school, which might get me thrown in a jail cell. "I guess so."

"Okeydokey, then." He leads me to the door and hands me a business card with a smiley face on it. "That there's my private number. I don't give it out to everybody, but sometimes the girls think of something after we've already chatted and don't have time to come back for a sit-down."

"Thank you." At least he's taking me seriously enough to give me his direct line. I pull out my phone and enter him into my contacts.

Staake smacks his forehead like he's forgotten something. "Totally slipped my mind—I bet you want to go and see the boy now, don'tcha?"

"Who?"

"Why Colt Widdacombe—the monster himself. Some of the girls have been eager to scream at him—blow off some steam and so forth." He pats me on the head. "I figure it's therapeutic—especially for you, given that he murdered your best buddy."

"Is that even ethical?" I hug my backpack to my chest. "I mean, what does Colt's lawyer say?" I think of Davey, sitting on his stoop with all that Beast, saying how the sheriff has a personal vendetta. Why else would Staake be urging me and all the other girls coming in to go and torture Colt?

"I'm giving you the opportunity." Staake frowns. "Now do you want to talk to him or not?"

The cell where they've got Colt isn't private at all; it's a barred-off portion of the courthouse employee snack room, which seems pretty merciless. Cops come in here on their breaks and probably taunt Colt over bags of Doritos. All day, he's got to stare at vending machines he can't reach.

Colt is doing push-ups when I walk in. "Hi," I say, just loud enough so he can hear me over his own counting. I expected to see him with a five o'clock shadow grown salty with tears. But when he glances up at me, he's the same old Colt. Hot as hell and looking somewhere between bored and pissed off.

"What is it?" He climbs to his feet and saunters over, bending his arms casually through the bars. Outside you can hear the protesters chanting his name. He shakes his hair out of his eyes. "You bring me a sandwich or something?"

"Ugh, you're so cocky."

"Quit being such a stuck-up virgin." He blows me a kiss and I roll my eyes, because I know he's making fun of me. I remember once I told Ruth that Colt wasn't the most kind or intelligent specimen, and she told me that was fine because he thought I was an icy-vaginaed prude.

"Yo." He reaches through the bars and tries to flick me

in the arm. "Seriously though, could you get me something from the vending machine? I'm starving and my parents aren't bringing me dinner for another hour."

I roll my eyes. I guess I sort of expected to stand here and know in my bones that he was a psychopath. But this is pretty typical banter for Colt and me and as far as I can tell he's just the same old asslord. I scan the vending machine for prices—and despite wanting to hate him I find myself rooting around in my backpack, searching for change. "Sorry, but I've only got enough for the breath mints."

"This sucks." He walks away from me and flops down on his cot.

"Sorry," I mumble. It's quiet for a second. "Listen, did you kill her or what?"

Colt rolls his eyes. "Oh, please."

"Did you?"

He points a finger at me, looking legitimately riled for the first time. "You shut the fuck up."

I shrug, trying to look casual. This is the only person who knew Ruth as well as I thought I did and for some reason I feel like I'm going to cry. "You weren't even at the memorial."

He stomps his foot. "Yeah, because they had me here. You want to know where I was when I found out about

Ruth? I was sitting right fucking here. They had me on vandalism for some mailboxes, and next thing I know they're telling me my girlfriend's dead and I did it. How do you think that feels? So don't you fucking tell me how to act—that I'm not sad enough or whatever. I'm not going to pretend to be some faggot crybaby like you just because that's what everybody wants." He rakes his fingers through his hair. "You'll think what you think, and my parents are going to get me a lawyer, end of story."

"You don't have a lawyer yet?"

"It's not exactly an easy case, is it?" He throws his hands up. "Someone planted a bunch of evidence in my car and they found my shotgun—well, guess what? I didn't shoot Ruth. Ruth and I didn't pull guns on each other. We *fucked*."

My palms are sweaty. He thinks she got shot. "Colt, that isn't how it happened."

"Nobody tells me anything," he shouts. "I sit here, and nobody tells me shit. Meanwhile I'm going hoarse saying, 'Yo, shitheads, everyone around here keeps a shotgun in their car.' I'm going, 'Yo, assholes, the night you have me murdering, I was actually rolling around Fang Road shooting up mailboxes.' And they're like, 'Stop calling us assholes,' and I'm like—"

"This is very cut and dry, Colt." I'm about to explain

that it's a big deal that he doesn't know how she was killed, and so he should probably tell a lawyer that—but he cuts me off by making a fart noise. Then he gives me the finger.

I sigh, feeling a little nauseous. From what he's saying, he definitely sounds innocent. But at the same time he's still so mean that it's a little hard to say I'm on his side. Regardless of where Colt falls on the line between asslord and murdering psychopath, he's still a total jerk.

"Listen, Tits McGhee, if you don't believe me go check it out yourself." He laughs. "Go talk to the witch—Klitch the witch—she'll remember. I got her so bad her mailbox looks like a warzone, like fucking Afghanistan. She came out and screamed at me and I was yelling all sorts of funny shit at her for almost an hour. She was drunk but she'll remember me." He smiles. "Nobody forgets the Honey-comb."

On the way out, I try to ask Sheriff Staake about the fact that Colt says he doesn't know any of the details of Ruth's murder. But Staake keeps cutting me off, looking more and more annoyed.

"Now I'm a thinker, see," he says, leading me to the exit. "And I'm starting to wonder whose side you're on—because you know what? I heard some of what you said up there with Colt and it didn't seem like you were on the town's side. No, ma'am." He spins me around so we're facing each other. His breath smells like bubble gum. "My daughter was right. You're an outsider. And a rebel without a cause in my professional opinion."

"Your daughter's a hoochie mama," I blurt. "And you're just mad because Colt did it with her."

Staake doesn't say anything. Just keeps a firm grip on my jacket all the way to the parking lot.

BUCKSHOT

Mrs. Klitch lives in a creepy house on an otherwise deserted street, and has all these homemade sculptures of dragons and dinosaurs and children in her yard. Kids call her Klitch the Witch. Well, kids and Colt call her that, I guess. It's not very polite. I once had this sort of hippie teacher, Miss Winston, who was always teaching us about art, and equality, and recycling. After she heard us saying Klitch the Witch, Miss Winston decided to take us on a field trip to Fang Road so we could do a tour of Mrs. Klitch's sculptures and come to know her as an artist. The only problem was that when we showed up, Mrs. Klitch was sick or something and wouldn't come outside. Kids kept screaming that they could see her peeking out at them through the windows, casting spells. The whole field trip was over in about ten minutes.

I park near the edge of Mrs. Klitch's property. Her mailbox is set back from the road, right next to her front gate. Over the years Mrs. Klitch has had to turn her house into sort of a fortress because kids like Colt kept vandalizing her statues. She's added a steel gate, who knows how many alarm systems, and a ten-foot-tall fence—with shiny barbed wire coiled on top. I slam the car door. On the other side of the fence, a crudely made brontosaurus stares at me with eyes made of blue-and-brown sea glass.

I hear coughing and startle to see Mrs. Klitch sitting on a folding chair in the shadows, like, twenty feet away. She's dressed for cold and sipping on a can of Beast. She looks ninety years old, all brown and crinkly, and her eyes are black and beady, sucked into her face like raisins on a Danish.

"Hello, Mrs. Klitch. I'm just going to look at your mailbox a second, if that's okay?"

In response, she burps, tosses her empty beer can on the grass, and crushes it under one of her snow boots— proving to be surprisingly strong for someone who resembles a mummified corpse.

"You should come in and have a drink with me," she snarls. "I'll tell you stories. I know everything about everything."

"No thanks!" I shudder and make my way toward the mailbox, half expecting Mrs. Klitch to throw herself against the fence like a wild animal and coil her tongue between the chain links. "Actually, though, Mrs. Klitch, do you remember—" I stop in my tracks. The mailbox is riddled with holes. Its metal is bent and pockmarked with shotgun-shell-size craters.

"Looking for these?" Mrs. Klitch digs into her snow pants, bringing out a handful of shotgun shells. "Last Friday, eight p.m. These shells were full of buckshot, and that boy was over raising hell against my property—that Lightning Bolt Skiddercrumb, or whatever the glory heck his name is. I was trying to watch infomercials."

Friday was the night Ruth died. Eight p.m. was when she was supposed to be at my house—which means that if Colt was over here at eight o'clock he could never have intercepted her on Route 51. My stomach hurts.

"Someone should arrest him," Mrs. Klitch snaps. "I told the cops but nobody believes me—not the witch!" She cackles a loud, witchlike cackle. I run back to my car.

"Balls!" I hurl myself onto the driver's seat and start banging on the steering wheel, accidentally honking the horn. Then I lock all the doors. "Balls," I hiss again—because, yeah, so sue me, but part of me was relieved for this to be over, just like Staake said. Then at least we'd all be safe. But now there's a killer on the loose, and Davey's not crazy like I told him he was, and no one at the police department wants to listen to reason. And all we've got for evidence is the word of a juvenile delinquent/alleged killer, the gut feeling of an attractive war veteran who probably technically has severe PTSD, and an alibi that consists of a certifiably crazy lady with an obvious drinking problem and a reputation for casting spells.

I look out at Mrs. Klitch laughing in her folding chair, gleefully kicking her boots against the cold grass. Certain people might be able to ignore this, but I can't leave Davey alone with the knowledge that things aren't right—because he isn't crazy, and it'd be mean to pretend he is just because that's easier.

But what do I do? Because honestly I don't even know what I'm after or up against here. I mean, the cops won't listen and everyone else has their heads inside their butts trying to be polite. Not to mention, Friendship is actually way less boring but maybe also much more weird and creepy than I thought it was, and nobody really prepared me for that.

I guess the real question is: How would a professional handle this? I know that if I were Diane Sawyer, I'd be serious and focused and composed and beautiful and perfect—wait, I'm getting off track. The point is that I've got to handle it correctly. Because who knows? Maybe if I do this right, and get to the bottom of things, it could be the sort of masterpiece that might even make Diane Sawyer cock her head and say, "Hey there, who the heck is that?"

SINGLE SHOOTER

Part of me wants to go straight from Mrs. Klitch's to Davey's and apologize—only we're not exactly on a drop-by basis, I guess. Plus, last time I was there I yelled at him, so he probably doesn't want to see me. I watch Mrs. Klitch's concrete monsters dwindle in my rearview mirror, and decide to do what I do every time I'm not sure what to do. I head to Ralph's.

I've never been very good at being alone. When I was little, I'd wake up in the quiet morning thinking Dom had left me. I'd collapse at the top of the stairs bawling, unable to go down to the kitchen and confirm my fears that the house was empty. He'd hear me crying and come running up the steps, lift me off the ground, and squeeze me until

I believed with my whole body he was there again. Looking back, I think it had something to do with Mom being gone—but after a while you're supposed to get used to that sort of thing, and the truth is that, for me, the fear of people disappearing never went away.

Probably the most hurtful thing Ruth ever said to me, actually, was that she preferred to be alone sometimes—which is weird, because there were moments when she straight up called me a snob or a prude or a know-it-all, and you'd think that would hurt more. I guess I was jealous of her ability to just be by herself and like it. Even though now I know that she had this whole secret life to comfort herself. I never had anyone but her and Dom and Ralph, like, ever.

And recently, like in the past year or so, it was mostly only her. In part because Ralph got really into video games I didn't know how to play—there were always like a million button combinations for shooting all the different kinds of guns—and also because it'd started to feel weird talking to Dom. I could sense him getting nervous about me getting older, or maybe it had to do with me being a girl in the first place or something, I don't know. There's a lot I can't put into words. And I guess in a way I looked to Ruth to fill the space, to be my everything, and probably that wasn't okay. I never wanted to kiss her like she sometimes joked about. But in a way it was like we were two girls clinging to each other, trying not to drown. No wonder she sometimes got annoyed with me.

Anyway, all I'm saying is that doing things on my own has always been hard, because if there isn't someone there to watch me, then how do I exist? Even if I'm doing my homework by myself, there's that want for a person near me, just for the body heat, just for breathing the same air.

"No matter how lonely you get, you will never be alone," Dom told me once, picking up on my inner workings with that ESP he has sometimes, though he has it less and less often these days. I think I ignored him when he said it. It can hurt to have someone see exactly what you're feeling, especially when part of you knows it's sort of narcissistic or dumb.

And that's something Ralph's the best for, come to think of it—a way for company and privacy simultaneously. Someone to just be around, someone who knows a lot, and knows me, and likes me anyway. Plus, Ralph can keep a secret. I mean let's be serious, who would he tell? Plus, he's always half-preoccupied—playing Total Escape 3 or Enemy of Death 5, or whatever—and not having his full attention makes it easier to work through your feelings out loud without getting embarrassed that technically someone else is listening.

The Johnstons' house is an olive-green bungalow. I've always been jealous of the redbrick walkway (ours is concrete) and how the only upstairs window has a green-and-white striped awning. The house faces the street like a friendly Cyclops with a half-shut eye, its redbrick tongue unfurled to the sidewalk.

I'm standing on Ralph's front porch kicking at his front door because my hands are busy warming up in my pockets. The doorbell stopped working a little while after his parents died and he hasn't gotten it fixed yet.

"You should tell your boyfriend to paint the house a nonpuke color," Ruth said once. "If the guy spent some money on remodeling instead of buying all that *Star Trek* shit, he could have a right little bachelor pad."

"He's not my boyfriend," I told her, in this pleading voice that I hated.

"I know." She smiled and linked her arm through mine. "But doesn't that word sound great, *boyfriend*?" She ruffled my hair. "We'll get you one at some point." She really did want that for me—a boyfriend. I think part of her felt bad about my singleness when she started dating Colt.

Ralph answers his door holding a *Star Trek* mug of what I'm guessing is hot chocolate. He's put so many marshmallows on top that they're falling off the sides.

"Jesus, Kippy!" he says, one eye pointing behind me at the darkening sky, the other at my face. "Would you come in already? You'll catch your death."

Ralph's living room is warm and well lit, with peach-colored carpeting and two fake leather Barcaloungers facing a roaring fireplace. In the corner, there's a TV attached to a video game console and a nest of cords. Shelves line the walls and are piled with stacks of trading cards and shopping bags. In the middle of the room is a TV dinner tray with a laptop on it.

Ralph sold most of his parents' stuff in garage sales after the funeral. I don't like going any farther than the front room because of how crowded the back hallways are with the stuff he's bought since they died. I even keep my eyes half-shut whenever I have to use the bathroom because that way I can barely see all the boxes and bags and stuff back there. I can't even imagine what he's got upstairs. And I don't like to think about it. The good thing is that according to the internet, Ralph doesn't qualify as a hoarder because (1) the hallways are walkable, (2) the front room is pretty uncrowded, and (3) there aren't any fire hazards in the kitchen or anything. They have a checklist for that kind of thing.

"It's great you're here, Kippy. Is it all right that I'm enjoying my cocoa in front of you?" Ralph asks. I'm sitting in one of the Barcaloungers and he's standing over me, slurping at his mug. "I would offer you some except I used all the marshmallows. It's been a long day."

I smile at him. "I'm fine." My phone buzzes in my pocket. It's a text from Dom:

Dom (Mobile) Received @ 5:15 PM:
EVERYTHINGOKAYCOMEHOMESOONOKAY

For a while, Dom wouldn't text at all, so I finally had to stop answering his calls in an effort to drag him into the twenty-first century. Now he sends messages without any spaces. Baby steps.

Dom (Mobile) Received @ 5:15 PM:
ICANSEEYOU

I look out Ralph's window and glimpse Dom waving frantically at me from our kitchen.

To: Dom (Mobile):
Calm down/I'll be home soon

I got a text from an unknown number earlier that turned out to be Libby, saying, "Hey honey, here's my #

call anytime! G'bless. —L." I'm not sure why she's being so nice, but then again Libby's moods fluctuate pretty rapidly. Once when we were in kindergarten, the teacher fell asleep during naptime and Libby cut off another girl's braids and glued them to the class bunny's head. She kept screaming, *"More pretty! More pretty!"* Of course everyone forgot about that little episode once she grew D cups. And now she's the most popular girl in school.

Anyway, for a split second after getting her text, I genuinely tried to imagine her and me being friends—because whatever, maybe I'm lonely enough to consider it. The furthest I could get was picturing us sitting silently in my living room. One look at taxidermied Mother Peanut Butter and Libby would probably be screaming *"ewwww!"* and running for the door.

"Can I talk at you about something?" I ask Ralph.

"Of course." He sits down on the carpet. "But just so you know I have to play my game soon."

"Right." I take a deep breath. "So you know Mrs. Klitch?"

Ralph blinks at me sleepily. He has a hot-chocolate mustache.

"Here, go ahead and put in your game, it'll make it easier to talk," I say. I slide down in my chair and kick him one of the controllers.

"It's fine, Kippy," he says, looking at his watch. "I don't have to start playing for eighteen more minutes. I'm hoping to set a world record by playing for one hundred thirty-six hours straight."

"That's quite a schedule you've got planned out." If Dom were here he'd probably be concerned by the idea of 136 hours in front of a television, but I kind of feel like until Ralph's parents have been dead a whole year, Ralph should do whatever might make him happier. It took Dom and me a full year to start acting like human beings again. For ten whole months I just pored over this book called *When Animals Attack*, planning for the next emergency, I guess, and wouldn't talk to anyone. The only reason Ruth and I even became friends is that she saw me reading it at recess and came over going, "Oh my God, did you know a chimp is so strong it can pull your foot off? Like right off the bone?" It was the only reason I let her sit down next to me on the grass and pull the book across both our laps.

Anyway, Ralph probably won't even go through with it. The 136-hour thing, I mean. He has a lot of trouble finishing what he's started.

I crank open the footrest on the Barcalounger. "Okay, so I've got eighteen minutes." I chew on my tongue for a second like I'm getting ready to give a speech and then launch into the thing about Sheriff Staake and Colt's alibi and my visit to Fang Road. I end with the part about how Mrs. Klitch said Colt was there that night, but how no one will believe her. "I mean, seriously," I say, watching Ralph blink at me nonjudgmentally from the carpet. "It's like a horror story. In forty-five minutes I've got to go eat hot Italian sausages with Dom like nothing is wrong." I roll my eyes. "Because you know if I mentioned any of this to him he'd just think I was having some grief-stricken psychotic break."

Ralph fiddles with the controller. "When my parents passed I got it into my head that deer were evil creatures planning to take over the world. Eventually I came to terms with how irrational that was, but it took a few weeks—and I have to admit, it felt good to have an explanation for what had happened."

I make a frustrated noise. "Ralph, are you even listening to me?"

Ralph's mouth hangs open as if he's considering this. "Kippy, do you remember when they came to get Ruth from the field?" He studies my face, his one wobbly eye creeping more and more toward his temple. "I just want to make sure you remember because it wasn't so long ago."

"God, I'm not, like, in shock or anything." I pull my knees up to my chest and play with the bottoms of my feet. Ralph doesn't usually talk to me like this—like some kind of parent. And of course I remember that moment—the ambulance lights hitting our kitchen walls, alternating emergency colors on the refrigerator. When I saw them pull up I screamed so loud because I knew that she was hurt—but I guess Dom already knew it was worse than that, because he dragged me into the living room and literally sat on me so I wouldn't see them load her in. I was lying there on the couch screaming with him pinning me down when they finally drove away. I'll always feel like maybe she still could have heard me if I had wrestled my way out to the ambulance and shrieked her name.

I don't remember telling Ralph about it so I guess Dom must have.

"Kippy—"

"I remember!" My mouth tastes like metal and I know I'm going to cry. "The whole reason I came over here is because you're supposed to be the one person I can talk to." No matter what crazy stuff she put in her diary, I can't get around the fact that Ruth's the one person who would have trusted me on this—who would have said, "Wait, that's batshit, what the fuck is everybody waiting for? This town is fucking crazy." The hardest thing to get through to yourself about death is also the most obvious thing: that the person is really gone. That you can't talk to them about anything anymore. That they're not coming back. I burst into tears.

"Kippy, please." Ralph cringes. "I'm just trying to help."

"I know how this looks. I'm not stupid." I press my palms into my eye sockets until I see stars. "Dom printed out the seven stages of grief and put them on the refrigerator. The first stage is denial, and it's easy to say that's what this is."

"Kippy, that's not what I mean at all." Ralph sounds sad. "I was just going to say it seems like you're hoping for a revenge mission of sorts—like in Total Escape Three—"

"Druid Mountain, I know." I hiccup and blink my eyes open. Tears roll down my nose.

"There is a multitude of evidence pointing to Colt. You and I both thought it made sense back at the Great Moose. But I can see how you might want to create another problem to solve—you know, to do something for her." He glances at his watch. "Is it that you feel scared? Scared that someone capable of gruesome violence might still be—"

"Obviously I'm freaked, okay? Obviously that's part of it. But the creepiest thing isn't that someone's still out there, it's that everyone's ignoring it." *Aside from Davey*, I almost add. But I'd rather not mention that in case Ralph gets up on his high horse about the mental health of veterans. My chest is tight and I can feel tears sliding down my chin. "Just never mind." My voice is soggy. Ralph's closer to my age than Dom's but when it comes to this he's more like a Dom than a friend, and I can't blame him for that. He's just trying to protect me. "I'll deal with it on my own."

"Kippy, stop it." Ralph reaches for my foot and gives it a squeeze. "If you really feel scared, I have some things that might put your mind at ease. I know how important it is to feel prepared."

"So you don't think I'm crazy?" I wipe my nose and try not to look too petulant.

Ralph sighs. "I think you're ignoring some important facts. But if you're having some itchy paranoia—well, I understand that. And it can't feel good. And if you truly think there's a killer out there, you should do whatever it takes to feel safe." He smiles at me. "Okay?"

"You mean I should look into it, right?" My heart races; he's on my side. I need to go talk to Mrs. Klitch again, I realize—just brace myself and go back there and bring a tape recorder this time. And I should talk to Jim Steele, too, obviously, come to think of it—and whoever else—

"No, I mean you should arm yourself," Ralph says, interrupting my racing thoughts. He leaves the room before I can answer and comes back in dragging a giant machete with a handle the length of a baseball bat, and a large can labeled *Ursidae Eye Gas*.

"It's up to you, Kippy." He sighs. "You can either borrow the two-handed machete—a collector's item (four hundred dollars plus shipping from eBay.com)—or my bear spray, which I got for twelve eighty-nine at the Buck Fleet." He screws up his mouth. "Given the costliness of the machete, I would have to charge a rental fee, is that all right?" He yanks the machete across the carpet, balances it on its head so I can get a better look at it, and wiggles the Ursidae can in his other hand.

I take the bear spray from him and put it in my backpack.

Uggggh, Ruth here. Sometimes I get up and it's, like, sad or something, how beautiful I am. Because you know it's only going to go away at some point and I'll end up looking like Mom, and even if I don't have children, I'll get chubbier and wrinkled and my boobs will sag. I'm just saying, it's a lot to lose.

Based on how much more attention I get, I'm pretty sure Kippy's jealous (who isn't?). And I'd feel worse for her on that point, because there are a lot of girls I look at and go, "Oh you poor, poor thing. You're you"—except if I were going to be jealous of anybody—and let's face it, I'm not—it'd probably be Kippy, just based on how different she looks from me. She's basically the yin to my yang. Like she's totally flat chested and superpale, but the real reason no one's ever asked her to a dance is because she wears those turtlenecks and screen-printed sweatshirts with stuff like ducks or elk on them. Plus her pick-up lines need work—the other day I literally heard her telling her lab partner, "Tommy Jenkins, I truly appreciate your skill with the Bunsen burner"—and she could stand to wash her hair more often. Sometimes she literally has dirt on her face and I'm like, "Grrrrl, seriously. If this is just the tip of the iceberg, I worry about your vagina."

But, like, it's all stuff she could correct if she really wanted to. Cuz really she's got nice skin and these gray eyes, and whenever she gets angry or embarrassed her cheeks grow red circles like some kind of fucking china doll. Oh and she's a proper goy, my Mom says—as in, her hair's actually blond even when she needs to take a shower, and not just some shitty light-brown color, like all those girls who say they're blond just because they were when they were babies—so booyah, wannabes. Probably in New York they'd call her exotic or something. But we're here, obviously, so people mostly tell her to eat more and whisper a lot about whether she's albino. Albinos have red eyes, motherfuckers, go read a goddamn book.

ANIMALS ATTACK

At school the next day, a lot of people are wearing black armbands, which is pretty annoying. What email list am I not on that I'm not getting the memos about vigils and coordinated grief gear?

The worst part is that it actually occurred to me to wear some black today. Last night I read another diary entry—which was superlong, and took me forever to decode and transcribe—and it had a nugget of niceness in it, which turned me into a major crybaby and made me want to do something cliché in Ruth's honor. Like, root around in my drawer for a black turtleneck. I even had it laid out on the carpet so I wouldn't forget. But ultimately I decided it'd be too obvious to wear something like that the first day back and that everyone would think I just wanted attention—like, "Look at me! Look at me! My friend died." So now here I am prowling the hallways in a rainbow turtleneck while everyone else is dressed up like yesterday was 9/11.

As I walk to first period I see that someone's put Ruth Fried Foundation Brigade posters on all the lockers. Ruth's school picture takes up most of each page, and then underneath it says:

MEETING TONIGHT
AT 6 AT COURTHOUSE
SAME SPOT!! SAME WINDOW!! SAME GOAL!!
(Bring markers and donations.)

It's crazy that they think they're honoring Ruth's memory by terrorizing Colt.

The bell rings for first hour and I duck into AP Chemistry. As soon as I walk through the door, the whole room goes quiet. Every person at every lab table is staring at me behind their Bunsen burners. In a way it's sort of reassuring. Part of me thought nobody would recognize me without Ruth around. I guess there are perks to being the dead girl's friend, even if you're the only one not wearing black.

Right away I feel evil for thinking that and remind myself that most of my classmates probably saw me give that speech at Ruth's funeral, which sort of makes me want to crawl into one of the Bunsen burners. If I had known there were going to be nice parts in her diary, I would have talked about the year we went as the couple from *American Gothic* for Halloween, or when we won the fifth-grade cake walk and made ourselves sick eating the entire prize in one sitting, or the time we went sledding one winter at the golf course, and I veered off the path into the pond and fell through the ice, and it was just the shallow part but she trudged in wearing her snow pants and dragged me out by my foot.

If I could talk to Ruth right now I'd tell her sorry about that eulogy and that I don't care about the diary or that she was annoyed a lot. *I'm afraid I'll never meet anyone like you*, I'd say. *And maybe that's sappy, but could you please just be alive? Please.*

I plop down in the front row. There's whispering behind my back but it's interrupted by an announcement over the loudspeaker. "Kippy Bushman, please report to Mr. Jake's office."

If I were being ushered to Principal Hannycack's office, then at least the whole class would treat me normally and go, "Oooohhh." But nobody ever makes any noise about Mr. Jake, because the only people who get sent there during class time are the cutters and the anorexics—or else the

ADHD kids, like, if their parents call because they've forgotten to take their meds at breakfast. You'd think that being the daughter of a school psychologist would make me less prejudiced about going to see my own school's guidance counselor. But someone has to kick my chair before I even leave my seat.

Dom says he and Mr. Jake have differing viewpoints on what it means to be helpful. I think they're competitive. For instance, Dom goes by Mr. Bushman, thinking kids need a friendly authority figure, whereas Mr. Jake goes by his first name, thinking it's better for students to see him as a friend. Up until now, my only interactions with him have been when he gives presentations to our health class. Last time he was there, he kept talking about how to use sex as a "relationship builder" instead of "orgasm teamwork." I watched him from the back row while Ruth and I stepped on each other's feet and tried to keep from laughing.

When I enter his office, Mr. Jake spins to face me in a magenta swivel chair and taps the floor with a yardstick, which he's holding like some kind of cane. Mr. Jake is bald with a goatee. He's also wearing a tie with a turtleneck, which I don't really understand.

"Hey pal." Even he's got on a black armband.

The room is wallpapered with motivational posters,

which all have a lot of dolphins on them for some reason, and each piece of furniture is a happy color, including
the three bookshelves, which stand in a rainbow against
the wall and hold a wide array of self-help books. *Think
and Grow Rich. Crazy Sexy Diet. The Fine Art of Flirting.* Mr.
Jake uses the yardstick to gesture toward a bright-yellow
couch where Libby Quinn is perched with her arms and
legs crossed, wearing an armband. "Hi *Katie*," she says,
crossing her arms and puckering her lips. Sure enough,
she's switched gears since her text message yesterday and
is now furious for some reason.

"Oof," I whisper.

"Or maybe I should call you *Traitor*." She twirls her
hair around her finger and I smile, trying to look friendly.
If I were an animal in the wild, I would be the kind that
rolls into a ball in front of predators. Or maybe the kind
that's objectively very pleasant but secretly poisonous.

"Wow, I really like what you've done with your armband," I blurt. "It's, like, way different from all those
other ones, in my opinion." She's decorated hers with a
pink crucifix.

Mr. Jake gestures again at the couch. "Why don't we
get started?"

I try to sit as far away from Libby as possible, but
this proves to be difficult, as the couch is actually a love

seat. No matter what I do, our legs are basically touching. There's a tissue box on the coffee table in front of us, and Libby plucks one out and presses it to her face. Is she actually crying?

"Wow." I let out a big sigh and look around, trying to seem impressed. "Well, thanks a lot for inviting me."

Libby sneers and rolls her eyes. "Stop trying to act like you don't know what this is about, Katie. The entire RFFB—excuse me, Mr. Jake, I'm talking about the Ruth Fried Foundation Brigade. Well, our email list got this thing saying you're basically trying to barricade our whole goal for justice. What are you doing going to the witch's house and asking her to give an alibi for Colt? Doris Klitch is a known alcoholic for goodness' sake! Why would you ever expose yourself to her insanity?"

How does she know I went to Mrs. Klitch's? "Wait, what email?" No wonder everyone was staring at me in chemistry.

"You know exactly what I'm talking about." She shifts so that her boob is smushed against my shoulder and our thighs are touching all the way to the knee. "I've decided you're not accepting what's what, and it isn't healthy." She looks down her nose at me. "I notice you've got your belt back on."

It's true. I'm wearing my utility belt again. I used to wear it a lot in elementary school because I was always drawing animals back then and it was a way to have constant easy access to my markers. Also I may or may not have thought I was Batman.

"So?" I mumble. This time the belt is for my Dictaphone. Oh, and some pens and Ruth's journal in case I think of something related to the case. I guess it's kind of weird to write in a dead person's diary—because maybe you're desecrating something? But I want to keep all the evidence in one place. Like Ralph said, I've got to arm myself. Plus I'm planning to work up the nerve to interview Mrs. Klitch after school, and it'll be easier if the Dictaphone's in my belt. Having a recorder on a table is distracting, I decided. Hands-free conversation is more personal.

"That's so gay," Libby mutters. "Not like *gay* gay—I'm not a bigot or anything—I mean like retarded gay."

"Libby, come on." I try to shrug her boob off me but it's too heavy. "What do you mean you got an email about me?" The only person I told about Mrs. Klitch was Ralph—unless Mrs. Klitch sent the email. I guess I also emailed Colt's parents about what I'd found out. I just thought they should know.

"Shh." Libby pats my hand. "I'm here to help."

Mr. Jake smiles from his chair. "Libby would like to stage an intervention."

She nods. "The thing is, Ruth is *dead*, honey. It's time to accept that and start doing charity stuff." Her lip curls sympathetically. "Let's start the intervention by you remembering some good things about her—just get it off your chest. Then we can light a candle and you never have to think about her by yourself ever again and you can start coming to RFFB meetings. So go ahead. Say a memory out loud."

I think about Ruth and I holding hands at the elementary school Halloween parade. The two of us at the end of her driveway dancing for cars that never stopped. "It's none of your business," I say.

Libby looks at Mr. Jake and raises her eyebrows. "Do you see what I'm dealing with here?"

Mr. Jake taps his fingers together and puckers his lips. "Tell me, Katie: Do you feel like an orphan?"

I pull the hem of my turtleneck over my utility belt. You'd think he would know my name since he and my dad are basically rivals. Am I really so invisible? "How long do I have to stay here, exactly?"

Libby presses her boob harder into my arm. "I mean, let's count this out, shall we?" She holds up a finger. "One. You give a really weird speech in front of everyone (that was the funeral, obvi). Two. You invent some fantasy world and crawl around on your hands and knees looking for something that doesn't exist so you can try and help a *known killer*. And Three"—Libby points her chin at me—"I care about you."

She's looking at me so intently that I feel I have to say something. "I care about you, too," I babble.

"Brava!" says Mr. Jake.

Libby raises her hand and waits for him to call on her. "Mr. Jake, I think Katie should probably *have* to come to the brigade meeting tonight. Personally, I think it would give us all some closure." She turns to me and smiles. There is glitter on her front tooth.

"Now I'm no rule enforcer because I'm not a regular teacher—I'm a cool teacher, don'tcha know," Mr. Jake says. "But what do you think, Katie? Could you hop on board that meeting? Bring a bit of the so-called verve?" He definitely uses those teeth-whitening strips.

Libby is smiling, and looking really nice all of a sudden—and even though I know she probably doesn't actually care, I still don't want to hurt her feelings. "I'll try," I announce.

Libby stares at me with a vacant expression that's probably linked to her learning disability. It's true she's going to have to pull some pretty outrageous stunts if she wants to get into Madison. One time for English class, she literally did a current events presentation on aliens invading because she didn't know the difference between tabloids and regular papers.

"'I'll try' is what a bitch would say," Libby whispers in my ear. "Make it yes, or die."

"Whoa, Libby . . ." I glance at Mr. Jake but he seems not to have heard.

"I'm done!" Libby chirps, batting her eyes at Mr. Jake. "I feel like I got everything off my chest."

"Well, okay," Mr. Jake intones, opening his arms for what looks like a hug. Libby leaps to her feet and actually embraces him, then grabs me by the elbow and drags me into the hallway, jabbering about RFFB members' dues and poster parties.

"Let's turn over another new leaf, okay?" she says. "Even though I think it's *totally* weird how I caught you hanging out with Ruth's brother like the second she died." She elbows me teasingly. "You little slut."

"We're just friends."

"Oh totally." Libby turns and grabs me by the shoulders, her eyes sparkling. "But watch out because love can make you do crazy things, Katie, believe me." She links her arm through mine and continues walking down the hall. "I'm just saying. Plus you're, like, an important mascot now for the group!" She's got the biggest smile on her face and keeps intentionally swinging her ponytail from side to side. "Colt deserves to rot for what he's done." She squeezes my arm so hard that I yelp and pull away. When my mom died, Libby and all the other girls in my grade besides Ruth were always descending on me in front of teachers, trying to braid my hair or tell me I'd done a good crayon drawing, or whatever. They were only seven but they'd seen enough TV to want to be part of my drama—be mothers to me, I guess, like I was a doll to practice on. They all got bored with it after a few weeks and started ignoring me again. But this time the attention feels different somehow. Creepier.

"Why do you hate Colt so much?" I ask. But instead of answering, she throws her arm around me and starts talking about getting me my own black armband and helping me "bedazzle" it. I tense up under her embrace and fight the urge to toss her off me. It's not like I love Colt, now, or anything. I just can't help but feel freaked out by the uproar. Dom told me that some judge in Madison is still deciding whether to allow the whole shebang to happen in Friendship. "Wouldn't that bias all the jurors?" I asked. But Dom just shrugged.

"People in this town will do the right thing," he said.

I look at Libby, who's still talking, swinging her

ponytail even faster. Nobody could accuse her of being on the wrong side—I'm the one who's technically supporting a bad guy, or whatever. But still, it makes you wonder. All her tenacious philanthropy—not to mention her predilection for threatening me if I don't want to do something as superficial as attend a meeting for a made-up club with no purpose. Regardless of how Christian Libby is, I probably shouldn't rule her out as a suspect.

I pluck Ruth's journal from my utility belt and flip to an empty page, groping for a pen.

Libby Quinn = sociopath?
Reasons:
I know she has some kind of serious learning disability but she really seems to have it out for Colt.
Grief gawker. Made up a fake group thinking it would get her into college and pretends to be Ruth's friend even though she wasn't. I was.
She basically just threatened me (scary!) and she's really strong.

I mean, Libby's probably not tough enough to drag a body, but I'm not a scientist so I can't say for sure. And as long as she's leading the charge against Colt, I'll have to keep an eye on her.

First things first, though: I've got to talk to Mrs. Klitch, get her testimony on tape, and find out who told everybody I went to see her in the first place.

BEAR SPRAY

After school, I text Dom.

To: Dom (Mobile):
Hanging out with some girls, home 4 dinner

The excuse comes out of nowhere and I realize I'll probably be lying to him a lot from now on. I'm pretty sneaky now. Like an actual fox. Today at lunch I even made an appointment to meet with Jim Steele.

"To discuss legal matters," I told his secretary. As far as I know, Ruth might have just been one more animal for him to stuff. At the very least, I feel like someone should confront him about their sex relationship and see how he responds. Better yet, I'm going to get the whole thing on tape.

"Okay, honey," the secretary said. "How about we have you come after school tomorrow?"

"I'm in tons of trouble with the law," I explained.

"That's just fine," she said.

When the bell rings I go to my locker and call Ralph, thinking we can talk before I head to Mrs. Klitch's.

"Hello?" He's slurping something. Cocoa, probably.

"Ralph?" I'm suddenly worried about offending him. "Hey! I thought you were doing your one-hundred-thirty-five hour marathon."

"One hundred thirty-six."

I fiddle with my combination. "What?"

"The world record is one hundred thirty-five, so I would have to play another whole hour to beat it in any memorable way." He gulps some more cocoa. "Anyway I decided against it. Maybe I'll try again this summer when I'm not so busy."

I lug out my backpack. "Right." Probably someone saw me there, or Mrs. Klitch called—but still I've got to ask. "So I know this is probably totally ridiculous, but did you, like . . . email Libby and tell her I'd gone to Mrs. Klitch's? I got this weird confrontation smackdown thing today and—"

"Yeah, I did that." He says it like this is completely normal.

"What?" I can't believe it. "Why?"

"Oh. Well, currently I am setting up the website for her RFFB thing—you know, the blond girl with the orange face?"

"Libby," I correct him. "Libby Quinn—and it's self-tanner."

"Leaving the house that day of the protest was hard for me so I told them that from now on I'd be fulfilling the rest of my duties from home. I'm the webmaster. Did you know we already have over one hundred fifty contacts on the email list?"

I swallow. "Yeah, no offense but that doesn't explain your tattling on me to a bunch of people I go to school with—I mean, you don't even know them."

"Kippy." He takes another slurpy sip. "How could I *not* have told them? The more I thought about what you had said, the more I thought it was something that our town should know—and the RFFB mailing list is the only way I have of getting in touch with that many people."

"I don't get it."

"It was about making sure people were informed. Technically I think it's all pishposh and that you're going through the motions of a grief debacle, but I thought to myself, 'Ralph, someone else out there might agree with her, and it's best to let them decide.' I thought maybe it might garner you some support."

I take a deep breath. The thing about Ralph is that he thinks everyone's as nonjudgmental as he is. Anyone who got that email is going to think I'm a total freak—and I know Ralph didn't know that would happen, but still. If he weren't such a good guy I'd be pretty mad at him right now.

"Are you mad at me?" he asks.

"No," I blurt. "You were . . . you were just trying to help." I slam the locker.

"Want to come over?"

"I'm staying after school. I actually gotta go."

"Okay. The door's unlocked and I ordered more hot chocolate off the internet if you change your mind."

I decide to leave my car in the parking lot because the sun's out, and I've got Ralph's bear spray on the off chance the killer decides to strike in daylight. Plus, walking to Fang Road will give me some time to think about what I have to say to Mrs. Klitch. I mean, I know she'll let me in to talk—she basically begged me to join her last time—but the question is whether she'll be too drunk to speak coherently. If I can just get her to lay off the Beast and practice her version of things a little, then maybe I could take her back to the courthouse and get the police to listen to her one more time. Or else we could make a YouTube video and get news programs interested in how the case is being "mishandled." That would really blow things out of the water.

I pull the back of my hat down so it meets my scarf and buckle my backpack straps in front so that they don't slide off my shoulders. Most of the trees on Fang Road are going bald, which means that soon it'll start dumping snow. It's slightly warmer than it was yesterday, seasonable enough for wool socks and a down coat, but Mrs. Klitch isn't outside this time. Her gate is closed and her tiny pink car is outside next to one of the cement dragons, so I know she's home. I smack the bell but nothing happens. So I reach up and smack it again.

"Hello!" I call.

The kitchen light is on, and I edge along the fence, taking out the bear spray just in case someone lunges from the bushes.

That's when I see someone standing on the kitchen table and recognize Mrs. Klitch's snow boots. At first I think she's standing up there dancing in tiny circles. But then I realize her feet aren't touching the tabletop at all. Her hands are hanging down by her sides and she's spinning very slowly. I tighten my grip on the bear spray and my world explodes in orange smoke.

"It's obviously a suicide," a voice says. "Nobody could have gotten through all of this security. More barbed wire than a prison. This woman was a true weirdo and that's part of why she hanged herself—oh look, our new hoodlum is snapping out of it."

I blink a few times and realize Sheriff Staake is talking about me. My back is drenched with sweat and I can barely see. Everything's so fuzzy. "How did you even get here so quickly?" I hear myself ask. Someone is pressing an ice pack against my forehead. "Hold this," they say. "It'll help with the swelling."

"What were you doing hanging around here in the first place?" Staake shouts back. "With bear spray to boot— and for your information we got an anonymous tip that some girl with white-blond hair was wandering around town with Ursidae gas. We put two and two together pretty quick and put a patrol on you. Followed you all the way from the high school." His face is blurry and his voice sounds far away, but if I tilt my face toward the sky, I can tell he's looking at me. "Where'd you even get that kind of weapon, I'd like to know?"

"Um." I don't want to get Ralph in trouble. "We had it laying around, I guess, like most people." Who would have seen me with it? "You never know with bears."

Staake sighs. "You look like crap, Bushman."

I start pointing to the mailbox, where the bullet holes should be. But as the world comes into focus I realize it's gone. There's just a wooden post with nothing on it.

Someone took the frigging mailbox. "Whoa."

Sheriff Staake tilts his head at me. *"Hello?"* He grumbles something underneath his breath. "Hey you, ambulance driver lady, get her a blanket. The kid's stupid from shock and looks like an Oompa Loompa." He snaps his finger and someone puts a blanket around my shoulders. A radio crackles somewhere. "Patrol units, lost dog on Elm Street. Repeat." Staake sighs and shuffles toward the noise. "Duty calls."

"You know, Bushman," he says over his shoulder. "My daughter's on RFFB, and I heard about that little email notification. I'd suggest you keep your nose where it belongs—last warning."

"Was Libby the one who saw me with the gas?" I clench my teeth—she's such a nosy jerk, and I wasn't exactly careful about hiding it—but right away my mind wanders: What if this is a double homicide? So many people probably read Ralph's email. The killer would have known that Mrs. Klitch could clear Colt's name and probably came lickety-split to wipe her out. "Hey Sheriff Staake, you should check the autopsy and make sure she actually killed herself. Ruth got hanged, too, you know— we could have a serial—"

"Oh, get off my butt about it," Staake snaps.

"Seriously?" There's a light in my eyes and the

ambulance driver takes me by the chin, peering at me from the other end of a flashlight. My whole face feels like it's sunburned shut.

"Who knew this spray stuff came out so orange," she says kindly. "Now where's your cell phone, missy? It's time we better call you a ride, don'tcha know."

Yeah, because there's a riled-up murderer on the loose. I root around in my back pocket for my cell and hand it to her.

"What's the name I'm looking for?" she asks.

There's only one person who I know for sure will believe me. "It's under Davey," I say.

MOUSE HOUSES

Davey arrives in less than ten minutes. Friendship is pretty small, but I'm pretty sure that getting across it that fast is some kind of record.

The whole thing is sort of a blur. I know that when Davey shows up, he puts his arm around me and he doesn't stare at my orange, inflamed face like I thought he might. He talks to the ambulance driver, then Staake, and by the end of it Staake sounds less stuffy. Then Davey leads me to his car and buckles me into his passenger seat. After that, things slow down and settle into focus. As we drive away I tell him everything: about school, and the armbands; how Ralph posted my business to the whole world; my conversations with Sheriff Staake and Mrs. Klitch.

"I think something bad happened to her," I say, holding

an ice pack over my eyes. "The autopsy report is coming back in a week—not that Sheriff Staake will want to tell me anything specific. But I'm going to follow up." I tell him about the missing mailbox. "Do you think Libby Quinn would have had time after school to get there before me—like in a car?" I suddenly imagine her snarling and wrestling the mailbox off the post. "I mean, she was angry about Ralph's email. Also, she gripped my arm in the hallway and she is incredibly brawny."

"No offense, but I don't think a girl could have tackled either of these jobs. Physically overpowering someone is hard work."

"How do you know? Oh right. Anyway." I explain that whoever killed Ruth might have easily seen or heard about Ralph's email. They discovered this loose thread, this possible tattler, and got to Mrs. Klitch before I could. There were ways, probably, to make it look like a suicide.

Davey tells me to slow down, breathe. But he doesn't question any of it—which feels new, and like such a relief I might cry. "Why didn't you tell me you figured all this out?" he asks. "You should have called me right away, you know."

I shrug. "It sounded crazy."

"But I believe you," Davey insists.

"The thing is there's nobody to help—the police are

basically stalking me—and the whole town is starting to feel weird and creepy."

"I'm not going to let anything happen to you."

I can barely hear him, his voice sounds so far away. Outside, the sun is setting in the trees. "So we're doing this," I whisper.

"I guess," he says.

"A real investigation." I feel for the vanity mirror on the sun visor and stare at myself. My eyes and nose are all swollen and sunburned-looking from the bear spray, and there's still some orange in my hair. The ice pack starts to leak on my lap.

I hear him take a deep breath beside me. "Hey, remember when you and Ruth used to make forts when you were like eight? You'd pull apart the whole couch for cushions and all the blankets would be missing from our beds. What did you call them?"

I smile. "Mouse Houses."

"Right. You were hilarious. I'd come in and knock them over with you guys in them and you would scream and scream."

"The sneaking up part was the best."

"You guys were inseparable. My parents used to think maybe it was unhealthy, how you couldn't be apart."

"I know." It's been hard to remember in the midst of all this but it's true—how before she started dating boys and had so many secrets, Ruth and I were pretty much attached at the hip. I mean, even as recently as last year we'd literally link ankles while doing homework at the kitchen table. Then Colt decided he'd hooked up with everyone else worth doing and sauntered over to us in the hallway. "What's your name again?" Colt asked. And after that it was all Colt this and Colt that, and *get off my nuts*, and *why haven't you had sex yet, Kippy?* Even though a few months earlier we had both been virgins.

"Hey . . . quick question," Davey says. "This sounds so gutless." He licks his lips. "Fuck it, listen, how soon does this get easier? Like how long does it take?"

"Dude, I've never done a murder investigation before." He doesn't say anything and my heart starts racing. "Wait, you mean with Ruth? Are you asking me about grief?"

He still doesn't say anything, and part of me feels like I shouldn't have said Ruth's name. Like we can only talk about her so much. "Shoot, Davey, I don't know. Just because my mom died doesn't mean I'm some kind of expert. I mean, you were the one in the war, right? People died over there, too, didn't they?"

"Ouch."

"Well, you're the one who said so and I'm sorry but it's not like I'm some kind of professional survivor or something." I turn away to hide my blush, which he probably can't even see behind my orange face.

"Listen, I'm sorry," Davey says. "It's just that, with war, you go into it knowing that sort of thing is going to happen so you're sort of braced for it and . . . I mean it sucks but . . . Anyway I just thought maybe you could give me some insight into the timetable, or—"

"Draw from your own frigging experiences," I blurt and cover my face with the ice pack. I have no right to be mad at Davey. He basically just came and rescued me, and also I'm never this testy with people I don't know—I was never even sassy with Ruth, really. In our animal rapport, I always played beta dog. It's just that I hate talking about Mom, I guess—like ever, basically. At least to anyone but Dom. Because when he and I say stuff about her, it's stuff like, "Hey Dom, remember that time that Mom caught you shaving your shoulders in the bathroom?" Or, "Remember when Mom chased raccoons off the porch with a spatula?" Like she's gone on vacation and we're just passing the time. With anyone else, it comes off sounding like a book report. Like she was never real and I'm just making stuff up and trying to get a good grade.

Luckily, my eyes are too dry from the bear spray to make any tears.

"I said I'm sorry," Davey pleads.

"It's fine, it's not your fault. Don't be sorry, okay?" I don't want to look at him because now I'm embarrassed about my face again. So I grope blindly for his shoulder in order to pat it reassuringly. "I just don't know what to say, that's all."

If I were honest, I'd say it only sort of gets better. That there's always this part of you that got carved out. It's a physical thing, I swear to God, and it's the part that swells right before you cry. Eventually you stop hoping and start to fill it up with memories.

"It'd probably really help, actually, if you could tell me about those people you knew in Afghanistan," I offer, trying to change the subject. "I mean the guys who got all violent, or whatever, and creeped you out." I reach for my pen. "Maybe it'd help us think of suspicious people around here?"

"Shit, I don't know," Davey says quietly. "I have trouble remembering that stuff. It gets lost in the noise."

I slap him in the arm with my ice pack.

"Ow!"

"You said you had all this experience, which made you some kind of expert," I snap. "And you said that's why you knew Colt didn't do it—and also just now you said Libby couldn't have done it because—"

"Okay, fine! Geez, Kippy—did you ever think maybe I just don't want to talk about it?"

"Under any other circumstance I would be respectful

of your psychological triggers, but we've got a killer to find." I tap the pen on my leg. "So what are they like, these wacko murderer types?"

"I don't know . . . Hyper. Angry. Sort of thrilled by the sight of their own blood . . . Wait." Davey gapes at me. "Is that . . . are you wearing a special belt for notebooks?"

"Eyes on the road—anyway I still think we should investigate Libby."

"Well, sure, that girl's awful." Davey raises his eyebrows. "But like I said, I'm not sure a girl could do what was done to my sister."

"Hm." I think about Libby's strong grip in the hallway—and the way I saw her hoist another girl onto her shoulders with such ease at last month's pep rally. I want to tell Davey this is no time to be sexist—but he gets there first.

"I'm not being sexist," he says. "If you want me to extrapolate from my experiences, I'll tell you right now that a girl didn't do this shit." It's quiet for a second. "So where's your car?"

"School . . . but—"

"Do you want to drive some more before I take you to it?"

"Yes."

We don't say anything—just drive around making

unnecessary turns. I watch the digital clock on the dash. "I told Dom I'd be home for dinner," I say finally. "Twenty minutes."

"Gotcha." Davey veers right, heading back toward school. "What are you going to tell him about your face?"

"Um." I slap down the vanity mirror again. "I have no idea. Maybe that I went tanning? Girls do that, right?"

"I don't know. It's not that bad. It looks fine, sort of."

"I'll just tell him I was crying. He'll like that." I scrub my face with the ice pack, trying to wipe away the orange. "He wants me to start going through the stages of grief in order, I think."

"I never cry about her," Davey announces. He pulls into the school parking lot. "Well. Except for at the memorial service, but it was, like, contagious there." He sighs. "I don't know why I said that."

"I think it's normal. Hey, listen. There's something I have to say." I stare between my feet at my backpack and tell him about the Jim Steele thing. My appointment tomorrow.

"What?" he says, like he's about to throw up. "What do you mean, 'sex relationship'?" He shakes his head. "Who says 'sex relationship'?"

"Well," I say, sounding parental. "That's what it was. I told Staake and he said she was eighteen and—"

"Jesus!" Davey starts punching the steering wheel and I pull my backpack into my lap for a hug. "He's an idiot— they're all idiots!"

"I know," I say, squeezing my own fingers.

He pulls up alongside Rhonda and parks, slapping the wheel one more time. "I'll go with you tomorrow but I've got to wait in the car or else I'll kill the guy. I will fucking kill him."

"You're coming?" I fiddle with one of the zippers on the backpack.

"Isn't that what I just said?"

"Really?"

"You're not going alone!" He looks legitimately pissed. "I already said I'd protect you and that's what this is, okay?" He crosses his arms. "Besides, I've got a certain amount of expertise when it comes to stakeouts. You should know that about me. You'll need a wingman."

I shrug, trying to look laid back about the fact that he's just agreed to be my sidekick. I don't have to be alone. "Okay, I'll pick you up after school." I prod my utility belt, wondering how to say good-bye. Do we hug? "So do you think this is really dorky?" I jiggle the belt.

Davey glances at my waist, then stares at me, looking stern. "Preparedness is never uncool."

I want to throw my arms around him, but instead I

reach out for a handshake—totally forgetting that he's got the bandage. "Oh." I wave instead and duck out of the car, hitting the back of my head on the way out. "See you soon, okay? I mean, I will, because we already planned on it. 'Kay, bye!"

BATS AND SNAKES

"Oh my God! Hey!" Jim Steele's secretary lets me in the side door of Jim Steele's four-story Victorian. It's surrounded by giant, animal-shaped bushes. Everyone called Mrs. Klitch a witch for her sculptures, but for some reason no one makes fun of Jim Steele. What would you even call him—a wizard?

"Sorry, but Uncle Jimmy doesn't like clients coming in the front for some reason," she says. She smiles. I recognize her from school. I'm pretty sure she graduated two years ago and used to be on the cheerleading squad.

"That's okay," I tell her.

"So, wow," she says. "You're, like, that dead girl's friend, right? What was she really like? Never mind, don't tell me, it's probably better in my head." She leans against the doorframe. "Isn't this a sweet job, by the way?

Jealous, right? Like, I barely just graduated and already I've got a profession—in this economy? Please." She flips her brown, curly hair over one shoulder. I never noticed it before, but she kind of looks like Ruth. I wonder if that's why Jim Steele hired her.

We stare at each other for a second. "Come with me," she says, waving me through the door into a tiny vestibule. The office is nothing like I imagined it; in the corner there's an actual child's desk, the kind with a flip top.

She plops down on the tiny chair. "You can go ahead. His office is right over there."

I look down the long hall, which leads to the front door, and wonder how many times he brought Ruth here, to his office. It's probably one of the tallest buildings in Friendship, come to think about it—the kind of place that most business owners would split up into multiple offices and rent out. Did Jim Steele get off on telling Ruth he owned the whole building and only used a quarter of it? I wonder if she came in the side door instead of the front, like clients, so people wouldn't notice. I wonder if that ever made her feel ashamed.

I got an email this morning from her mom:

Dear Kippy,
How are things going with the journal? I know

the handwriting is difficult (she gets it from her
father). I was wondering if you could send the
redacted version to me here in Canada so I can
use it in my therapy sessions. If not, no worries.
Sincerely, Mrs. F

She wrote "gets" instead of "got," like Ruth is still alive.
In my head I sort of do the same thing sometimes—refer-
ring to Colt as her ex-boyfriend, like maybe she broke up
with him instead of died.

Dear Mrs. Fried,
I am not ready yet.
Love, Kippy

There are taxidermied animals all around his office:
pheasants and foxes wearing sunglasses, a deer lying on its
side in a sexy pose, propping up its head with its hoof. Jim
Steele is sitting behind a big, shiny red desk. He's tapping
his fingertips together, which is kind of gross, actually,
because he's got these superlong fingernails shaped like
guitar picks. I try staring at the giant dream catcher on
the wall behind him.

"Welcome, young cub!" he booms, gesturing for me
to sit. He's got bright-blue eyes above a salt-and-pepper

mustache. "I hear you've gotten into a bit of trouble—what was it, trespassing, loitering, public urination? In any case, you've come in need of Big Bad Uncle Jimmy's legal advice. Please, sit." All of a sudden I picture him and Ruth making out. Him chomping on her face with his furry mouth. "Ms. Bushman, are you ill?"

"So basically I'm doing this yearbook page for my best friend Ruth Fried and was wondering if I could get a quote from you," I blurt.

He taps his fingernails together. "Essentially, you came here under false pretenses."

"Well—"

"Do you know how much my time costs?"

"No." *But I know you knew my friend.* He glances away and I turn on my Dictaphone.

He smirks. "In New York, I would charge seven hundred twenty-five dollars per hour to deal with your bullshit."

"Your secretary didn't say anything—"

"In Friendship the first visit is free, otherwise no one in this godforsaken town would show up," he snaps, frowning.

"So then after that is it seven hundred twenty-five dollars an hour?" I ask, curious. "I just don't see people around here paying that—it's as much as a four-wheeler—"

"I said New York, for God's sake—what is the point of this?" He bangs his fist on the table, and I jump. He's got some anger issues.

"So—" I glance at my belt to make sure the Dictaphone is really on. It is. He's on the record now. I'm pretty sure if Diane Sawyer were here, she'd say, *Kippy Bushman, you are an actual genius with incredibly smooth moves.*

I smile. "You're a pretty important man, huh?" Davey and I practiced with the Dictaphone before coming over and you could hear stuff really clearly even when one of us was speaking softly. "An important man with tons of fancy money, am I right?" Best to start with compliments. Loosen him up.

"I'm a great man." He smirks again. "Many people think this means that I should be like Jesus and welcome every visitor with open arms—that I should sit and listen patiently to every question about every bullshit subject in the universe." His yellowing fingernails click against the red enamel. "Are you in trouble or not, Bushman? I only want to talk to you if you're damaged in some way and can pay me—does that make sense? This is not a Girl Scout welcoming center. I do not want your cookies."

"Um." I'm pretty sure that these metaphors are nonsense and Jim Steele is a crazy person, but I try to keep him talking. "I've been trespassing a little."

His face softens. "Did you bring cash for a retainer? How much is the fine? My secretary tells me everyone you've ever loved has died—forgive me, but high school gossip can be beneficial." He gestures at the reclining deer. "I like to think nothing ever really dies. But there is no better weapon than tears, Ms. Bushman. You'll end up paying me more than the fines to get a clean record, but it'll be worth it for things like college applications—does that make sense?" He smiles at me.

I wriggle in my seat, suddenly very uncomfortable, and try to stick to the script. "By trespassing I mean I know about you and Ruth. I want to get a nice quote from you about her for the yearbook or else I'll tell everyone about the . . . sex things you had together." I can feel my face getting red.

I expect him to slam his fist on the table, or at least to clear his throat, but instead he busts out laughing. "Oh, you little bitch," he says.

I reach into my bag and grab Ruth's diary, which I put on my lap. "I have proof right here, in Ruth's journal."

"Give me that." He folds his hands together on top of his desk, waiting for me to pass over the diary. His eyes are hard and cold, like a stuffed animal's. The irises are huge. "What do you want from me, money?"

I touch the Dictaphone. "So you admit it? And now

you're trying to bribe me so no one finds out?"

He wheels his chair a few steps over and pushes the office door shut. "How much money is it going to take, sweetheart?"

I sort of want to see how much money he would actually give me, but I'm on record, too, and it's best to sound squeaky clean. Last night I did a bunch of Googling, researching investigative tools and strategies. I'm starting to think I could be more than a journalist even. Like maybe I could out–Diane Sawyer Diane Sawyer. "That's not what I'm after," I snap. I riffle through the journal to the dog-eared pages that mention his name. "Here, look."

Jim Steele yanks the diary from my fingers, looking tense. He plucks reading glasses out of his shirt pocket and unfolds them with one shake. "Hm." He gazes intently at the entry, then grins. "Are you kidding me with this?" He removes his spectacles. "I can't even tell what language this is in. It's illegible." He stands and goes to the window, dropping the diary in my lap as he walks by. "I know the law, Ms. Bushman—and this diary doesn't mean shit." He starts pacing, chuckling under his breath. "Ruth was eighteen. She could make her own decisions. Not that anything happened." He stops pacing and glances at me. "Now get out before I call the police."

I can feel sweat slip down my biceps. Time to bluff.

"Quick question: How does it make you feel that I've got proof you weren't just sexing with her but you killed her, too?"

He charges toward me, and when he reaches down into my lap I scream, thinking he's going to rape me or something. That's when I see him grab the Dictaphone and smash it in one fell swoop against the desk.

"There we go," he says, shaking pieces of plastic off his bright red palm. "I don't need that chicken-scratch diary because it's inadmissible—and I'm offended, I'm deeply offended that you would accuse me of something so craven." His eyes are red. "Ruth . . . I . . . it's none of your business." He clears his throat, smooths his tie, and crosses to the door. "Time to leave now, I think, little bear. Our time together is past."

He's opening the door for me to leave—and I want to, believe me. But I'm stuck here in my chair. Nobody's ever gotten violent like that with me before and I can barely move. I look up to see him gesturing for my exit and manage to rise shakily to my feet.

"You came here without any trouble, Ms. Bushman." I can see the muscles tighten underneath his beard as he smiles. "But it seems you will be in trouble soon, very soon, if you are not more careful."

The door slams in a flash.

．　．　．

As I approach the secretary in the back corridor, I force a smile and shove my hands, which are still trembling, deep into my pockets. "What's Jim's schedule like?" I ask quietly, trying to sound pleasant. "He said to ask you about another appointment. Sorry about the loud noise."

"Oh, he's always slamming his door—so, today's Thursday." She thumbs through a planner. "Generally any time after school works . . . except for all day tomorrow." She nods. "Yeah, Friday is Jim's day with his nieces and nephews, and also he goes to the gym, and he also does other things, so, like, he's not here at all tomorrow, apparently."

"Thanks," I say, moving toward the door.

"Wait, you don't want to make an appointment?"

"I changed my mind," I tell her.

Outside, across the street, Davey is sitting in Rhonda's passenger seat with the window rolled down, using the binoculars I brought along.

"He basically threatened me," I blurt. My hands are still shaking. "Tomorrow I can break in through one of the rear windows."

"Wait, what?" Davey leans out the window. "What do you mean he threatened you?" He peers over my shoulder with a menacing look. "I'm going in."

"No," I tell him, remembering Libby and the recycling bin—not to mention Jim Steele saying he'd call the police, with whom I've already got a pretty unstable relationship, let's be serious. "It's fine, I mean, the guy just plays hardball." I take a deep, uneven breath. "I didn't get any actual evidence that he did anything. Honestly, I don't even know what I'm looking for, really. Which is why we've got to come back tomorrow when he's not here."

Davey gestures at my waist. "Can I listen to the recorder?"

I finger my utility belt. "Not right now," I say, and pull the hem of my sweater over the empty spot. If Davey knew about Jim smashing the Dictaphone, there's a chance he might throw himself through Jim Steele's office window and strangle him. "But I might have to run some things by you as far as, like, murderer behavior." I rack my brain for anything concrete. "What about long fingernails—like extremely, disgustingly long?" I'm kicking myself because I can't remember much besides those fingernails and the sight of Uncle Jimmy destroying my Dictaphone. "Does that remind you of the killers you knew?"

"Soldiers," he snaps.

"But do you see similarities?"

He flops back into the passenger seat. "Listen, I know I had some opinions early on. But I just don't know if I can go there, okay?" He looks pale, angry.

I walk around the van and climb into the driver's seat, waiting for Davey to yell at me—he looks so mad. But instead he reaches over and ruffles my hair. "We'll get better at this," he says. "You photocopied the journal, right?"

"Yeah, of course. I know what I'm doing," I respond, wanting him to touch my head again. "So, tomorrow I'll skip school and we can break in while Uncle Jimmy is off with his nieces."

"You're not scared at all, are you?" he says. "This is like a fantasy for you."

I bite my lip. "No, it's real," I say. "It's perhaps the most serious thing in my life, actually."

Davey flops his head against the headrest, and the sun falls on his face in a half circle. "For me, it's like a video game again."

I remember Ralph telling me once that army people get trained to kill by playing video games. "My neighbor says sometimes he thinks life is a video game," I blurt, suddenly missing Ralph. I never stay annoyed at him for long. "When he's playing he'll start talking like the characters." I smile.

Davey shakes his head. "I don't trust my brain sometimes."

My smile trembles and my stomach kind of lurches. "I

wish you wouldn't say that." It's not that he's got a temper, or even what Ruth said in her diary about him crying on the letters he sent her that makes me nervous. But here's Davey telling me again he can't count on himself, that he's on some kind of slippery slope, maybe. And if that's true, then maybe he'll take me down with him.

I keep opening my mouth and shutting it. I want to tell him, *You know how my mom died, right? She went crazy and I was scared of her at the end. Please don't make me scared of you.* But that's my own stuff. I already gave him some of that in the car last night on the way back from Mrs. Klitch's. So instead I blurt, "You're fine." It comes out sounding like a promise to us both.

Davey doesn't say anything.

"Listen, do you maybe want to come over for dinner?" My heart is racing. "Dom's making something called Hot Dog Jumble—I think you'll like it."

Davey nods and I tell myself that he got home from the war in time. That other people might be scarred for life, but not us. Not if I have anything to do with it.

Basically, the story is this: my mother died of brain cancer. Before she got sick, she collected wind socks and made pancakes and thought I was the funniest person in the universe. But for the last few months of her life, before she went into hospice, she was a raving lunatic. Her brain was cobwebbed with plaque and tumors. She'd see alligators in trees. Bats and snakes flew out of walls at her, and she'd scratch herself trying to get them off her face. Cutlery would turn into slugs on her plate and make her vomit. Once they brought over the hospital bed, Dom started sleeping on the living-room carpet right next to it, because he thought it made her feel better. But then one night she woke up and thought he was some kind of monster. Only by that point she couldn't articulate much at all, so we never found out if he was a hybrid jaguar-lion, or a serpent with a boar's head, or what.

"Big," she kept saying, trying to explain. "B-b-b-i-g."

She wore her delusions like a mask, and after a few weeks they were our nightmares, too. It used to be that I'd have bad dreams and she'd reassure me that none of it was real. After she got sick, I couldn't even talk to her. She was so afraid, and I found myself sneaking into the living room at night to make sure she wasn't convulsing with night terrors. Dom would lead me back to my room, but I kept trying to see her monsters out of sympathy. I imagined them living in a creepy castle surrounded by storm clouds, and visiting our house in shifts. I spun my brain creating them, squinting until bright spots formed behind my eyelids and I could carve out creatures with the stardust. I'd pretend so hard that they were real—mostly to pretend she wasn't crazy, which she was. I tried so hard to convince her she was sane that I sort of went crazy, too.

After she got moved to hospice, Dom dragged the sleeping bag back upstairs, and I slept in it on the floor next to their bed, which was now his bed. The beasts I'd created all retracted their claws. Their fangs fell out and their eyes dimmed. I started making cribs for the imaginary creatures out of towels and putting them to sleep at night. In my mind, they were dying with her. And after a few more months, we got the phone call that she'd stopped breathing, and they were gone entirely. But I guess I still have this fear that you can catch invisible things from other people. That someone else's insanity can creep under your skin and fry your brain.

SHELTERED

Having people over has always been kind of an issue because of Dom. There's always the chance that you'll come in after school and he'll be wafting incense into his face at the kitchen counter while watching the Oprah Winfrey Network, or doing half-naked yoga on the floor in the family room. Ruth was used to him and she was about as far as I got in terms of after-school playdates. Only I'm pretty sure you don't call them playdates once you're sixteen. Plus, I've never had a boy over.

I remember once saying goodnight to Dom when I was like eight, and asking him if he thought this boy Steven Daniels liked me back. Dom didn't know anything about Steven—it was the first thing I'd ever said about him— but I was young enough that I still thought Dom shared all my thoughts, that he and I had some kind of ESP that only went one way.

And of course Dom acted like he had all the information. He said of course the guy probably *adored* me, how couldn't he? I was wonderful. It didn't seem like a true kind of answer because it wasn't based on anything real. It meant Dom liked me, not the boy, and Dom had to because he was my dad.

"But how do you make a boy like you for real?" I pleaded. "I mean, what do you do to make it happen fast?"

I was hoping for some kind of ritual—a magic séance or a trick I could play to get what I wanted. Dom just smiled at me and promised that it would happen someday, when it was meant to, and without any effort on my part.

"I'll have to be a different kind of dad then," he added, seeming sad. "You won't like me as much."

When I open the front door I try to be really loud so Dom'll know I'm not the only one here. *"Hello?"* This is starting to feel like a big mistake for a lot of reasons. Once I came home from school and Dom was literally in his bathrobe, pretending to ballroom dance with dead Mother Peanut Butter because he knew I was coming and wanted to make me laugh. Also I'm starting to wonder if Dom is going to get genuinely riled up about a boy being over, especially since he was already a little weird about me hanging out with Davey. And, like, maybe I should have considered that before I made it seem to Davey like my dad was all laid back and totally normal and made great Jumble, or whatever.

Davey shuffles in behind me. "Hello?" he calls, mimicking me—and I elbow him in the ribs to be quiet. In the other room I can hear Ralph's video game beeping.

I glance up at Davey. "Just so you know, my neighbor Ralph Johnston is over and he's pretty much my second best friend. He was a few years above you in high school. He's great."

Davey shrugs. "Cool."

"Kippy, is that you? Welcome home!" Ralph calls. "My MMO buddy, Daugon, is sick or something. Do you want to be my second player?"

"Daugon?" Davey asks.

I smile way too big. "Oh, it's one of his online role-playing games," I whisper. "I hardly ever play." I just remembered Mother Peanut Butter's on her favorite chair and I definitely need to hide her before Davey sees and thinks we collect dead things. "Um, Davey, why don't you go way over there real quick to the refrigerator and get yourself a glass of milk or something—"

"Kippy?" Ralph calls. "Are you coming, because I'm sort of raring to go—is that all right?"

"Ralph, I'm kind of busy now because I have a guest!"

"Oh, I'm sorry—hello, guest!" More beeping. "No worries—I'll get in touch with Alagos, then. Or Goat-fist27."

I glance at Davey, searching his face for signs that I might be a weirdo.

"It's cool that you're friends with your neighbor—I don't know any of mine." He smiles. "I'll pass on the milk, by the way, but where's the bathroom?"

Good, I think—Davey's being in the bathroom will give me some time to find Dom and prep him and make sure things are normal.

"Is that my Pimple?" Dom calls down the stairwell.

"Go!" I hiss at Davey and shove him toward the bathroom. It's just in time because right then Dom comes down the stairs wearing only his bathrobe, with a towel wrapped around his head like how ladies do.

"Dom, you have to put some clothes on," I say quickly. "I have a guest and you can't be naked."

"Oh!" Dom mouths, and steps backward up the stairs. "Who's here? One of the girls you were hanging out with yesterday?"

"No, um. One sec." I run into the living room, leaping over Ralph's prostrate form to grab Mother Peanut Butter. "Who's here?" Ralph asks as I hop back across him.

"Listen, we have to be normal, okay?" I tell him. "I have a boy over."

"Miss Popular!" he calls after me admiringly.

I slide across the hardwood floor in my socks and thrust dead Mother Peanut Butter into Dom's arms. "Here," I say. "Put this—her—somewhere. And go upstairs and put on some normal clothes." Dom has mostly all normal clothes but for some reason I'm not sure he'll know what this means, so I tell him, "Your dark khakis and that gray sweater with either your brown shoes or your reddish penny loafers."

"Very fancy," Dom whispers, and makes his eyebrows dance. "Who's the boy?"

So he heard me. Not like I was going to be able to hide it for long anyway. "Davey."

Dom's smile fades. "Kippy."

"Dom, please be cool, please," I beg. "I never ask you for anything." I make my eyebrows dance, too, trying to make him smile again. "Please?"

He turns around without answering and retreats up the stairs.

"So Davey!" Dom is frying hot dogs in mayonnaise and butter, breaking up white bread into a bowl with his free hand. "Long time no see! When do your folks get back? Kippy never told me they were gone or that you'd been unchaperoned this whole time, including when she went to visit you." He glares at me.

Davey shrugs. "I'm actually not sure when they're getting back, sir."

Dom forces a smile. "We're all friends here. You can call me Mr. Bushman." He fluffs his apron—one of Mom's old frilly ones. "So you're in special ops—when do you go back, if you don't mind my asking?"

I roll my eyes. What a stupid question. Davey's knee is bouncing a million miles per hour. I almost wish Ralph would come in from the other room so we could talk about video games or computers or whatever.

"Never, sir—I mean, Mr. Bushman," Davey says. He raises his bad hand. "Not really going back at all."

Dom smiles. "I was just wondering because we would have gladly driven you to the airport."

"Dom!" I roll my eyes again.

"What? I'm just telling him that we're here to help." Dom stares at Davey. "You look swell, kiddo."

Swell? Kiddo? I have to stop myself from groaning. Dom should have said, "You look good." Or else nothing at all.

"Ork?" Ralph shouts. "More like dork!"

"You look . . . swell, too," Davey says. He's paging through some pamphlets on the counter. "So, uh, are these from your work?"

Dom beams, looking genuinely friendly. Finally. "Yes,

sirree. Area support groups. Good stuff. People coming together helping people."

I reach over and grab a couple from Davey. *Alcoholics Anonymous. Unemployed (and Unashamed). STDS ARE NOT A CURSE!*

Then I see an old, familiar pamphlet—*Non-Violent Communication Group (NVCG): Learn How to Speak Giraffe*—and turn bright red. NVCG was my support group after Mom died—back when I was so convinced everyone was going to die that I kept accidentally hurting people. I'd hold on too tight or forget not to use my nails when I hugged. Throw myself at people. Knock them down. It was a complicated mental process that Dom has since explained to me.

"Did you really have to have these on the counter right now?" I ask.

"Gold!" Ralph cackles in the other room. "You can keep your crystal, Mr. Goatfist, because I've got buckets and buckets of gold."

Miss Rosa, the NVCG group leader, must be in her fifties now. When I was little, I remember thinking she looked exactly like a troll.

"What's the issue, Pickle?" Dom says, trying to barge in on my thoughts.

"Nothing." I turn the pamphlet over in my hands, recalling all the different violent personalities I met at

NVCG back when I was just a kid. It didn't seem fair that I had to go there so young. But then again Dom has always gone to extremes to ensure that I'm mentally healthy. "Just looking."

Anyway, I wasn't studying their behavior at the time, so I can't really explain what to look for in violent personalities—that's what Davey was supposed to be for. But if I really want to figure out what to look for in my investigation—what sorts of personality traits could make someone like Jim Steele more suspicious, for instance—well, I could easily go back.

Dom scrunches up his face. "Is that the NVCG one you got there?" He smiles. "Remember when you graduated from NVCG? You were the youngest one. Ralph and the Johnstons and I were so proud—Hey Ralph! Remember—"

"Dom!" I slap the pamphlet on the counter. "Are you kidding me right now?" I can feel Davey looking at me. Dom is the worst when it comes to bringing up private stuff in public. Doesn't he know that it's only funny to joke about NVCG when we're alone? When he turns his back on us I shove the pamphlet into my pocket.

"You feel free to take any one of those, Davey, okay? Any which one," Dom says to the smoking Jumble. "Things can't be easy on you right now. Anytime you need an ear—"

"I'm doing okay," Davey says. "But thank you, Mr. Bushman."

"He's fine," I snap. I'd like to tell Dom to shut up and go watch TV in his bedroom—I'll handle the hot dogs— but I don't want to look like any more of a brat in front of Davey.

"Okeydoke." Dom pours the hot-dog mix over some plates and nods at me. "And how was school today, Lovebun, any better?"

I think of today during last period, when I was mentally preparing to go to Jim Steele's and still thought I was so close to solving everything. Dom's staring at me, waiting for an answer, and I'm so eager to break the tension that I burst out in a fit of nervous laughter. "Let's just say no one was wearing armbands for Mrs. Klitch, am I right?" Even before no one else laughs, I feel a little sick for having said it.

"That poor woman," Dom says, squirting more mayonnaise on the hot dogs. "That poor, troubled soul."

After dinner, I drag Davey up to my room and slam the door. "I don't know why Dom was being that way."

"No worries." Davey shrugs. "Seriously, it was nice not eating alone." He looks around at my bedroom walls— obviously awestruck by all the pictures of Diane Sawyer

I've printed out. She's pretty awesome—let's face it. But unfortunately we don't have time right now for admiring iconoclasts.

"Hey." I snap my fingers to get his attention. "So tomorrow we're going to Jim Steele's—but after that, you know what we have to do, right?" I pull the NVCG pamphlet out of my pocket. "This is the next step in our investigation, Davey. This whole time I've been wondering how we might get inside the murderer's head—and no offense but you haven't been entirely helpful in that regard, which isn't your fault, it's just certain psychological roadblocks have gotten in the way." I nod. "And besides, you and I are after the kind that hide, and that's new to both of us." I flick the pamphlet. "So what do you think?"

Davey just stands there, scratching underneath his bandage. "You're smiling funny."

"Davey! Come on!" I start pacing back and forth in front of my bed. "We have to come up with a strategy— you know Kim Jong Il, that North Korean dictator? Apparently he always wore platform shoes because he was, like, supershort, and he wouldn't be around women who were any taller than him because he had this humongous inferiority thing, like Napoleon, which meant Diane Sawyer couldn't interview him, even though she really wanted to, because did you know she's really tall? Like a beautiful giant. But she found a way around it—I mean, she didn't just sit around eating hot dogs—she had casts put on her legs and got rolled in on a wheelchair! That way she'd be shorter than him, get it?"

"Why are we talking about Diane Sawyer?" Davey asks impatiently.

"Exactly, we're past her—she reports on stuff, she doesn't solve it. What about Agent Scully in that one episode where they need to uncover—"

"Kippy, out with it."

I flap the pamphlet. "This is the key to our case—if we find the secretly violent, figure out their tendencies, pretend to be like them, then we find out traits of possible killers. Tomorrow Jim Steele is gone for the day so we'll sneak in there—"

"You mean break in."

"Right, and then the next day, it's the weekend, and it's straight to NVCG!"

Davey looks surprised. "You're talking about going undercover?"

"Yes! You and me are the newest addition to the underground club of self-loathing bloodthirsties."

He raises his eyebrows, teasing. "But won't they know you? At this violent club place? Your dad said you went there."

I shrug. "The instructor'll just think I've relapsed."

"You really do know a lot of psychobabble, don't you?" Davey smiles with his eyes. "What were you there for anyway?"

Oof, I think, remembering my Banzai phase. Not even Ruth knew about it, actually. I mean, she'd heard about the thing that got me sent there because everyone at school was talking about it, but I never told her that I went to the church basement twice a week for a year to attend a support group for violent people struggling to overcome their urges. It just wasn't relevant.

I kind of bite my lip and roll my head around, hoping Davey will change the subject, but he doesn't.

"I used to be a biter," I murmur. "Um"—I start counting on my fingers—"and I jumped on people, and I hugged too hard, and—" I put my hands behind my back. "It was lots of things."

He laughs through his nose, still staring at me with his eyes all soft. "That's not so bad." He reaches out and squeezes my shoulder, and before he gets a chance to take his hand away I touch his fingers.

"You better have that bedroom door open," Dom shouts from downstairs.

Davey looks embarrassed. He clears his throat. "I should probably go."

"Don't walk home," I blurt. I don't want him to leave. And I don't want him to hustle down that stretch of highway like Ruth did. What if something happened? I could offer him my reflective safety vest but it didn't do any good the last time someone wore one. What is he trying to do, torture me?

"Geez Louise, calm down, Bushman. When did I ever say I was going to hoof it home?" He reaches out like he's going to squeeze my shoulder again, but then looks at the door and just grazes my arm. "Just give me a ride, okay?"

So I do. The ride is quiet but not in that buzzy, awkward way. I even manage to give him a parting hug without injuring either of us.

But probably the best part about saying good-bye to Davey is when he tells me, "See you tomorrow." I think the thing about being a team is that you have to be clear what your schedule is.

When I get home, Ralph is gone and Dom starts yapping my head off about open door policies and having boys upstairs. "Remember what happened with the last boy you liked?" he says, crossing and uncrossing his arms. "Well, do you?"

He means Steven Daniels. One day I crept up behind him on the blacktop and tackled him, and when he tried to get away I yanked him by his rattail until he held still, wincing, and let me kiss him. He ended up moving to Oregon and occasionally I still worry that my ritualistic rape-dance on the blacktop had something to do with it.

I kick at the carpet, feeling mortified and furious and antsy. Why did he have to bring up Steven? "I don't *like* Davey."

"My foot," Dom snaps.

It doesn't feel fair that he's making this so embarrassing. He didn't used to be like this. I mean, Dom was the one who talked me down about Steven Daniels for cripe's sake. After the school called home about what I did on the blacktop, Dom was nice about it and even said I didn't have to try so hard—that kissing was fine and natural but I was too young—and when I was old enough it would happen on its own, and I wouldn't have to attack anybody. I took his advice and have never experienced physical contact with a boy since.

So why is he having such a heart attack and treating me like such a freak when I'm not even doing anything wrong? "It's not cool of you to try and manipulate my insecurities," I shout. Dom gives me a stern look and I groan. "Is this because I brought him upstairs where the beds are? It's called being friends, okay?"

Dom rolls his eyes. "Why else would he come over

and eat hot dogs with you if he didn't have amorous intentions? Tell me that."

"Because we're hanging out, that's all!" I shrug. "I remind him of her. I remind everyone of her." My eyes feel hot. I hadn't thought about it until I said it, but now I know it's probably true—maybe the only reason Davey wants anything to do with me is because he misses Ruth.

"Kippy . . ." Dom opens and closes his mouth a couple of times. "I'm worried about you. There, I said it."

"Oh, like you haven't said it a million times already in all sorts of ways. Geez Louise."

Dom wags his finger at me. "You know, Ralph feels the same way. He told me so before he left—and he doesn't trust this Davey, no sir. We care about you, Kippy. I wish you'd talk to me—"

"What do you even know about grieving properly? You're the one who went into your room after your wife died and couldn't even take care of your own daughter."

Dom looks disgusted. "It's not like you to be mean."

"Mean?" I throw my hands up. "Everyone else is mean, okay? Not me. I'm just some nice girl trying to be nice."

He crosses his arms. "There's a point here, and it's that Davey is a lot older, Kippy Bushman—twenty-one, that's a *lot*." His face is splotchy and I can see sweat on his upper lip.

"Oh calm down—Ralph's even a little older than that, and you're, like, sixty." Now I'm just listing ages.

"I'm forty-nine!"

"Whatever!"

"Don't you get snippy with me, missy, I'll tell you right now." He wipes his forehead. "I don't like it—any of it—yesterday you come home with a fully orange face and no explanation—no sir. Am I mad right now? You betcha."

I roll my eyes. "I already told you the stuff on my face was paint from making posters."

"Bull crap!" Dom explodes about Davey's parents being out of town and my having a car and not enough monitoring, and how he doesn't trust me, and even though he's screaming and it should be emotional or something, I'm not really listening. He goes on and on, and then all of a sudden his face trembles and he looks pale and deflated. The only other time I saw him like this was after Mom's funeral when Mr. and Mrs. Johnston used to come over to drag him out of his room.

"I don't know how to handle this stage in your life," he says. "I haven't even ordered the right books yet." His lips tremble. "I keep wishing your mother were here—"

"I wish she were here too," I snap. "I'm sick of it just being you and me."

LOOK OUT

The next morning I want to get an early start. So instead of driving to school, I pick up Davey and have him phone Principal Hannycack's office, pretending to be my dad.

"She's sick," Davey says in a lower-than-usual voice. I mime explosive vomiting from the driver's seat and gesture that it might be coming out the other end as well. "Lots of barfing and shitting," he adds. "I mean, diarrhea. Yeah, it's totally gross. Thank you. Good-bye, sir." He hangs up and hands me back my phone.

I beam at him. "That was good."

He shrugs. "What if your dad finds out? I want him to like me."

"Forget him," I snap, remembering last night. "Plus, it's unavoidable. Plus, I've never missed school before or been irresponsible, like, ever, so it's not like Hannycack will call him. Plus, we're close to answers, I can feel it." I start the van.

Davey cocks an eyebrow at me. "You're getting bossy."

My stomach burns because Ruth used to say that all the time when we were kids. "Sorry."

He makes a face like *whatever* and taps my arm gently with his knuckles. "No, it's fine," he says. "I like it."

Davey waits in Rhonda while I slink around the back of Jim Steele's building. I've got my cell phone on vibrate in my utility belt, and Davey's supposed to call if he sees anything. It's good to have a lookout.

Jim Steele's doors are locked, but sure enough all the back windows are cracked, to let in autumn air, I guess. You'd think Jim Steele of all people—being from big bad New York City, or whatever—would have some kind of security system. But in Friendship I'm not sure they even sell those things—I mean, Mrs. Klitch had some gnarly stuff, but she probably had to send away for it.

I shove my way between two of the rabbit-shaped bushes, yank open one of the first-floor windows, and climb through, finding myself in a bathroom. I've got to be quick in case he comes home unexpectedly. So I duck into the hallway and race around the first floor, doing one preliminary investigative loop. Nothing really catches my eye; the whole thing's empty—no furniture or anything—except for that stupid child's desk and Jim Steele's office and tons of terrifying taxidermied animals. There're even raccoons flashing what I can only guess are gang symbols. I go through the secretary's stuff and find a stopwatch, laxatives, and baby-scented perfume—nothing, in other words—then duck into Jim Steele's office and riffle through one of his desk drawers: eye drops, lozenges . . . a mustache trimmer? All old-man stuff. The other drawers and file cabinets are locked, and his computer is password protected so I can't search his email. I try *guest*, and *password123*—and *Ruth* and *RuthFried* and *Ruthbaby* and *SexyRuth* and *I_want_to_kill_Ruth*—but none of them work. This sucks.

My phone buzzes and it's a text from Davey.

Davey F. (Mobile) Received @ 8:35 AM:
don't 4get to check all floors.

To: Davey F. (Mobile):
Good thinking

I decide to do the basement next—the one that Ruth was so afraid of. I open the door and peek down the stairs; it smells wet down there and it's dark and I really don't want to do this. But somehow I force my legs onto the creaky steps, inching down into the darkness. After what feels like forever there's cold, hard cement under my sneakers. I can just make out a hanging lightbulb to my right. I tug the chain and it flickers on. There's a giant freezer in one corner and a table crowded with bottles and various half-stuffed animals. Some of the stuffing is scattered on the floor. I touch it but it's sawdust, not straw. I look at the freezer and swallow hard.

It makes a sucking noise as I open it. Inside is a single, frozen fox. I exhale and snap some photos with my phone. A rat skitters by my ankles and I scream. Who has rats in their basement? Unless it's one of Jim Steele's projects that managed to escape from the icebox? I take a few deep breaths and look around. There's also a Fleetwood Mac poster above the washer-dryer. I've never heard of them, but by the looks of the bubble letters used to spell their name, they're probably some kind of satanic band. I take some pictures of that, too.

To: Davey F. (Mobile):
basement+first floor=finished

I bound back up to ground level and do preliminary laps around the second and third floors—both of which are totally empty, just hardwood and sunshine—but then

I go to the fourth floor, where there's a bedroom. Or at least a king-size bed in the middle of a giant landing. Creepy. Does he sleep here, too? But then why isn't there any furniture, just dead animals and cough drops? I mean, he's lived in Friendship for like five years, and if he used to charge $725 an hour for his services, you'd think he could afford a couple rugs, or whatever. It's all very suspicious. I take some more pictures.

I tug on the latex gloves I brought and roll back the covers, which smell like men's deodorant. There're no strands of hair or anything that I can see. But when I get down on my knees and peek underneath the bed frame, I notice a balled-up piece of fabric among the shadows and dust bunnies. I shake it out and realize it's Ruth's underpants. I know they belonged to her because this summer, she got really into wearing "days of the week" undies after seeing it in a movie or something. This is her Friday pair—bright yellow with *Friday* printed on the front in rainbow colors.

Friday was the day she died.

To: Davey F. (Mobile):
found something, cover me

I've seen on crime shows that seminal fluid is supposed to be obvious—detectives on cable TV are always picking up underwear or stockings or something and saying, "Yep, look at that—we all know what that is. Send it to the lab!" I'm not exactly experienced with semen, and this underwear looks clean to me, but it's still probably enough to place her here the day she was murdered.

"You're going down, you old furry-faced butthead," I mutter, and slip the panties into one of the Ziploc bags I brought. Whether or not there's any DNA is for science to decide.

That's when my phone buzzes. It's probably Davey wanting to know what I've found.

"Hello?"

"JS at twelve o'clock," Davey whispers.

"We probably should have just come up with a code word, because I don't know what you're saying."

"Evacuate!"

"Oh!" I shove the phone and plastic bag into my backpack and barrel down the flights of stairs. I pitch myself through the first-floor bathroom's window and land facefirst in the bushes just as a car door slams. As I creep around the corner of the house, shaking leaves out of my hair, I lock eyes with Jim Steele, who's in the process of locking up his bright-red BMW. Beyond him, a few blocks down, I can make out Davey's binoculars, aimed at us from Rhonda's passenger seat.

Jim Steele crosses his arms and stares at me. In an effort to intimidate him, I grab Mom's old makeup brush from my utility belt and begin rapidly dusting his car. "Just checking for fingerprints." I squint at him. "I've, uh, already done the whole *outside* of the house, so." At this point he's probably very frightened and desperate to outwit me. I brace myself to be strangled in broad daylight, reassured by the fact that Davey is just down the road and trained to do worse.

Jim Steele shakes his head. "You're *such* a loser."

It takes me a second to register this. "Yeah?" I blurt. "At least I'm not the one who had an affair with a high school student."

He shows me his teeth. "Yes, I can tell you probably don't have very many relationships with your peers." He turns away, humming to himself, and I wonder with a sinking feeling if Ruth told him I'm a virgin.

"For your information, that's because I don't want to!"

"If I find anything missing in the house, I'm phoning the sheriff," he calls over his shoulder. I can't help but smile; yeah, right, he'd have the guts to admit he was missing a dead girl's underwear.

"Ha!" I shout. But then that sinking feeling returns— because now that I think of it, I still don't have any actual evidence. Yeah, the underpants in my backpack say Friday, but even though Ruth was superstitious about her undies and always wore them on the right days, I have no actual proof that she was actually wearing the Fridays on a Friday. Also, who am I kidding? I don't have access to a DNA crime lab, and it's not like Staake's going to put me in touch with one.

Still, what I've discovered is more than enough to keep Jim Steele high on my list of suspects, and hopefully going to NVCG tomorrow will help me figure out what to do next.

Davey honks at me from the car, and I run toward Rhonda.

Ruth here. It's officially August 20. Happy birthday to me. Another year older, another year closer to death.

As of this week it's been nine years since Kippy and I started being friends. Not that I, like, remember our anniversary. I just know that one of the first things I ever told her was that it would be my birthday in a few days, and she convinced me to have a party at the bowling alley, and so we had this really lame just-the-two-of-us birthday experience that we were dumb enough to think was awesome.

Even back then I felt a little funny having a younger friend. It's gotten weirder as we've gotten older. I mean we're in the same grade. But recently she's started studying SAT vocab words, which is, like, kind of a slap in the face because I haven't started doing that yet, and what is she trying to prove? The other day I was saying how everyone at school should stop calling me the Jewess. Even if it's just because they think I'm pretty or whatever, it's still anti-Semitic. But then Kippy's all, "How bad of an epithet can it be if it makes you sound like royalty?" Epithet??? I was like, get off my nuts, girl. Stop trying to rub it in my face just because I got held back a grade and meanwhile you're some Type-A personality genius motherfucker.

Anyway, just because it's basically our anniversary doesn't mean I'm gonna go making her some BFF card with horsies and flowers on it. If I absolutely had to do something like that, I'd probably tell her thanks, you know, for everything, because otherwise I'd be the only one in Friendship without a single friend. But come on. She'd hate it. Any self-respecting person would. It's like, "Oh, friend, you fill my heart with smiles, let's hold hands and dance." Better just to write it down and get it out of my system.

Anyway, Kippy and I are having a sleepover so I gtg. The girl's all right—let's be serious, I love her—I just wish she'd play it fast and loose instead of perfect all the time.

QUIVER

The story of the NVCG begins with me tackling a principal. In elementary school they had us do these stranger drills. The whole exercise was built upon the psychopath-enters-building-with-gun scenario, which had started happening around the country at the time. Basically the sound system would beep and the Friendship Elementary principal, Mr. Weiner, would say, "Code Stranger. I repeat: it's a stranger." And then our teacher would lock the door and draw the blinds and we'd hunker down under pillows in the reading nook and wait.

Anyway, the first time we did this drill, I thought it was real. Dom attributes it to the fact that Mom had just died, but I don't know. At the time, I remember really wanting to be a hero. To protect someone. Anyone. I was also pretty obsessed with Batman. Hence the utility belt. I had dreams and stuff about everyone being shot and me getting some sort of superhuman strength and carrying people stacked like firewood to the hospital. Or else the fantasy would be me getting shot (I practiced dealing with the pain of this by pinching myself a lot), and Mr. Weiner, who I had a crush on, would rush out to the playground and carry me.

So that first day, when Code Stranger started, I thought: this is it. I'll either save an entire classroom of people, or else get shot doing so and have to be carried out by Mr. Weiner. It was a win-win situation. While the teacher was burying everyone else under pillows, I snuck out the door and crouched behind the lockers. I listened for the stranger's footsteps, and then I leapt onto his penny loafers and sunk my teeth into his ankle. I thought it was a pretty good strategy.

No matter what anybody said afterward, I didn't expect "the stranger" to be Mr. Weiner. Yeah, part of me wondered why they had the same penny loafers, but the other part thought whoever belonged to this foot was a maniac and needed to die. Even when the maniac tripped over me and squished my head, I held on.

At the time, I thought the cracking noise was me, that I had broken something and would get to wear a cast for the rest of the year. I was less excited when I learned it was the sound of Mr. Weiner's teeth on the linoleum. He hit his face so hard the front ones just snapped off. Dom got a hefty dentist's bill and I was urged toward counseling. I could never look at Mr. Weiner again without cringing at his replacement teeth, which were bigger and whiter than the old ones. I don't remember this, but apparently I wouldn't talk after that. Dom tried everything—home sessions, trust-building sessions. He tried psychiatrists, psychologists, art therapists—even this red-haired woman who called herself a healer and made our whole house smell like sage. I took baby-size antidepressants, but they just made me loopy. I took vitamins, but still I wouldn't say a word. I guess in the end Dom thought the only option was group therapy—whether or not the group included actual criminals didn't seem to faze him at that point. He was all by himself and afraid I'd be silent forever. He was desperate.

My first day at NVCG, I was superexcited. I remember dragging out my favorite ensemble: some long-sleeved shirt with unnecessary buttons sewn on and matching leggings, all in a gray-and-purple floral pattern. When I arrived in the basement of Friendship Church, I looked around at these huge guys—all muscles and wrinkled tattoos and cigarette-stained fingers, all squashed into

Sunday-school desks—and decided I had to seem tough. I launched my backpack into the nearest chair, promptly knocking it over. "I'm a biter," I shouted. "And a hugger, and a mayhem maker. Everybody calls me Banzai because of how I pounce." Nobody called me that, obviously, but it was part of my game plan. I thought it'd be good to go into that room with a fierce-sounding nickname.

After that the rest of the group—mainly wife beaters— sort of took a shine to me. Most of them I'd never seen before; it turned out they'd come from the next town over because they didn't want to get saddled with recognition on top of whatever guilt they were feeling. Even at that age, I remember being able to tell that they were pretty lonely, and didn't see themselves as big or strong, not at all, actually, even though they were.

"There's some kind of animal inside me, you betcha," one of them sobbed. "Like a rabid opossum or a dog that needs to be put down."

The instructor, Miss Rosa, told us we needed to grow more space between our brains and hearts. She said that we were hyenas, and that she was there to teach us how to speak giraffe.

Even Miss Rosa had a history. She didn't really go into it, and her Polish accent kept us from understanding most of it, but everyone caught on to the fact that she'd probably been arrested before.

"Once I raise the puppies for money," she said. "The splendor make me wild. I squeeze too hard—poof!—many dead."

Maybe I was lonely at the time for Mom, but part of me warmed to Miss Rosa despite her violent history. She was shaped like a bowling ball, with this particularly soft, bread-loaf bosom. One time during a meditation session I let myself fall asleep on her shoulder and she pinched me. "Don't be closer please," she said. "I am wanting for to strangle."

I ended up graduating as part of this little ceremony in a Sunday school classroom. Dom came with the Johnstons and took pictures. I found them a few years ago and threw them away.

Anyway, it's one of those secrets I try not to think about because it makes me wonder if it had anything to do with Ruth being my only friend. It sucks to think that your actions have consequences, and that you might be sad or lonely because of one mistake. I said that to Dom once in a moment of weakness and he told me it was part of growing up, learning to be lonely. It might have been one of his moments of weakness, too.

CAMOUFLAGE

When I go to pick up Davey for our NVCG meeting, he's dressed in his army uniform. He looks great but I'm trying to be practical.

"Maybe you should wear regular clothes," I explain. "Just because otherwise they might think 'Oh, violence,' and 'Oh, an army uniform,' and send you to some other group that's only for PTSD people."

"I do have PTSD," he says.

"Right." I'm kind of trying not to listen.

At some point Davey must have gone to a doctor or something because his bandage is gone. There's still a little bit of his finger left; it's sewn tight across the top with black thread and is sort of a funny color, like how skin gets after you take off a Band-Aid. He still hasn't told me what happened and I really want to ask.

"Nice finger," I blurt.

Davey frowns. "Thank you."

The good news is he looks pretty tough, like he got it doing something really violent, which I guess he did. It'll definitely help us blend in at NVCG.

I clear my throat. "They've just got to think you're hitting me for the regular reasons. Otherwise they won't relate to you. Do you want them to think you're my abusive boyfriend or what?"

Davey starts unbuttoning his army shirt and sits down at the computer in the Frieds' kitchen. Behind us, the counter is piled with dirty plates and old, goopy casseroles that couldn't fit in the fridge. It smells like rot. "Here, look at this," he says, and brings up something on the screen. I notice that a bunch of the frames and even the pictures on the refrigerator have gotten turned around. I know they're all of Ruth, but I wonder if any of them have me in them, too. Mostly, I'm distracted by the fact that Davey is pretty much getting naked in front of me.

"Sit," he says. His shirt is all the way open now. He stands up and gestures to the desk chair. "I'll go change."

It's an email from his mom. Apparently they're extending their stay in Canada.

Davey,

I know we left things on bad terms and you won't
be happy to hear we're staying with Families
Aggrieved Retreat Together for three more weeks.
WE LOVE YOU FOR GOD'S SAKE, remember that,
and don't be stupid, we just need more time.
Your father cries every day because our leader
told him it's therapeutic. It's driving me crazy.
Pray to God that he stops so that I don't drown
and our carpets stay dry. (This is a joke. Our
leader told me it's good to make them.)
Your Mother

I hear Davey come down the stairs.

"The name of their group spells FART," I call.

"I know," he says. "It's ridiculous."

I turn around and see him reaching underneath his gray sweater to tuck his blue plaid shirt behind his tan belt. "I like your finger," I blurt.

"You mentioned." He raises his eyebrows. "Thanks."

"You're very welcome." It comes out sounding too loud. Something about Davey makes me want to raise my voice and talk in all caps. Like, NO MATTER WHAT I'M SAYING I JUST WANT YOU TO KNOW I'M HERE AND VERY EXCITED.

I gesture at the computer screen. "Thanks for letting me read this. It's important to be able to trust your investigative team, even with things like personal emails. I particularly liked the part where she tells you she loves you in all caps. It reminded me of this one time that Ruth and I were in the grocery store parking lot and saw this woman screaming at her three-year-old kid. She kept shouting, *'Why you crying? I love you.'*"

"I didn't show you the email because I wanted to talk about Ruth," Davey says, not looking at me.

"Oh." I blush. For a second I let myself pretend he's trying to tell me it's just me and him, and there's no one dead between us, and we would have started hanging out no matter what, because he would want to be my friend forever, no matter if any of this happened.

Really I think he just doesn't like to talk about his feelings.

"I don't know," he says. "Sometimes crazy stuff happens—like this email—and you need to share it with someone, otherwise it's not real."

"Yeah," I add hopefully. "And maybe sometimes you share things because of the person and not because of the things that are happening."

A group of four people, one of whom I'm pretty sure I recognize as a lunch lady at our high school, is standing with Miss Rosa right next to Friendship Church's yellow school bus. I notice the engine is running.

"Hi!" I call.

Miss Rosa looks exactly the same. Big Coke-bottle glasses that make her eyes look like an owl's, witchy hair pulled back tight into a ponytail that's as skinny as a pencil. She's got on corduroy cargo pants with an elastic waist and orthopedic shoes.

"Hm!" Miss Rosa grunts. She waddles over to me. "Your face is seeming very familiar to mine." She squints up at me suspiciously. Behind her, three men I've never seen before and the lunch lady smoke cigarettes in silence.

"It's me, Kippy Bushman," I tell her, smiling sweetly. "I came a really long time ago for . . . overexcitement, remember?" I gesture to Davey, who's holding a tray of peanut butter tasties. They're all black on the bottom, but they're homemade and in Friendship that's what's important. "I brought snacks."

"Banzai!" Miss Rosa grins. Her hands jerk up in front of her as if she's going to grab me, but then she frowns and murmurs quietly to herself, "No touching."

"What's Banzai?" Davey whispers in my ear.

"I'll tell you later," I hiss.

"Please, welcome—*welcome*." Miss Rosa wiggles her shoulders and makes a sort of gurgling noise, like a pigeon. "So you are experiencing the relapse, eh? Pouncing everyone every place, am I right? Squeezing . . ." She strokes her hands excitedly and does a little hop. "Who have you bitten?"

Before I can explain, she turns to Davey and hunches her top lip toward her nose, squinting again. "You." She points a finger at him and draws a little circle in the air. "Who is this? Hm. Boyfriend perhaps? No spying at NVCG. Safe space for hyenas—in this case relearning giraffe." Her English has gotten a lot better.

"Actually, Miss Rosa—"

"You are good to Banzai, no?" Her eyes expand behind her glasses. Behind her, the smokers toe out their cigarettes. "You treat her with the respect?"

Davey looks around nervously. "Not exactly," he says.

Miss Rosa bares her little teeth.

"No, see, Davey and I are having some problems," I say quickly.

"I keep hitting her," he says. "But I want to stop."

"You can't see the bruises because they're underneath my clothes," I add.

"Geez the Louise!" Miss Rosa is pointing frantically at Davey's bad hand. "Banzai! You have bitten off the finger."

Davey and I exchange a look. "Exactly," he says.

Miss Rosa licks her lips, her eyes swimming behind

her glasses. "Simple relapse, we are here for to help." She whistles at the group behind her, then points at the church bus. "You will come with us then," she says to Davey and me. "Today is maze day."

We're going seventy miles per hour down Route 51, the same rural interstate that runs between Ruth's house and mine. One of the group members is driving. His red, braided ponytail is so long he's literally sitting on it.

"I used to truck," he barks when Davey asks if he's qualified to operate a bus.

There are three other guys aside from Davey, and then the lunch lady from school. Each of us has to sit in our own seat. ("No sharing!" Miss Rosa instructed. "No touching!") Davey is across the aisle from me. The bus belongs to the church and is wallpapered with Jesus posters: *JESUSAVES* written in red, white, and blue graffiti-like script; *40 THINGS THAT PROVE GOD CARES ABOUT GIRLS*, including *He made babies so cute!* and *He invented Australian accents!* and *There are no diets in heaven!*

"NVCG is now field-trip based," Miss Rosa says, turning around in her seat to talk to me. She crosses her arms over the seat back and rests her chin against her hands. "Too much basement makes for crazy."

"So where are we going, exactly?" I ask.

"It's fuckin' maze day," the driver booms.

"We go to cornfield maze," Miss Rosa clarifies. "Many cornfield mazes in Friendship, but are closed currently, so we must go more west."

The lunch lady clears her throat right behind my ear. I spin around to see she's leaning over the back of my seat, listening to our conversation.

"I know why they're closed," she says. She's got a really deep voice. "It's because of that Jewish girl's murder."

Davey's looking at his hands, playing with his stitches.

Even though everyone around here makes Jewish jokes, there's something about the lady's tone that sounds different. As if people shouldn't be so worked up about Ruth, or that it would make sense shutting down the cornfields for a Friendship Church person, but not otherwise. I guess I should be mad but I'm more curious. I get out Ruth's journal and start a list on the inside cover, where I can access it easily.

Potential suspect types
1. Racist-ish

"You know Miss Rosa is Jewish," Miss Rosa says, peering at the lunch lady.

"I knew her," the lunch lady adds in a bragging voice,

as if having seen Ruth once or twice in the cafeteria means she can say whatever she wants. She stares me down. "You knew her, too."

I shrug. "I mean, we went to the same school." Before we came here, I told Davey that if the Ruth thing came up we should downplay it as much as possible. The point was to figure out their secrets, not to steal the show with ours.

"Terrible, terrible." Miss Rosa stifles a burp and raises her eyebrows in apology. "We hear about this murder all the way in Nekoosa, where I live."

"My folks heard about it all the way in Milwaukee," says the driver.

The lunch lady grunts. "I think we should let alligators eat her boyfriend's balls off. That kid was always asking for meat loaf on non–meat loaf days, like I'd go and make it for him just because he was pretty."

"They must have been in a real fight about something," says a man sitting behind Davey. "He probably had a reason unless he was, you know, special needs."

"All he can hope for is an insanity defense," says the driver. "I've used it before. Lesser charges, obviously."

"Insanity?" The lunch lady grunts. "Having spent time at Cloudy Meadows, I'd say crazies prefer the term *misunderstood*." Cloudy Meadows is an insane asylum about an hour away. Everyone knows about it.

"Can we talk about something else?" Davey asks.

It's quiet for a moment and I can feel myself sweating. Silence with these people is full of tension; so many bullies on one bus makes for possibilities like random wrestling matches or just getting punched in the face out of nowhere.

"Yes," Miss Rosa says. It comes out as "Jayse." "We will talk about reasons." She turns her head the other way against her hands, so that she's looking at Davey. "Tell me, why you are violent?"

"Because she a bitch," booms the driver. We all jump in our seats.

"That is very good with feelings, Marion," Miss Rosa says. "But we are talking Davey's reasons, not Marion's." She gestures toward me. "Banzai has bitten back, amputating Davey's finger with her teeths." The other members of NVCG make a collective, impressed noise, as if watching fireworks. "But why you have provoked her, Davey? You knew these risks, no?"

Davey shrugs. We talked about his demeanor in the car. None of the wife beaters come in repentant. I'm pretty sure that Miss Rosa takes it as a challenge.

"I'm not sorry," he says.

More oohing and aahing. A small smile creeps across Miss Rosa's face.

Davey reaches across the aisle and squeezes my knee. "This little tiger gets me all bent out of shape. Maybe if she weren't so naughty——"

"No touching," Miss Rosa snaps.

"Perhaps Davey could better articulate his reasons if other people went around and shared first," I offer, my leg all hot where Davey's fingers were. "I mean, maybe he just doesn't know how to put it, or feels embarrassed and alone."

In the rearview mirror, I see Marion nod soulfully.

"Yes," Miss Rosa says. "For example, once when I am fat, I join sex dungeon to be spanked for problems. I am ashamed, for example." She lifts her hand straight above her head and flicks her wrist. "Please, we begin. Reasons. Marion?"

Marion clears his throat. "Well, thanks a bundle for sharing, Miss Rosa. I want to apologize for using my man voice earlier. Sometimes the yelling just explodes and I feel like a broken lawn mower." His voice is friendly now, slow like syrup. He reaches behind him for his ponytail and puts the tip of it thoughtfully into his mouth. "I suppose I stand by that, though——what I said——Jennifer does bring a lot of it on herself. She nags and screeches. The lady is like a velociraptor."

"But Marion." Miss Rosa moves her hands in front of

her as if packing a large snowball. "What is inside you for this? For example, there is no contract saying, 'If you are like dinosaur I smack you.'"

Marion gnaws harder on his ponytail. "I guess the thing in me would be that hyena you're always talking about."

"Very good—next!" Miss Rosa nods at the lunch lady, who looks nervous.

"This is all confidential, right?" she asks, staring straight at me.

Miss Rosa makes an exasperated sound. "Mildred! Yes. To NVCG we only bring secrets and trust."

"Okay." Mildred sighs and flops back into her seat. "Most of the reason I buy antique dolls on eBay and blow them up in my yard is for reasons I can't understand. All I know is it's getting expensive. The shipping and handling and cost of dolls, that is. Not the explosives because those are homemade from ingredients at Walmart."

Miss Rosa raises her eyebrows. "It is satisfaction you are wanting. You destroy into pieces for wholeness."

Mildred looks like she's going to cry. "I'm a monster."

"Next!"

I reach for my pen. It seems like they all think someone or something else is triggering their outbursts. I guess the conclusion here, so far, is that whoever did this thing to Ruth thought they couldn't help themselves, or that she deserved it, like that guy behind Davey said.

I guess it could have been another girl, like Libby, maybe—someone jealous of her. Someone who wanted Colt. But why would a girl have fiddled with her bra like Sheriff Staake pointed out?

Potential suspect types
1. Racist-ish
2. Can justify what they've done
3. Homicidal lesbian?

"Hi, I'm Jason," says a guy with greasy black hair. "The two of you new kids can call me Big Jason. And my reason for violence—most of the time—is just to get my wife to look at me. That's why I grab her by the hair. To position her head better." He nods, satisfied, and rolls his T-shirt sleeves up higher over his muscles.

"Welcome home, Miss Rosa," says Marion. We pass a large wooden sign, painted black, with *NEKOOSA* in white block letters. Pretty soon there's smog from smokestacks rolling across the sky. Friendship is known for good corn and good schools. Nekoosa's known for less good corn, due to its primary industry: paper mills.

"I'm Luther," says the last guy. "I brought an ax to the grocery store and attacked a watermelon display."

"But why?" Miss Rosa asks, once again packing an invisible snowball.

Luther gives this some thought. "God told me to do it."

"So Luther," I say, tapping my list. "What are your hobbies, exactly?" I need more attributes for my list and "delusional" won't cut it. Too vague.

"I am group leader!" Miss Rosa slaps the fake leather upholstery and wriggles angrily in her seat. *"I ask questions!"*

Davey and I jump.

"Yeah and how come she gets to take notes?" Mildred asks.

"I always write things down," I blurt. "It's, uh . . . so I can remember all the insightful stuff people said. And as for the question I asked—I'm sorry, it's just maybe Davey has some of those hobbies and should cut them out so that he doesn't end up ax murdering a bunch of fruit—no offense, Luther."

Luther says, "None taken. It was the lord's work."

"I'm this close to axing the watermelons," Davey says. He pinches together his thumb and what remains of his forefinger and winks at me. I giggle despite myself.

"You guys seem pretty in love to be at NVCG," Mildred says grumpily.

"What?" I blush so hard my ears pop. I try to catch

Davey's eye, but he's gazing out the window.

"We're here," Marion barks.

I hear the clicking of the bus's turn signal and look out the window. The smog in the air is hanging over a large cornfield, set back behind an empty parking lot. Next to the entrance is some kind of observation deck, and a large red sign that says *MAZE OF TERROR* in green, dripping letters.

"Fantastic!" Miss Rosa says. She slides off her seat and glances at me. "No worries about the interruption, Banzai.

"But no more interruptions," she adds quietly.

Marion cranks open the door and Miss Rosa turns and hops down the steps on her stumpy legs. I let everyone pass by me down the aisle and click my pen nervously, looking after them.

"You coming?" Davey asks.

"Hold on a second," I say.

Potential suspect types
1. Racist-ish
2. Can justify what they've done
3. Homicidal lesbian?
4. Doesn't like interruptions.
    Wants to be in charge

. . .

I can't see anything and all I can smell is cornfield. Apparently this is supposed to build trust or something—teach us that it's okay to get bossed around and to rely on people. Those of us in the cornfield are not allowed to speak or remove our blindfolds. If we do, we won't be getting any of the M&M'S Miss Rosa keeps in her pockets.

"I am promising you candies," she said, shimmying back and forth so that the loose M&M'S in her cargo pants started clacking. Then she handed us bandannas to cover our eyes and had our partners lead us out into the cornfield.

"You okay?" I asked Davey before we got led in. He looked a little funny. I'm not sure where he is in relation to me now.

"Hey Davey, where are you?" I shout.

"No talking! Last warning!" Miss Rosa calls. She and our partners are watching us from the observation deck, which I guess is where field-trip leaders usually go if they need to spot lost children. Maze of Terror seems like the sort of place you bring a field trip of kindergarteners.

Davey is partners with Marion. Luther's with Big Jason. I got paired with Mildred, the lunch lady. Neither of us is doing very well, it seems.

"Keep walking, you stupid animal!" Mildred calls to me. "Now stop—no, not yet!"

I hear Miss Rosa saying something to her.

"You're doing okay I guess!" Mildred adds.

It's hard to hear her voice specifically above everyone else's—not only because everybody's screaming, but also because her voice kind of sounds like a man's and blends in with the rest. Luckily, a few minutes in, she comes up with a nickname for me so I can pick her out.

"Hey Fart Muffin, *Left, I said. Goddamnit, left.*"

Marion keeps calling Davey "dumbass."

"Jason, you shriveled dick, move your ass!" Luther screams.

I wish I could take off the blindfold for a second and write in Ruth's journal. I'd add that violent people tend to name call when they're frustrated.

"Davey?" I say softly.

I didn't think it'd be so weird to be back at a cornfield. I mean, it's not as if it's the same one where they found Ruth. But the smell is really getting to me.

"You dumbass!" Marion booms. "Quit spinning in circles like a dog and walk toward me, goddamnit!"

There's the sound of leaves crashing somewhere far behind me.

"Not through the fucking wall, dumbass—find your way around it," Luther yells. Luther shouldn't even be talking to Davey because he's technically Big Jason's partner.

I put my arms out in front of me and try to follow Mildred's instructions: "Left—*lefter*—no, now straighter, Fart Muffin. *Try a diagonal.*" There's another crash somewhere behind me.

"He's lying on the ground," complains Marion. "The dumbass isn't moving."

"Hold up, Big Jason, I gotta talk to Davey—*You have to play the game, Dumbass,*" Luther booms. *"It isn't fair if you don't play."*

"Give me . . . a second," Davey yells. He sounds out of breath.

"No talking!" barks Miss Rosa.

"I'm not . . . okay," he says. He's not even shouting and I can hear him, so he must be close.

All of a sudden I get that old hero desire again. I want to be the one to help. I imagine myself carrying Davey up a mountain to a hospital amidst crowds and cheers. I rip off my blindfold. "Davey, where are you?"

"Banzai!" shouts Miss Rosa.

"Here," Davey says.

I go crashing through the corn-maze wall, following the sound of his voice. "Partners stick together," I am saying over and over, keeping my knees high as I run. Leaves are slapping me in the mouth and getting stuck to my hair. All of a sudden my foot catches on something and I fall flat on my face.

"Ouch," Davey says. He's on his stomach with his head in his hands. He's still got his blindfold on. I must have tripped right over his butt.

He isn't crying or anything, but he's holding very, very still.

"Sorry." I brush dirt from my face and crawl over to him. "Hey, take this off, it's fine. Is it the smell? The corn smell? I don't like it, either." I untie the bandanna behind his head but it's still stuck between his face and his fists.

I lean down and get close to his ear. "Is it Afghanistan memories?"

Without warning, Davey reaches out and grabs me around the waist, pulling me onto the ground next to him. I'm so stunned for a second that I just lie there, with my back to his chest, letting him spoon me, feeling warmth through his thin jacket. I squeeze his arms. There's something nice about being held so gently by something that could easily kill you. It feels good to touch him, like touching a lion.

"Okay," I say. I'm afraid if I hold on too long he might pull away first. So I scootch and stand up and pull him to his feet. As we walk out of the corn he reaches for me, keeping his hand cupped around the back of my neck. The stitches on his finger are tickling my hairline. I shiver.

"Will you tell me how you got that someday?" I ask, reaching back and tapping the back of his hand.

Davey gives my neck a little squeeze. "Soon."

The maze is easy with your blindfold off, obviously. No one's yelling at us anymore, but Davey keeps his eyes on his feet, probably anticipating reprimand or epithets, or maybe he's embarrassed at how easy the maze is once you can see. I'm trying to make out people's expressions on the observation deck. I'm feeling pretty proud, actually. Part of me expects them to clap.

"Is he okay?" Mildred calls, and I nod.

"I wish someone would hug me like that," Marion shouts, frowning.

Miss Rosa has climbed down and is waiting for us at the exit of the corn maze. She's got her back real straight and her heels together, and for a second I'm afraid she'll put us on time out for cheating.

"Sorry," I tell her, walking a little faster. "I forgot that Davey's allergic to corn."

She cocks her head. "It is okay, this touching. Maybe later you will kiss instead of hit, no?"

Back on the bus, we pass around the charred remains of my peanut butter tasties. Everyone's being pretty nice to Davey, trying to make light of what happened, even though they saw him freak out in a child's corn maze.

"You did okay."

"I get claustrophobic, too, buddy."

"It's hard to put your destiny into the hands of others—especially a dumbass like Marion."

"Hey!" Marion says.

"I could give you my number, like if you ever get bored of my cornfield maze partner and want to go on a date or something," Mildred says seriously.

I laugh out loud and click my pen.

Potential suspect types
1. Racist-ish
2. Can justify what they've done
3. Homicidal lesbian?
4. Doesn't like interruptions.
   Wants to be in charge.
5. Likes calling people names
6. Likable

Everyone's telling stories of the last time they "clammed up" or "freaked out" or "messed themselves over nothing, in front of everybody." But the goodwill only lasts until the bus breaks down. The scenery starts to slow through the windows. The engine rattles and the laughter stops.

"You were driving it too fast!" Mildred scolds.

"I'll squash you like a watermelon!" Big Jason yells.

In the rearview mirror, Marion's face is growing red. He turns around, looking dangerous. "If you're going to sit there and pretend this doesn't always fucking happen, then I will crush your skulls."

"*Control,*" shrieks Miss Rosa. Her shoulders are hunched. She's anticipating mayhem. "We push. Like always." She adjusts her glasses. "Together. Banzai, you press pedals."

I look past Marion at the controls. "But I don't know stick shift. Why don't I help push? I'm like a foot taller than you anyway."

Miss Rosa rolls the sleeve of her turtleneck up over her bicep, then flexes—her flabby arm popping into a veiny muscle. It's amazing. "You are delicate and dainty, Banzai." She winks at me. "The way you help is for to turn the ignition. You are not a fighter."

"But I'm in NVCG—"

"I know why you are here really." Miss Rosa nods seriously. "And it is for Davey."

I blush.

"Jayse." Miss Rosa makes that gurgling sound. "Delicate flower." She reaches for me, then slaps her own hand. "No touching."

I laugh. No one's ever called me delicate before. Most of the time I go around feeling like an old man on roller skates. I guess it comes from being the clumsy, food-on-the-face sidekick of the most beautiful girl in school. Or from having a dad who's got aprons more feminine-looking than anything in my own closet.

"Fine," I say, unable to hide the sound of my smile. "I'll stay put." *Delicate.* I wonder if Davey thinks I'm delicate. The rest of them shuffle off and I lower myself delicately into the driver's seat, just to see how it feels. My feet are dangling in front.

"We'll get her to pick up speed and once you're moving, you turn the ignition," Marion says, popping his head back in. "Go ahead and put it into neutral."

"What about you guys?"

"We got a system."

The emergency door at the back of the bus is all Plexiglas, with a handle near it. In the rearview mirror, I can see them pack in side by side to brace against the bumper. Davey is right up front—pushing with his shoulder, holding his bad hand to his chest. Miss Rosa has disappeared. She's so small she must have her hands on the backs of someone's knees.

Davey's face is serious and strained, and I can feel the bus start to move. He's probably helping just as much as any of them. He's probably just as strong, just as powerful and dangerous. He could fight any of these guys, not that he'd ever want to. And once again, there's something romantic about that. The fact that he's gentle and careful, even though he could be lots of things.

BLOOD

Usually Dom's idea of "personal space" entails texting me every five seconds and sitting very close to me on the couch but not so close that our bodies are touching. ("What! I've given you a whole cushion. It's not like your tushy is very large, Pickle. You don't need a whole love seat, don'tcha know.") So it's surprising he hasn't bombarded me once over the course of Miss Rosa's entire field trip. Or really even tried to talk to me since our fight, come to think of it.

Anyway, I'm starting to feel sort of guilty about giving him the silent treatment. So on the way back from Maze of Terror, I text him saying I'm out with NVCG, finding closure "on my own terms" (he'll like that)—and also, I'm sorry for not telling him sooner about NVCG, but I was mad at him about our fight because I'm a teen-ager and "sometimes I have hormones" (he'll understand that, too)—and can I please stay out past eight o'clock tonight—please? Maybe even ten thirty?

To: Dom (Mobile):
Ice cream+emotional debrief with my SUPPORT GROUP
2 discuss healthier coping strategies!! ☺

Really I just want to hang out with Davey.

Dom (Mobile) Received @ 5:30 PM:
THANKYOUFORTELLINGMEIHAVEBEENSOWORR
Dom (Mobile) txt cont.
IEDBUTWANTEDTOGIVEYOUSPACEYESTOICEC
Dom (Mobile) txt cont.
REAMITRUSTYOUSWEETHEARTTAKEYOURTIME
Dom (Mobile) txt cont.
XOXOXOXDOMMY

After "conquering" the maze, Davey and I head back to his place to debrief about what we've learned. We pull onto the gravel and jump out, and sure enough, there's Marco Baseball, basking in the fading sun. He hears us walking over and lifts his head off his paws—his top lip stuck behind his crooked bottom teeth—then raises his eyebrows at my phone, which has started buzzing again. Apparently Dom has not finished what he set out to say.

Dom (Mobile) Received @ 5:40 PM
ALSOIMADEUSBRATWURST!!!SOIWILLPUTYO
Dom (Mobile) txt cont.
URSINTHEFRIDGE? ☹

"Did your dad just send you six texts in a row?" Davey asks, handing me a beer.

"No spaces still, but he's learning to use punctuation." I tell Dom "yes please" about the brat, then turn off my phone and stuff it in my backpack.

"That's progress." He wraps a scarf around my neck. "My mom refuses to text at all."

"Cheers," I say, and our full beer cans make the dull sound of bumping fists. I take a sip and wonder how many mouthfuls will make me drunk—and will I be able to notice? I'm not exactly an experienced party animal. The only other alcohol I've ever had was a couple of those tiny rum bottles, which I split with Ruth one night after we discovered them in the cabinet next to where her mom keeps the board games. I threw up after the first sip but that probably would have happened anyway because earlier

I'd eaten a whole thing of cookie dough.

"So why don't you tell me about your hand now?" I ask. I've been staring at his stitches for the past fifteen minutes, trying to think of a smooth, conspiratorial way to put this. But like all my questions, it comes out vomitous.

Davey sort of laughs—at my tone maybe, or at the very idea of telling me, I don't know. "It's not a very good story."

"I don't care." I imagine him waving his men over some kind of mountain and catching sloppy sniper fire like a touchdown pass—or meeting some sadistic Afghanistani colonel and having to sacrifice his finger as ransom for a prisoner of war. "I won't tell," I add. I pinch my thumb and pointer finger together and run them across my lips. "Zzzzp!"

Davey squints at me. "What was that?"

"I was, uh, making a zipping noise." I take a sip of Beast. "You know, like 'zip the lips' . . . or, 'I promise I won't tell'?" I reach for his good hand and try to finagle a pinkie swear through our mittens.

He smiles, breathes. "Okay. So, we were in the mountains, right? I'd just found out about Ruth and they weren't going to let me come back. They said we had a war on our hands. 'Sorry for your loss, son.' There were probably other steps I could have taken, I don't know, but I'd heard of other guys doing it."

I put down my beer and pull my arms into my coat for warmth. It's getting colder by the second. "Doing what?"

Davey blinks at me. "Shooting yourself, taking off a part of yourself. Hanging up your hat, or whatever . . . Punching out permanently." He rubs his palms on his knees. "I'm not going back to the army because they won't take me, okay? I got dishonorably discharged. I shot off my own finger. My parents both think I'm a lunatic fuckup." He takes a long sip. "The end."

I try to picture Davey taking aim at his own hand. Did he use a pistol or a shotgun-type thing? A bayonet? How did he protect the other fingers? Did he flatten his hand against a rock? Did pieces of the rock fly up and kill somebody? Did the finger only come off halfway, hanging from some skin and flesh, forcing him to yank it off like a Band-Aid? I have so many inappropriate questions.

"The guys I knew won't even talk to me. I shoot them emails and nothing, no response. They think I'm pathetic."

I wrestle my own fingers back through my coat sleeves and throw my arms around him, knocking his beer out of his hand and soaking both our coats with Beast. "I think what you did was brave," I mutter. "Who has the guts to shoot themselves just to get home?" Our cheeks are touching, and he's clasping me so tight I can feel his nails on my back, through all those layers. Jacket, sweater, turtleneck. The air around me vibrates, and I can feel everything—every muscle in his cheek, the slightest bit of his lip brushing my ear.

"You are very brave," I whisper. I'm worried I might be misunderstanding—that at any moment he'll pull away and say *what are you doing*? But then there's this: the slightest movement from him, and I turn, and we knock heads—and suddenly my hands are on his chest and he is reaching up my shirt. I throw a knee over him, straddling his lap. My utility belt is pressing into him, and he spins it around my waist so that the pockets are in back, to pull me closer. His tongue is on my teeth, his fingers are struggling down the back of my pants—which are too tight, I realize—I wish I didn't even wear pants, I wish society didn't condone it. And the dogs are barking and beer cans are rolling off the stoop, soaking our knees and ankles— and I am trying so hard to be gentle, to kiss softly and passionately like in the movies. But I want more, I want his tongue to touch my taste buds.

Davey yanks away, his lip bloody. My stomach drops. I've bitten him.

"Sorry," I blurt. Do we have to stop now?

He licks the blood off his lip and reaches for my knees.

"I've seen worse," he says, leaning in again. His tongue is metallic now—bleeding against mine. And my stomach is all hot soup and firecrackers—I feel like I'm dripping—because this might sound weird but I think tasting the inside of Davey's mouth is probably the most exciting thing I've ever done.

"Kippy." He kisses his way from my mouth across my neck, up to my ear, hugging me tight. I hold my breath, wanting him to say my name again—wanting his tongue in my mouth so badly I can barely sit still. "Do you think she'd care?" he asks.

I wriggle away, gasping like a person who's nearly drowned. "Why?" I yell. "Why is it always about her?"

Davey shakes his head. "Wait, what?"

"Before you wouldn't even say her name!"

"Kippy—"

"Do you even like me?" I feel like I'm going to cry. "Or are you just trying to . . . I don't know, feel close to her."

"Kippy." Davey scootches toward me. "I shouldn't have . . . I'm sorry—for a second I just felt guilty." He squeezes my knee. "I want this—you—I have for so . . . it's just—I just . . . I thought you could reassure me—it's just for a second I thought, *What if she could see us?* You know—"

"Well, thanks, because now *I'm* thinking it," I snap, struggling to my feet. I dust off my coat and yank my utility belt around my waist so it's facing the correct way. "And I'm thinking that we—that *I* need to focus on this investigation more so maybe we should take a break." I swallow, trying not to cry. "Is that what people say? 'Take a break'?"

Davey stares at me, looking sad. "How should I know?" he asks. "I've been living in the sand for three years."

I want to crawl back onto his lap and tell him to squeeze me as hard as he can until we both feel better. But now, like him, I'm imagining her seeing this. How does that even look? Me with her brother. Squashing him— but, like, in a sexual way. Spit everywhere and sucking face instead of crime fighting.

I'm possibly the worst friend ever.

"Kippy," Davey says again. And even though hearing him say my name still makes my scalp tingle, I am traipsing toward Rhonda. The gravel is crunching underneath my shoes and I am stuttering good-byes.

Ruth here. If Lisa Staake comes up to me one more time in the locker room and says, "So how's Colt?" I'm going to bash her teeth in. There should be some kind of respect for older grades. When I was a sophomore I'd have never had the guts to go up to a junior in my push-up bra and say that kind of shit. It's like, yeah bitch, I know my boyfriend fucked you when you were, like, fourteen, now get off my nuts before I rip your tits off!

Sometimes I wonder if Colt is maybe seeing her again. I mean, he's already cheating on me with Libby Quinn. I saw them kissing in the parking lot the other day. I'm biding my time to confront him about it, but part of me doesn't even really care. There'll always be something between us and besides, I know I've got the upper hand. Big Daddy says this whole town's just too polite to ogle me like they want to. Sometimes it's like there's something huge inside of me. Like there's something waiting to happen. Things are going to be so much better at college, I just know it. I can't wait.

Still there's something nasty about that girl Lisa. Like, you know she does it with everyone on the football team, but she pretends she's some sweet virgin, and then when she gets close to me in the locker room it's like she's gonna bite. And I think she probably cried to her daddy about her and Colt hooking up. Colt said the sheriff walked in on them making out one time and probably guessed the rest. His knowing they fucked is the only thing that explains how often Colt gets pulled over and blamed for things he didn't do. That whole Staake family is a bunch of dumb crooks.

SCENT

After getting back from Davey's, I go straight to my room and lock myself in there and lie facedown on the carpet to plan all the next steps. I only come out to use the bathroom and scavenge the fridge for bratwurst—and even then I maintain such utter single-mindedness that I manage to ignore Dom as he follows me around asking whether the support group helped and also is that beer he smells on my jacket?

"No, I must be imagining it—sorry about that, Pickle, I said I trust you and I do, I really do. Now will you talk to me please?"

"Not now, Dom."

The next morning, I slip out before Dom can bother me about breakfast. I've got a busy day planned, and first up on my list of things to do is to see if Sheriff Staake will let me talk to Colt again. Last night I managed to get through a whole diary entry saying there was something going on between Colt and Libby—and I think it'd be worth it to get a sense of whether Colt thinks maybe Libby could have gotten jealous enough to hang Ruth like a buck from a basketball hoop. I mean, she's pretty batshit, there's no denying that. But I don't have enough to confront her with yet besides the fact that she's mean and kind of moody and was doing it with Colt.

Anyway, speak of the devil—because lo and behold, when I pull into the station, there's Libby, storming out the front doors. She looks almost naked without any of her usual protest accoutrements—she also looks like she's been crying. I slam my car door and as she tries to barrel past me I grab her by the arm. "Hey, wait a second, Libby." I've never seen her like this before—she seems legitimately sad—and for whatever reason that riles me up, gives me guts. "What are you upset about?" I ask. "Colt?" I want to feel bad for her, honestly—I mean, she looks terrible. But even though Davey was probably right about Libby not being strong enough to kill somebody by herself, there's always her horde of equally tan teen-girl followers. Heck, they come along and strike her poses, parrot her expressions. She could probably get them to do anything she wanted—even if it meant yanking Ruth's hair out and choking her with straw.

"Oh my Gah." She wipes her cheeks and tries to edge by me. "Just leave me alone for Gah's sake."

"Libby, I need to talk to you."

She rips her arm away with surprising force. "I've got work to do, Katie."

"Well, me, too!" I yell after her. "And by the way it's Kippy—my name is Kippy Bushman!" When she doesn't turn around, I get out my phone. It's easier to be confrontational via text.

To: Libby Q. (Mobile):
I said my name is Kippy Bushman and also I know about u+colt . . . what's the RFFB rly 4, neway? Covering ur tail? From, KIPPY BUSHMAN

I barge through the station door and at first it seems like Sheriff Staake isn't even going to let me see Colt. Good thing I've got a plan.

"Please," I beg. "I totally believe you guys now and I found this really mean note Ruth meant to give Colt, and I want him to know all the bad things she said about him, so that he knows that she's hating him from heaven."

"You're a weird one, Bushman." Staake licks his lips. "Ten minutes."

It's not a pretty picture. The last time, Colt was like some kind of Ken doll with Tourette's, all inappropriate and mean. But it must have been some kind of denial stage in his grief process because this time, he literally looks like a zombie. He hasn't shaved and there's food caught in his creepy beard. His eyes look red and wrinkled, like maybe all he does is cry. I shake my braids off my shoulders in an effort to refocus. "I know about you and Libby," I snap. "I read it in Ruth's diary."

He doesn't answer and right away I revert to feeling bad for him—blabbering away, asking about his mental health and whether there's any evidence he might've thought of. "I mean, okay so you made a mistake—you came in here and acted all superior and now nobody believes you—but do you think that Libby might have had a motive to kill Ruth—I mean, aside from the fact that setting up some charity in her honor might help get her into college? Because we could use that stuff, Colt, we really could, I think. Sex makes people crazy, right? I mean I wouldn't know, but, whatever."

He just looks at his feet and for a second I think he might actually be asleep. But then he glances up at me with bloodshot eyes and says, "They're letting Jim Steele prosecute me. You gotta get me out of here, okay? He and Ruth were fucking. He's going to tear me to shreds."

"I can't— Wait, how did you know about them?" I

ask. "What exactly do you know—that might help, too. Did you try telling your lawyer?"

"Ruth told me. She rubbed it in my face to get back at me for Libby." He looks at his sneakers. "And I fucking hate my lawyer. My parents got him because he represented that cannibal guy from the eighties."

"Oh, him. Yeah, that didn't end very well." The cannibal guy ended up in a maximum-security prison, getting his skull crushed with a pipe.

"This lawyer's superexpensive, and I'm telling you, he's horrible. He won't listen to me about the Jim Steele thing. He's too busy trying to spin my case into something like—I don't even know, a crime of passion or self-defense or something. The only thing he's good at is pushing back my trial. He barely talks to me. He thinks I did it."

"Geez Louise."

"Kippy, please." Colt's literally sweating. His skin is pale, gray almost. "I thought this was cut and dry, but even my parents are losing it. The other day, my mom brought over some kind of federal-prison life coach. He was prepping me on worst-case scenario stuff—like what to do if someone tries to stab you in the shower. Apparently you're supposed to get in a fight your first day so that no one will mess with you."

"Geez Louise." I'm repeating myself. I don't know

what else to say. Colt reaches through the bars and even though I can hear Sheriff Staake coming up the stairs, I give him both my hands. He's not all bad.

"Bushman." He tugs me toward him. "Please," he says, reaching around my waist, pulling me closer to him against the cold steel bars. And then, who knows why— curiosity I guess? Proximity and opportunity? But I kiss him. Nothing explodes inside of me and I don't feel any- thing, really. Nothing. But I stand there and we kiss.

"Kippy Bushman, you climb down off that boy this instant!" Sheriff Staake shouts from the stairwell. I see him charging toward us. He has his hand on his gun.

"Uh—" I shove off the bars and pretend to be reading from the hate letter I pretended to have brought. I can smell Colt's rank breath wafting up from his spit, which is all over my mouth. "'And that is the last reason that I think you're an asshole, Colt! Sincerely, Ruth'—"

Staake grabs me by the shoulder and leads me forcibly down the stairs toward the front door. I'm babbling false starts, unable to finish my sentences because I'm panting to keep up with him—and he's just about to throw me off the premises when I get the words out. "What about the possible double homicide?" If Colt couldn't give me any more hard facts, maybe Mrs. Klitch's autopsy can shed some light on all of this. "Wait, seriously, Sheriff

Staake—one sec—how'd it turn out with Mrs. Klitch?"

"What?" He yanks me to a halt. "You've got a morbid curiosity, you know that? She's over at the funeral home, for God's sake, resting peaceably."

"Her body, I mean." I smile and shrug, trying to look delicate, nonthreatening. "Didn't you do an autopsy?"

"The whole thing was open and shut, cut and dry—"

"But it could so clearly *not* be a suicide—"

"For your information, we didn't even need the autopsy. That's how good we are at what we do."

"But what about marks of struggle or violence, did you look for those? Or perhaps a time of death? That stuff is superimportant, you know. You shouldn't cut corners just because you think—"

"Oh, just can it!" He grabs me by the shoulder, but I dig my heels in.

"Think of how many people hated her, it could even be the same person who—"

"This isn't some crime show, missy!" He tugs me toward the door. "The only thing we've ever had to worry about is that juvenile delinquent Widdacombe, and now he's upstairs." He shakes his head. "You keep your mind off that boy—you hear me? All you girls coming in wanting the same thing. Pure sex on your brains. You're just hungry for drama, that's what this is. You and that crazy veteran, both. He bothered us at the beginning, too, just like you."

"Davey's not crazy." *And I'm going to prove it*, I almost add. But then I remember that this isn't supposed to be about Davey. I'm working alone now. I'm going solo and being professional and not getting distracted.

And apparently kissing other people, like Colt, who happened to be Ruth's boyfriend. My stomach drops.

Staake squeezes my shoulder and I lean into his grip, craving physical contact. Comfort. "And you better watch out, too, don'tcha know, because like I say: you go looking for trouble, it's gonna find you!" He stops and points at the cars outside. The front row is all cop cars, each with a smiley face on the side. "See how safe that is?" His tone of voice has changed to something fatherly. "That's because of me, Bob Staake. See my jeep in the back row? Nice and red and new and shiny? It's not even locked. That's what kind of town this is again. Because of me. Because of my smarts."

He opens the door for me and leaves blow in, whipping around our ankles. I'm just sort of standing there, blinking at the cop cars, all those smiley faces. When you're little, you think nothing bad can happen to you because if you fall out of that tree, a fireman will catch you, or a doctor will fix it—and if someone brings a gun to school, maybe it's okay to engage in dangerous heroics because an ambulance will get there soon enough. Now here I am with a sheriff whose first thought after a murder is *maybe I can pin it on that guy I don't like.*

"I'm a smart man," Staake adds sharply, sounding a little sad, and gives me one last shove out onto the pavement.

Luckily Cutter Funeral Home is open, even though it's Sunday. With a business like funerals, I guess it's statistically necessary to be ready for someone to croak at a moment's notice. Rob Cutter even lives right above the business, just in case.

My phone buzzes in my pocket and it's Davey calling. I press Ignore. I got three missed calls from him while I was at the station—and honestly, what am I supposed to say now? *Oh, hi—sorry about last night. I was freaked out because I've got issues related to people I love dying unexpectedly—oh, and I tasted Colt's tongue.* I've got heartburn just thinking about it.

Dom has called a few times, too, but I can't handle it right now. I obviously haven't told him about any of this investigation stuff because I haven't got any solid proof—and also if he knew everything I've been up to, he'd probably worry about my state of mind or think I was delusional. He might even do something drastic. Another support group or antidepressants again, or something.

I'll tell him everything later, I've decided. All of it. Once I gather a little more evidence, there's no way he won't believe me.

I ring the doorbell and kick my sneakers against the porch to get the wet leaves off. This time of year the leaves are coming down everywhere. I've got to take a broom to Rhonda later otherwise they'll rot against her roof and leave fossil marks.

My phone buzzes again and I turn it off without even looking at it.

Suddenly, the front curtains move and Rob's big pink face appears. He smiles at me and I wave, chewing on the inside of my cheeks. I've pretty much figured out what I'm going to say:

You might not have known or be able to believe this, Rob, but Mrs. Klitch and I were BFF. Any chance I could take a peek at her corpse, and also, was she murdered?

I practiced it a few times out loud in the car, so hopefully it'll sound very natural.

"Well, well, well. Kippy Bushman." The door creaks as Rob opens it. "I've been meaning to send you one of our specialty Cutter condolence cards. I didn't get to talk to you much at the Fried funeral, it was such a madhouse. I'm very sorry for your loss, you know."

I launch into my preplanned script and he stares at me a second.

"Well, sure," he says finally, and beckons me inside.

Mrs. Klitch is laid out on a metal table in the same high-waisted jeans and sweater I saw her swinging in. The whole room smells like formaldehyde.

"We couldn't change her," Rob explains. "Cremation takes place tomorrow morning. Don't know what else to do, frankly, since nobody's claimed her and the police didn't bring an extra set of her clothes. They said not to expect anyone, actually—she's alone, I guess—but I preserved her, and made her up just in case." He gestures at the body proudly.

I doubt Mrs. Klitch ever wore as much makeup as Rob has plastered on her. She looks sort of like a clown—an effect made scarier by the fact that he hasn't shut her eyes, which are cloudy and yellowish, like something from a zombie movie.

"You're the only person to've come by," he says. "According to Father, we buried her husband about fifteen years ago, no kids between them." He coughs on purpose. "So, not to be nosy, or anything, but how exactly were you and Mrs. Klitch friends, here?" He bites his lip and whispers, "From what I heard, she wasn't exactly supernice."

"She was tutoring me . . . in the ways of the world," I stammer. I'm not sure where that came from. "Also I talked to her sometimes about her sculptures."

"I could see that." Rob nods. "She had a unique personality."

I scan Mrs. Klitch's corpse for some kind of clue. "Hey, listen, Rob . . . you didn't find anything, did you? Like something that might have told you how she died?"

Rob laughs, like he's trying to be modest. "That's above my pay grade. I just prepare them for the last viewing, don'tcha know." He shrugs. "I suppose there's her wrists, but that could have happened during when she hanged herself. You know, perhaps she changed her mind, reached up and tried to free herself last minute." He sticks his tongue out the side of his mouth and rolls his eyes back, clawing frantically at his throat. Once he's done, he stands there as if waiting for me to applaud. I let out a tiny, nervous laugh.

"Anyway, sorry for your——" Rob scratches his head. His hair looks an even brighter shade of red under the fluorescent lights. "Well, it's just a shame you've had so many losses, Kippy Bushman."

"What do you mean, her wrists?" I lift Mrs. Klitch's arm, which is pretty heavy and stiff. As I do, her hand falls to the side at a strange angle.

"See?" Rob asks. "Broken."

"And the police didn't say anything about it?"

"No way, José."

Her skin is cold and feels a lot like the pleather on Ralph's Barcaloungers. I set her arm back down carefully on the table, and rearrange her hand so that it's straight. There are cuts around her fingers, I notice. Signs of struggle. I mention them to Rob but he just goes, "Huh."

I ask him if Mrs. Klitch had any personal effects on her when the police brought her in, and he points to a small table across the room, on top of which are some crumpled dollar bills and a set of keys. I tell him I need a minute alone with the body and he pats me on the head like I'm a dog. "Oh, Kippy."

"You're getting really pretty, by the way," he tells me awkwardly before shutting the door. "I bet you probably have a lot of boyfriends now, huh?"

I force a smile. "Billions." The minute he leaves the room I pocket the keys, which are on a pink rabbit's foot keychain, and pull my sweater down farther over the top of my jeans.

BANZAI

My heart still feels like it's bobbing in hot soup whenever I think about Davey. Like, how when I kissed him, there was this stomach drop, only I was filling up with stars and . . . I'm totally not describing it right.

Maybe Davey doesn't have to know about Colt. I mean, it wasn't really my fault—not entirely. Colt's like some kind of sex robot. You can't stop him.

And also, I don't know, probably part of him knew I was experienced finally, and that's why he reached for me. Maybe I'm just more attractive now because I've got that make-out glow, or whatever. Or maybe I just wanted to see how it would feel. Create a reference point. See if what happened with Davey was legitimately special.

Ugh. I did a bad thing.

Anyway, the fact of the matter is that I've got work to do, problems to solve, and a killer to find. I mean, every good crime drama has some dame slowing the whole thing down, right? And yes, I guess technically I'm the dame, biologically speaking. But the point is that Davey gets me all riled up, and how am I supposed to pay attention now that all I want to do is climb on him? I can do the investigation myself for a while, just for today, and tomorrow, maybe—just to get my head on straight.

Before I head to Mrs. Klitch's—aka, the latest crime scene—I have got to get to my locker. It has some stuff I need, including a box of disposable latex gloves and batteries for my flashlight. (The gloves were to deal with my sophomore-year aversion to communal bathrooms, a thing Ruth teased me about until I finally got over it. The flashlight batteries are obviously in case of a power outage, because preparedness is never uncool.)

The parking lot isn't totally empty so I guess there're probably some teachers inside working on lesson plans, or else an impromptu student council meeting. I've never been very into clubs, though Ruth and I started our own once for college application purposes. We thought it'd be better if we came up with something edgy, which is how I got to be vice president of the Anarchy Club. (Ruth was president.) In terms of official club procedures, we couldn't think of anything to do, really, except for smoke pot—and we only did that twice because I didn't like it very much. After we smoked it, all I wanted to do was go to sleep with food in my mouth.

"You've got to get better at partying," Ruth told me. "We're leaving for college in, like, two years, you know." Next year was supposed to be so much fun. Prom and choosing colleges and parties with beer kegs. A few days ago, Dom asked me if I'd given any thought to Ivy League schools and I barked at him to can it. I don't want to talk about leaving now that there's no one to be excited about it with.

I get the stuff from my locker, and when I come back down the stairs there's Libby Quinn. She's taking down the old black-and-white printouts of Ruth's school photo and putting up color fliers for the next Foundation Brigade meeting. It takes her a second to notice me.

TRIAL APPROACHING!!!
NOW IS OUR TIME FOR JUSTICE!!!
Come to Libby Quinn's house
11/1 at 3 p.m. 11 Elm Street.
Apple juice and carrot sticks available.
Bring anti-Widdacombe feelings and rally ideas!

"Hello, *Katie*," Libby says. "I got your little threatening text." She flattens one of the fliers against the metal locker and rips several pieces of masking tape from a roll with her teeth. "You're so delusional. And to think I thought I could get through to you." She shakes her head. "I could have really made something of you."

"Stop," I murmur. I want to punch her in the gut. I mean, even though Ruth harbored similar feelings about my needing a transformation, it's somehow more obnoxious hearing it from Libby's mouth. What was she imagining? Vigils and makeovers?

"Oh, *Katie*." Libby bats her eyes. "You need help—in so, so many ways. Like your clothes, for starters." She nods at my sweater, which is perfectly fine, though also plaid.

"Whatever, Libby, not all of us can shop on the internet, okay? Also my name is Kippy. I don't know why it's so hard for you to remember since our names are pretty much exactly the same."

"You're such a hypocrite." She sneers. "We missed you at that last meeting, by the way, even though you, like, basically promised to come." She presses loops of tape onto the next flier, keeping her eyes on me the whole time, and raises her eyebrows. "WWRT?"

"Excuse me?"

"What Would Ruth Think?"

I slip my thumbs under my backpack straps, trying to control myself, ready to pounce. Libby's tall and has a lot of repressed rage, and is also a potential suspect, I remind myself. She could easily murder me—or at least scratch my face really bad. What would Miss Rosa say again? *Think like a giraffe.*

Libby shrugs sarcastically. "Maybe you were too busy hanging out with Davey Fried? That's supernice of you, by the way. What'll you do next, date Colt? Everyone knows that's what you wanted the whole time." She uses her fingernail to flatten the edge of the flier against the wall. "Exactly how many ways can you betray her, Katie?"

"It's Kippy," I scream, and tackle her against the lockers. Her head hits the metal hard, and before I know it, I'm climbing all over her, tugging on her hair and raking my nails down her neck. By the time I realize what's happening, I'm sitting on her chest with her head between my knees and strands of her hair between my fingers, fighting the urge to scream "Banzai!"

"I know about you and Colt," I say, breathing heavily. "I have proof and I'm gonna show the police, how's that?" Libby lies beneath me looking stunned. I'm shocked, too, but mostly intrigued by my own behavior. Violence is sort of easy, I guess, if you think you've got some kind of reason for it. I shift my weight on Libby's chest and reach into my backpack for Ruth's journal.

Potential suspect types
1. Racist-ish
2. Can justify what they've done
3. Homicidal lesbian?
4. Doesn't like interruptions.
   Wants to be in charge.
5. Likes calling people names
6. Likable

I'm definitely a number two right now.

I was going to read Libby the journal entry about her and Colt out loud but instead I'm stuck on the list of attributes. "Hmmmm . . ." I tap my pencil against number six and peer down at Libby. She kind of fits every trait except for that one.

"WTF you crazy asshole!" she yells, tossing me off her and touching the back of her ear. There's blood on her fingers. "You fucking bit me!"

She's right—I didn't even know I did that.

"And I already told the police about me and Colt for your information!" she shouts. Her crucifix necklace slides off her neck onto the linoleum, landing in the shape of a snake. I guess I yanked on it and broke the chain.

"What?"

"You're a psychopath," she hisses. "I knew it—everyone always said you had problems." She's laughing but there are tears in her eyes. "Yeah, fine, I hooked up with him, okay? Like, a lot. Gah might not like it, but it's not against the law, you know." We're slumped side by side with our backs against the lockers. She slides a safe distance away, then turns to look at me and I notice there's blood trickling down her neck. "The whole reason I started RFFB in the first place was because I felt so bad about it. Are you happy now?"

There goes her motive. I guess I should take her off the list and maybe give her a hug or something. "Libby, I'm really—"

"*Crazy?* Believe me, I know." Libby winces, rubbing the back of her head. Unsettling scenarios spring to mind—a concussion, maybe, or court-sanctioned support groups and Dom breathing down my neck even harder than usual. I stumble to my feet, readjusting my backpack.

"I was just going to say, 'I'm sorry,'" I mutter. "That's all." Then I run.

In the parking lot, I'm barreling toward Rhonda when I hear someone call my name. It takes me a second to realize they've said "Banzai," not "Kippy."

"Banzai!" the voice shouts again.

I turn around and it's Mildred, the lunch lady.

"I saw what happened," she says, trudging toward me. "Here." She's holding out a sheet of paper.

"What are you doing?" I snap. "Are you following me now or something?" My words sound weird, like they're zipping out of my mouth. The whole world feels like it's in fast forward.

"No." Mildred tucks a strand of hair into her hairnet. "Head start on tomorrow's meat loaf." She smiles, waving the paper in my direction. "Listen, you don't have to like me—and I'm not here to scold you about what happened back there with that Oompa Loompa–looking girl—"

"It's fake tanner."

"Fine, I'm just saying"—she waves the paper at me harder—"listen, this here's the NVCG phone tree. If you need anything, you can call me."

When I don't take it right away she looks embarrassed. "Fine," she yells. And before I can pacify her, she crumples the phone tree into a ball, lobs it at my feet, and storms back toward the cafeteria.

"I'm sorry!" I shout after her. I pick the phone tree off the ground, shoving it into my backpack. I feel like maybe I should run after her and reassure her that I appreciate the gesture, but there isn't time. I've got to get to Mrs. Klitch's.

At first I think I'll have to climb Mrs. Klitch's fence. I even get one of the floor mats out of Rhonda to toss over the barbed wire. But then I remember there's more than one key on the rabbit's foot, so I try a couple till I find one that opens the front gate.

Bingo.

Inside, Mrs. Klitch's place is startlingly perfect, aside from smelling a little musty. The walls are bare and the carpets are straight. All her coats and scarves are on the coatrack. All her boots and sneakers are lined up by the door, by height. She might have sat outside in snow boots drinking Beast and made lumpy, childish sculptures out of concrete and garbage, but it looks like Mrs. K was a little OCD.

That is, until I get into the living room, where there're books flung around and a lamp tipped over on the carpet. It looks like someone tried to catch themselves on the bookshelf and took down half the library with them.

More signs of struggle. It's a crime scene all right.

Two cans of beer are on the coffee table in front of the couch, each of them on a coaster, as if Mrs. Klitch was entertaining a guest right before she died. I think of how she invited me in that time and my heart jumps, thinking about how her killer must have been the next visitor.

I go into the kitchen and grab some sandwich baggies for evidence, then kneel down by the coffee table and put on my gloves to investigate further. Sure enough, both of the beer cans are half-full. Mrs. Klitch was definitely not the kind of person to leave half-finished beers. One of these cans probably has incriminating fingerprints all over it.

Just then, there are police lights on the wall and I look out the window to see the sheriff's smiley-faced car approaching. There's no point in trying to escape. Rhonda's right outside and if I run they'll just tow her and keep her as collateral. So I walk out through the front door with my hands up in surrender, still holding the two beer cans. "Don't shoot!"

"Goddamnit, Bushman," Staake barks. "Are you drunk?"

"I can explain," I say, as he pushes open the unlocked gate.

"I can, too," he snaps. "Kippy Bushman, you have the right to remain silent, anything you say . . . blah blah blah." He snaps the handcuffs on my wrists, not even bothering to take the beers from me.

"Hey, what are you even doing?"

"Theft, obstruction of justice, breaking and entering, and battery—we got a call from Libby Quinn plus some hot tips from a concerned friend of yours. Looks like it's my lucky day. Gonna finally get you out from underneath my coattails, you gall-danged nut."

"Okay, I can really explain," I blurt, rattling the beer cans. "But first of all you probably need to fingerprint these. It looks like Mrs. Klitch had a visitor and—"

He snatches the beers from me and dumps their remaining contents onto my head, then tosses the empty cans into the bushes. Rivulets of old Beast sneak into the corners of my mouth, leaving a chalky taste. I can't help but think I might be tasting a dead lady's backwash.

"Why don't we add a DUI to the list of charges, eh?" he asks, licking his lips.

Which "concerned friend" called with the hot tip? Mildred? I didn't tell her where I was going, though. Did Rob notice the keys missing? No. It doesn't really seem like Rob notices much of anything. "What, were you following me again?"

Staake grunts. "Not this time."

The hair on my arms stands up. "Well, someone's definitely following me."

"Get in the car," he barks.

"There's a crime scene in there, you know," I plead, stumbling toward the vehicle. "One that you maybe should have looked at, if you cared about anything."

"Watch your head," he says, and cradles my skull as I duck into the backseat.

I bite my lip. I know that somewhere inside Sheriff Staake is an okay man, a father who doesn't want his daughter hanging around with guys like Colt. I know that Mildred's okay, too, and that Libby's probably fine in certain ways as well—or at least innocent—despite being kind of crazy. Not that I can really say anything about irrationality at this point, having tongue kissed two different boys in twenty-four hours, one of them being my dead friend's brother and the other her boyfriend.

But as I slump in the backseat of Sheriff Staake's car and try to wipe the stale beer out of my eyes with my shoulder, it occurs to me that there are just too many distractions—too many people who are mean or vindictive without being all the way evil. I mean, I've cleared Libby, who I really don't like—and I don't think Staake's guilty of anything except laziness, really. Uncle Jimmy's still dubious, I guess. But it still feels like I'm missing something. And, like, maybe no matter how hard I investigate, I'll never find one real murderer among all these decoys. There're just so many different kinds of bad.

Uggh, Ruth here. "Everyone is a bitch and I'm a sweetheart"—that's how Kippy acts. "Oh, I put my foot in my mouth sometimes and it's cute, look at me." It's so friggin annoying. She lets her dad control her whole life, but she and I could be such a dream team if she'd loosen up. We could dress up skanky and start partying, practicing for college, all the boys would friggin love us. Big Daddy says she's probably like everyone else in this town, brainwashed into being docile and polite, but the thing about Kippy is she's smart— like not just straight-A smart, but, like, sneaky smart, not that I'd ever give her that kind of compliment face-to-face. All I mean is, if she ever decided to kick the sweetie-pie routine, she's definitely got it in her to be a badass friggin psycho.

SNARED

I've been sitting in this cell for about an hour now and it's frigging cold. Luckily I've got my coat. The young guy at the desk even let me keep my backpack and stuff, though he did take away my cell phone, flashlight, and bear spray. "Attack objects," he muttered, sounding like a robot. Anyway, I've already finished all my math homework and now I'm decoding Ruth's diary, which is taking forever, but there's nothing else to do.

I've only made it through, like, one entry and I've already got to take a break. Ruth's handwriting hurts my eyes—but also, if Jim Steele was as obsessed with her as it sounds, all she had to do was reject him a little and his strings would snap. I'm kicking myself thinking I didn't look hard enough at his place because he definitely had something to do with this. He was probably the one following me around and ratting on me, too. He's a schemer with a temper. Ruth was probably just another animal for him to stuff.

I take off my scarf and wrap it around my legs to get a little warmer. They forgot to give me a blanket and the cot mattress is totally bare. But no matter how many times I yell, nobody comes to see me. Colt's up in the Lady's Cell—the one in the break room—for his own protection, so I'm down in the basement with the general population, which doesn't really make any sense. Granted, it's not like there're tons of prisoners rattling their bars like in some pirate movie. It's just me and Bart, the town drunk, who I hear gets put in here regularly for reaching behind the counter after bar close. He's sitting in the cell across from me with his elbows on his knees and his chin in his hands, staring at me.

"You're very pretty, Miss Lady," he slurs. "You betcha."

"Hi, Bart." I really need to go to the bathroom, but the toilet in my cell is out in the open and I don't want to pee in front of him.

I'm contemplating public urination when I hear footsteps on concrete and Sheriff Staake comes sauntering into view. "Well, well, well," he says. Looking at him, I just know he's pretending he's in some sort of old Western movie. "If it isn't Little Miss Diane Soy Sauce."

"It's Sawyer, for cripe's sake." I frown and cross my arms atop my knees. "At least I've got an icon worth emulating, Sheriff Staake. Who are your heroes?" I completely, 100 percent hate him now. A few hours ago, he failed my Breathalyzer test for me. I thought his red face was some weird lingering sunburn, but I guess he's just constantly intoxicated.

Staake makes a sound between *hmmph* and *pfft*.

"Diane Sawyer is gorgeous," Bart says, smiling.

I raise my eyebrows. "She is."

"Both of you shut up," Staake yaps. "Bushman, have you decided on a phone call?"

"Dom." I pretend to be engaged with my SAT flash cards. "That's my father." I give Staake the number, which he writes down. "You sure gave me long enough to think about it."

"That's right." Staake nods so hard his hair shakes. "And I can give you lots longer, if I want, because I'm in charge." He takes a step closer to my cell. "You know, Bushman, no matter who you get in here, we've got enough to keep you, so you're probably gonna have to spend the night. You and Bart can have a slumber party." He crosses his arms and rocks back and forth on his heels. "Hell! You and your dad might have to take out a loan after I'm done with you, between all the fines and the lawyer's fees."

I fan the SAT cards in front of my face to hide my expression. I didn't realize that this would turn into tickets and payments. I guess I was imagining something more along the lines of a slap on the wrist and community service. My misdemeanors feel a lot like Ralph's mail-order figurines all of a sudden. I sigh, trying to appear calm while I imagine Mom's life insurance money going up in flames.

"Leave her alone," says Bart sadly. But when Staake snaps at him to shut up, he begins to cry, then obediently flops onto his cot facing the wall. Pretty soon he's snoring.

Staake crosses his arms. "You need help, Bushman, you know that?"

"I'm not crazy," I yell. Then I don't know what else to do so I flip the cot mattress on the floor and kick it. It's a pretty stiff performance, but I'm tired and I used up all my tantrum energy on Libby. "Like, I don't know if you knew, but there's kind of a murder case going on, so you really shouldn't be so proud of yourself for wasting time on me."

"No time wasted at all." Staake beams. "The murder is all settled, see, and you're the only thing left to worry about."

I've got to pee so badly. I hop around trying to hold it. "I want to call my dad, right now," I say, trying to sound brave. Staake laughs.

. . .

"Where is she? Where's my baby?" I can hear Dom's voice from all the way down here. He sounds hysterical. Unluckily, I am right in the middle of peeing when I hear his footsteps coming round the corner. I've fashioned a little tent around me by wearing my coat backward.

"Oh geez," Dom says when he sees me. "Oh, Kippy Bushman." You know things are bad when Dom uses both my real names, and isn't calling me Big Tooth or some such.

"Dom, some privacy here."

He turns away and as he does, he sees Bart begin to stir on his bed. "Don't you look at her, Bart!" Dom snaps. "Don't you dare!" I've never heard him talk to people this way. Bart immediately starts weeping himself to sleep again, and while Dom issues embarrassed apologies, I shake off and flush, pull up my pants, and put my coat on right.

"Okay, it's fine now," I say.

"It is not fine!" Dom spins around. His face is pale and sweaty. "Your tickets are going to be astronomical, Kippy!" He shoves his arms through the bars of my cell and wiggles his fingers at me. "Come," he says sternly. "Hug." Dom's big thing is that discipline should always be paired with equal amounts of love. Still, he sounds like a gorilla.

"Some of the stuff I actually did," I tell him quickly. "But the DUI thing is one hundred percent false." I tell him about the Breathalyzer test. "He's a drunk, Dom, you've got to believe me."

Dom nods. "I believe you, I believe you," he says, but I can tell he's not really listening. He wiggles his fingers at me faster, and I walk toward him, sighing. The minute I'm within arm's reach he grabs me by the shoulders, yanking me against the cold metal for a hug. For a split second I'm reminded of Colt.

"What the heck is going on here, Kippy Bushman, hey?" He holds me out away from him, looks into my eyes, and gives me a little shake. "I call up Jim Steele thinking he'll help you, because the guy helps everybody for a price, and he says he wants nothing to do with you—says you'll know exactly what he means. What the heck is that, hey?" When Dom gets mad, his Wisconsin accent gets thicker.

"I can explain," I say dumbly. At this point I feel like I've been saying that my whole life. "After the funeral, I started thinking." I tell him about Sheriff Staake being out to get Colt, about Mrs. Klitch's death being a murder, not a suicide, and about Jim Steele being Ruth's lover. I outline the local corruption and disgraceful investigation standards. "It's up to me to fix this or else that psycho lawyer is just off hiding in a bush someplace, waiting for the next victim," I blurt. "I have to do this—ask Davey—don't you see, it's kind of like we can save her just by solving this?"

"So Davey's in on this." Dom's grip loosens. He's barely holding on to me now. "I should have known."

"I should have told you sooner," I offer.

It's quiet for a second except for Bart's snoring. Then, finally, Dom shakes his head, looking very, very sad, and lets go of me. "You're not well, honey," he says.

This isn't the answer I was looking for, but before I can say anything, he storms off. At first I think he's left me, and immediately begin to cry. Bart turns his face toward me from his mattress, and he starts crying, too.

He stops abruptly, squinting at me. "You look like your mom did."

"Thanks," I mutter, scared now. I've always been afraid to be too much like her.

For a second there's shouting upstairs—it's Dom, though I can't tell what he's saying. I hear footsteps on the stairs again and wipe my face. Dom lopes toward me, shaking his head and closing up his wallet.

"What happened?" I haven't even seen a judge, which means there isn't any bail—so why would Dom be giving money to Sheriff Staake? "Dom, you didn't give him any lucre, did you?"

Dom cocks his head at me, looking confused and exhausted.

"It's an SAT word," I explain. "It means, like, dishonest pirate money. Bribes."

"It's called negotiation, Kippy." Dom runs his hand through his hair, and I can hear someone coming down behind him, the jangling of keys. "We're getting you out of here."

In the car, Dom turns on smooth jazz, and when I try to change the station, he bats my hand away. "You need to relax, Kippy Bushman." He breathes in deeply, gesturing like he wants me to imitate him. "We're relaxing now."

I flop back in my seat and crack open the two-gallon plastic baggie they put my stuff in, reaching for my cell phone. "So do I not have any charges on me now? You lucred them and it's all, like, over, or something?"

Dom turns up the volume a little and grabs for his own cell phone, which has started vibrating in the car's unused ashtray. "Hi, Ralph?"

I roll my eyes. "Fine, don't talk to me." I flip open my phone and start texting Davey: Weirdest day ever . . . can you come over? Dom won't like it, but he won't say much if Davey just shows up.

My phone vibrates almost immediately.

Davey F. (Mobile) Received @ 8:25PM:
Nope.

My heart jumps a little in my chest. Maybe he misread the text or was taking a nap and just woke up or something?

"Yeah, there's been a bit of a mishap," Dom says into the phone.

"Can you keep it down please?" I blurt. I'm annoyed that he and Ralph are talking about me right in front of me like they're both my parents, or whatever.

Dom waves his hand at me for quiet. "I need you to drive over to Fang Road with me and pick up Kippy's car . . . Yeah, long story, thanks, buddy. Call you in an hour." He claps his phone shut. "What was that about, hey? You're in trouble, Kippy Bushman, and it would really reassure me, see, if you could think on that instead of getting so persnickety."

"Whatever." I grip my phone.

To: Davey F. (Mobile):
Is everything ok?? . . . I got in all this trouble . . . I need to talk to you about the next step in our investigation . . .

Davey F. (Mobile) Received @ 8:27PM:
Carl already told me bout ur troubles

To: Davey F. (Mobile):
Carl, like your contact at the station? Is he the guy that checked me in?

Davey doesn't write back.

To: Davey F. (Mobile):
WTF?? RU mad or something?

Davey F. (Mobile) Received @ 8:32 PM:
Is it true you hooked up w/ Colt

I close my eyes hard and slouch down in my seat.

Dom nods at me, not getting it. "That's it," he says. "Simple relaxation."

Davey F. (Mobile) Received @ 8:33PM:
Carl told me. Said Staake saw.

I could just lie, I guess, but then I'd be like everyone else around here.

To: Davey F. (Mobile):
no hookup, just kissed! Pls don't b mad . . . it wasn't my fault

He doesn't respond. I should have told him sooner about Colt. I should have said sorry about last night and that I think about him all the time, because it's true.

To: Davey F. (Mobile):
it was a mistake, pls, I need a wingman

Davey F. (Mobile) Received @ 8:35 PM:
ur on ur own. Cya.

I groan and thump my head against the headrest. I can feel my eyes burning. I've never felt lonelier.

"Hey, what's going on over there?" Dom asks nervously. He squeezes my knee, but I turn away and lean my cheek against the window. That's when I see that we're passing the sign for Nekoosa. We're driving in the wrong direction.

"Where are we going?" I snap.

"Now just you hang in there, Chompers," Dom says, gripping my leg. "You know I love you, right?"

"What's going on?"

"Listen to me, Kippy Bushman, you're going to be okay. This isn't permanent."

I bang my fist against the window. *Tell me what's going on.* My voice sounds monstrous—croaky and unhinged—like something from *The Exorcist*. I remember Mom all of a sudden, how she was right before she went to hospice: banging her way around the house, drooling, screaming profanities. I sound like her. I look like her and I sound like her.

"I told Sheriff Staake that you needed help, that's all," Dom says carefully. "But honey, I can't give you the kind of help you need—I got him to agree to put you into my custody so that I could bring you somewhere you could get that help."

My mouth feels dry. "So where are we going?"

Dom pats my leg. "Cloudy Meadows."

"No, Dom. Please."

"It's only ninety days."

All of a sudden I start screaming and won't stop. But instead of turning the car around, or at least pulling over like I think he might, Dom turns up the radio, drowning me out with smooth jazz.

Cloudy Meadows is surrounded by trees and flanked by a cow pasture. The building itself is gray stone slab and concrete, all arches and towers and steeples, disappearing into murky clouds. Shadowy figures move back and forth behind the dimly lit windows, pacing lunatics or nurses making their rounds. It's like the castle I imagined Mom's monsters in.

"Dom, please," I say. We're at the bottom of the hill, still, waiting for security clearance on the other side of the wall. The cows have crowded into the corner of their field and are watching us from behind the adjacent barbed-wire fence.

"It's going to be fine," Dom says. "It's all part of the agreement."

I'm too exhausted from screaming the whole way to even talk to him, much less fight. Mounted cameras swivel on the front gate, flashing skinny red beams across our windshield, scanning us like a barcode. The gate swings open, and before we can pull in all the way, clangs shut, thunking against the back bumper of the Subaru.

Cloudy Meadows Sanatorium

6459 Old Highway 13

Battle Creek, WI 53092

Patient 276

Kippy Bushman, 16 yrs.

Unit: Adolescent Female

Self-committed? NO

Seeking treatment for: Delusional thoughts, paranoid thoughts, obsessive thoughts, grief counseling

Approved visitors: Dominic Bushman, Ralph Johnston, Davey Fried

Check-in notes: Grief counseling sought for death of friend, Ruth Fried. Most brutal slaughter in state since who knows when (this doctor's opinion).

Check-in interviews:

Father, Dominic Bushman, distraught at check-in. DB describes feelings of self-doubt while expressing deep concern for daughter's mental welfare. When asked how long daughter had been expressing symptoms, DB responds, "I don't know, I don't know." Explains that daughter has always been private but has history of psychosis. "She's not a rabble rouser, no shenanigans, this is totally atypical—but after her mom died, yes, there was a period of obsessive thinking, tunnel vision. She technically assaulted someone—but I'm not convinced she meant to. Recently she's been preoccupied with Diane Sawyer. I'm not sure if she knows the difference between what's on TV or on the YouTube, and what's in her head." As a psychologist (self-described; works as a counselor in a middle school), DB was alarmed to find that the patient had constructed an elaborate fantasy world around friend's death, and committed several delinquent acts. DB seems to think that Friendship police will drop recent charges against patient in exchange for her seeking psychiatric treatment.

Sheriff Bob Staake. Interview sought upon patient's father's request. SBS says, "I'm not dropping the charges just because she's crazy. That girl's a pain in my tush, you betcha, no offense. Always sticking her nose in my case, she was. Basically threw herself at the murderer, don'tcha know. Walked in and they were playing tonsil hockey. Next thing I know she's conning undertakers and robbing dead ladies. I'm no doctor, but I'd say that young thing needs a good dose of Kick-in-Ass." (SBS laughs)

BOUND

Up until this very second, I've felt packed in foam rubber, like I'm floating around weighing five hundred pounds. I actually don't even know what day it is or how long I've been at Cloudy Meadows. But now, through the noise—metal spoons on metal trays, the squeals and gurglings of psychopaths—I'm beginning to make out noses and eye colors on what used to be a sea of featureless faces. I catalogue what I know: I am hungry. But then I remember: the pills make you hungry. There are pills in the food. I try again, rooting through my cobwebbed mind for memories or clues, the facts of my surroundings. Across the table from me, two blond girls are sucking on each other's hair while eating mashed potatoes.

"I told you it'd work if you stopped eating the food!" someone whispers cheerfully into my ear. "Not so blurry anymore, right?" It's squeaky, like a mouse's voice, and I'm pretty sure I hear a British accent.

I turn to address whoever's speaking and lose my balance, falling into a pile of yellow pajamas to my left. I'm wearing these yellow pajamas, too, I realize: yellow flannel, decorated in pink dogs. My fingers grab hold of a bag of warm sand draped in cloth.

"Hey," the pile of clothes says, turning toward me, coming slowly into focus. It's an enormous girl, maybe three hundred pounds, whose face and neck are dripping with burn scars. Her red hair is matted in places, singed looking, and she's eating ravenously off my plate. I'm holding on to her thigh. "Sorry," I mutter, but she clamps a large hand down on mine before I can remove it.

"We're wearing the same pajamas," she says in a low monotone.

"That's Jefferca," the first voice chirps.

Jefferca pats my hand and goes back to eating off my plate. I turn to my right and see a small, pale girl with freckles and light-brown hair, the one who's been talking to me in the British accent. She looks young—twelve maybe, or else a really young-looking teenager. Her pajamas are blue, with hippos on them. "Don't mind her," she says, and I can tell now that the British accent is fake. "Jefferca's helping in her own way. You should give her a hug! But watch out because she bites."

I have no idea what's going on. "Jefferca or Jessica?" I hear myself asking, because I think maybe I've gotten it wrong.

"Jefferca," Jefferca commands, and I can tell she'd be yelling if she had the strength to raise her voice. She looks at me through half-shut lids.

"And why are you helping me?" I ask Jefferca.

Jefferca shrugs. "Hungry."

The food smells nasty, but my mouth is watering. I reach up and feel how damp my chin is, and spongy, too, like maybe I've been drooling on it for days.

"Jefferca's on her own team," the freckled girl interjects, pinching my waist. "Hey, at least push your food around and pretend you're eating or Felicity and Barb will see you. It took you skipping breakfast and lunch to wake up this much. Keep fasting through dinner and we might be able to have a conversation. No more futzing around." She scoops up some potatoes with her spoon and dumps them back onto her plate just before the spoon touches her lips. "See? Jolly-ho!"

I cradle a fork with both hands and try to navigate it around my tray. It's like trying to eat with a small shovel.

Here's something: they took Ruth's diary away, first thing, after Dom alluded to the fact that it might be some kind of trigger. I remember that. I also remember realizing pretty quickly that if I fought with them about it—like, begged to keep it, or whatever—I'd only make them look more right. At Cloudy Meadows, I'm figuring out that the more you try and tell them you aren't crazy, the crazier you look. That's a thing I would write down if they let me have a pencil.

"You don't understand, this is what they want. Everybody just wants me to be in trouble so that I'll stop my investigation!" I pleaded at first. And these two almost identical nurses murmured, "Delusional, Barb," and, "Oh ja, Felicity, superparanoid," nodding to each other until someone barged in with a gigantic needle, and they had to hold me down. The nurses here dress like something out of a World War II movie: light blue women's dress suits with puffy sleeves under long white aprons.

That's basically one of the last things I remember clearly, though I'm pretty sure it happened more than once, judging by the track marks on my arms. I'm not even certain how long I've been here. I sleep a lot, and see everything through a kind of frosted glass. I've heard Dom's voice a couple times, so I guess he's come to see me—though based on how far away he sounded, I could have just been talking to him on the phone.

"That's it," the small, freckled brunette says,

pretending to feed me a mouthful of corned beef before smearing it across my face. She reminds me that her name is Sir Albus—she's told me before, apparently. "Yes, like the guy from *Harry Potter*, one of your typical British names, obviously. Okay, so just sort of scoop it onto your lap, if you have to. Lots of girls miss, so it doesn't look suspicious to be covered with food. Don't put it in your mouth, though! You and I'll be able to have a strategizing session in no time."

"I killed Ruth," I hear myself say. I try to remember, but my mind is a wet tunnel clogged with bricks and fog. "Wait no . . ."

"You didn't kill anyone," whispers Albus. "Quit saying that—you're a detective, for God's sake."

"But how do you know?"

Albus puts her little hands on my face and stares at me. "Because I'm not crazy, Corporal, and neither are you."

"Davey . . ."

"Shh. Don't worry about that, we'll fix that." Albus gives me a quick hug. All around us, drunk-looking girls cram glop into their faces. I'm reminded of the cow pasture that Dom and I saw on our way into Cloudy Meadows. Animals gnawing cud. I reach down and finger the snaps on the pajama pants, remembering how there aren't any drawstrings so that we can't hang ourselves. How they even took away my bra because of the straps. I reach up and instinctively cross my arms across my chest, trying to hide the outline of my nipples.

"Your elbow's in my mashed potatoes," Jefferca says gloomily. She looks like one of those melted clocks by Salvador Dalí, who we learned about at school before they got rid of art class because of the budget cuts.

"Sorry," I say, and move my arm.

Sir Albus pokes me in the ribs, reminding me to put some food on my face. Three tables over, a girl is squeezing her hands into a pair of powder-blue gloves and looking down her nose at those across from her.

"Who's that?" I ask, pointing. My tongue feels like it's wrapped in cotton.

Albus swats my fingers. "That's Brenda," she whispers. "She thinks she's the queen."

"What grade are you even in?"

"You and I are simpatico," she says, ignoring me, and tickles my knee under the table. "Luckily I'm the only sane person in here, and I'm your roommate, and I know all about your thing with that friend of yours, and I'm going to help you get out. Jefferca, well"—she reaches across my plate and taps Jefferca, who's in the middle of lapping up my gravy—"Jefferca's just ravenous."

"Won't they be mad that she's eating my meds?" I look

nervously across the cafeteria. No nurses in sight, just Queen Brenda buttoning her giraffe-print pajamas all the way up to her throat.

"Oh, Jefferca's always stealing someone's food. They stopped trying with her. She's surprisingly lucid for someone so medicated—then again, she's so big she could eat all our meds and probably still survive. The only way they'll care is if they catch you fake ingesting." Sir Albus rubs some mashed potatoes on her cheeks and raises her eyebrows at me to do the same. "If you're on drugs, this is what you'd look like after lunch anyway."

I vaguely recall some sort of deal made through a haze of downers, Albus and I pawing around in our individual fogs before we could find each other's fingers and finally shake hands.

"What's our plan again?" I say.

"We'll talk about that part in our room with the door shut," she says, cocking her head at Jefferca. "This one's not exactly a flight risk, but she might decide to copy us. Luckily, you've got an actual British police officer for a roommate. I'm the head bloke in district three hundred fifty-seven, and we all know how bad US cops are at their jobs. I totally believe everything you said about that Steak character." She winks. "I can't come with, mind you. The younger lads will be coming back to claim me soon. But you've got to get back there and fix things for the town! That's for certain, Lieutenant."

There's a tiny thrill in my heart to be finally believed, to know that I must have mumbled garbled versions of Ruth's story to this miniature person, and that she's taken it upon herself to get us both coherent. For now, I'm ignoring the fact that she seems to think she's a forty-year-old man.

"Oh no, Felicity and Barb!" Sir Albus springs to her feet on the cafeteria bench, looking around like some kind of prairie dog. "Quick, they've seen you!" she chirps. She collapses facedown into the food on her tray, and begins to snore loudly. I see that many of the girls at our table are already doing the same. "I'm going undercover, Sergeant!" she says out of the side of her mouth. "Don't copy me! You've got to think of something to say!"

I look up to see two nurses making their way toward us down the aisle. Their matching orthopedic clogs clack against the linoleum as they walk. Barb and Felicity. Soon, they're beaming down at me, looking extraordinarily friendly and wholesome. They've got long, athletic legs and the short blond hairstyles of soccer moms and Nazis. They could palm watermelons—and probably bake a really mean casserole, too.

"Hey there, why aren'tcha eating, Kippy Bushman?" croons Barb.

"Isn't the food treating you well?" adds Felicity.

"Any diarrhea?"

"Upset tummy?"

"We saw you giving yourself a little facial—"

"And wanted to check in what the matter was. The food goes in your mouth, don'tcha know—"

"You betcha!"

They're looking down at me batting their blue eyes. One of them plucks my bread roll from Jefferca's fat fingers.

"Because I'm anorexic all of a sudden," I blurt. "You know, in addition to whatever else is wrong, I'm very anorexic."

Barb and Felicity exchange a look. "You can see Dr. Ferguson now," they murmur approvingly, dragging me along. "Therapy wasn't any use until you could admit you had problems."

The crooks of my elbows are trapped between their meaty forearms and biceps, and my feet are barely touching the floor. As I look over my shoulder, I see Jefferca bending her face to the table, licking up the last globs of ketchup from my tray.

Even in the heat of a funny farm, with my body screaming *emergency* and my brain spinning with ways to bolt, there are still cool corners in my mind where the wind stops and where I think of Davey. And I can't believe I ruined everything.

Not to make excuses, but I've heard that half-orphaned children often have a hard time with romance. Dom once had a book about it in his bedroom called *Confused Love Seekers.* Apparently boyfriends and stuff make us terrified.

Now that I'm awake, I think of what I've lost and tumble between utter remorse and childlike hope, anxiously retracing all my wrong moves and praying for time machines. Part of me imagines clawing through the jungle surrounding this asylum, and crawling all the way to Davey—playing some kind of love song on a guitar outside his window, even though I don't know how to play guitar—and begging for his company back.

I need to get out of here.

Dr. Ferguson is wearing purple glasses on a chain around his neck and a light-gray lab coat. His face is sad and cavernous, like Abraham Lincoln's, and his long torso makes the metal desk he's sitting at look even smaller. When I enter his office, he's rearranging pens in a mug on the corner of his desk with the thoughtfulness of a florist, as if putting together some kind of bouquet.

"Ah, hello there, Ms. Bushman." The chain around his

neck jingles as he places the glasses on his nose. "What can I do you for?"

Something unexpected stirs in me. Now that I am finally alone with an actual psychiatrist, and not just Dom, I'm tempted to ask about regret. Like, how long do you kick yourself for when you feel like you've ruined something? I sit down and rub my palms on my flannel pajama pants.

"The nurses made it seem like you wanted to talk to *me*," I say carefully.

"Right! Because you were finally able to admit you had a problem. So why don't you tell me about your problem, then, hmm?"

Answers swirl: *My best friend was murdered; she died after having her teeth forced down her throat; I found I'm very skilled at investigative research, but no one will allow me to help; I sort of kind of cheated on someone because I wasn't sure he liked me, and now I'm pretty sure he hates me.* I notice an eight-by-ten gilded frame on the doctor's desk, next to the pen mug. It's facing away from me so I can't see who's in it. I wonder what kind of person is important to this man.

"I've been meaning to talk to you about these, for instance." He brings out the Ziploc bag containing Ruth's Friday underpants, and shakes the bag as if for emphasis. "What are these, Kippy?"

The back of my neck prickles. They must have gone through my backpack. "They're mine," I blurt. "I bagged them for hygienic purposes."

"Hm." He thumbs up the tag through the plastic bag, and sure enough *RF* is written in black Sharpie. "They seem to have your friend's initials on them. I'm interested to know more about your determining them a keepsake."

I can feel my face getting hot.

"Perhaps we can talk about that later." He smiles and puts the underwear to the side, adjusting his glasses. "You think you're some kind of elderly journalist, that's what it says here." He blinks at the page. "Oh, no, excuse me. Your journalistic ambitions have escalated into detectivelike pursuits, which is"—he looks up—"clearly not healthy."

"I just admire certain people."

"Hm," he says, like this makes zero sense. "Are you and Adele getting along? I thought you two should make fast friends as roommates. She thinks she's a British police officer, or some sort of military man, depending." He smiles.

"You mean Sir Albus?"

He looks vaguely disgusted. "We prefer to call her by her given name. It expedites the rehabilitative process, we've found."

"How old is she, anyway?"

He wags a pen at me, smiling mischievously. "This meeting is about *you*, Kippy. No wiggling. I've heard you're good at diverting people's attention." He wrinkles his brow, looking suddenly concerned. "You seem very . . . cogent, for this time of day. Have you been eating properly?"

My stomach growls loudly, as if on cue.

Dr. Ferguson raises his eyebrows. "Would you like me to have Felicity bring you some corned beef?"

I shake my head. "Dr. Ferguson, how long do I have to be here?"

"Based on some of the background we have on your case, that really depends on you."

"What do you mean? What are people saying about me?" I realize this sounds paranoid, maybe, and vaguely rude. "I mean, I'd like to know what my dad said when he checked me in. What people think of me, or whatever."

"That's good, that's good. Being concerned with other people's point of view demonstrates an interest in normalcy." Dr. Ferguson's brow wrinkles as he squints into my file. "Seems here that Dominic Bushman has been worried for your mental welfare because you haven't adjusted well to the recent tragedy." He lays the folder down on his desk. "You know, we heard about that Fried incident all the way out here at Cloudy Meadows. I'm told you two were good friends?"

I nod fast.

"Hm." Lightning cracks outside. "It's enough to make anyone crazy, I suppose." He shakes out the folder. "We also have statements from Sheriff Bob Staake, and a fellow named Ralph Johnston."

My pulse quickens. "Why did you call him?"

"Ralph? Oh, we didn't. He called us."

"What?"

Dr. Ferguson writes something down. "I know it can be shocking to hear that others worry for you," he says gently. He lays my file open on the desk and I try to read it upside down, but all I can tell is that it's typewriter font, with some of that slanty doctor's cursive in the margins. "As I said, you show rich cognitive promise simply by demonstrating interest in outside viewpoints." He folds his hands on the file, blocking its written contents. "That's a fantastic start."

"Does that mean I can go home now?"

"Oh no, no, no," Dr. Ferguson says, chuckling. "We've got more than two months ahead of us—and you've been skipping meals, Kippy. That's obvious even without reading the fax I received from the dining room."

"Two months?"

"We still have to see how you adjust to the medication."
He opens a cabinet under his desk and briefly removes a
two-gallon Ziploc—Ruth's diary is in there—to make
room for my file. Then he plucks a single key from his pen
mug, slides the file and Ziploc back into the drawer, and
locks it.

I pay close attention to where he puts that key.

Outside Dr. Ferguson's office, Felicity and Barb are waiting to escort me back to my room. On the way, they stop
at some kind of nurses' station, chattering nonstop in
their thick Midwestern brogues. Barb gets a note out of
her pocket, and I notice it has Dr. Ferguson's letterhead
printed at the top.

"Ooh, what's on the docket there?" Felicity asks.

"Quite a prescription," says Barb. "Hefty."

I remember Albus's and my plan to stay away from the
meds. How will I finagle this?

Felicity shakes three different-colored capsules into a
tiny paper cup and hands it to me. "Swallow, pumpkin,"
she commands.

My mind races with ways to get out of swallowing the
pills—I mean, I've seen this part in movies all the time—
mental patients trying to avoid taking their meds—and
I've always thought about how I'd get around it: pretend

to swallow, keep the stuff under my tongue. But it's a hard thing to get away with when you've only got so much room in your mouth, and there are two gigantic women staring at you. If I resist they'll just stick me with needles again. I don't know what to do—so I smile as sweetly as possible and scramble for a question.

"May I please have a glass of water?" I ask quietly.

Felicity playfully smacks herself in the head and Barb chuckles.

"Oh boy, we're getting old," she says. "Of course you can."

"Forgot the water—geez Louise!" adds Felicity.

They lead me down the hall to a bubbler. But when I try the nozzle, no water comes out.

"Gosh darn this building!" Barb complains bitterly—her tone suddenly frazzled.

"Oh, Barb!" says Felicity, rubbing tiny circles on Barb's back. I think maybe I'm going to get out of it—but then Barb pipes up again.

"We'll take you to the ladies room," she assures me.

My hands are sweating as we enter the bathroom because they're watching my every move. As I scoop water from the faucet, they stand so close to me our hips are touching. The pills are huge, and I manage to swallow them only a little bit, so they're basically lodged in my throat. You'd think this would be more obvious. I mean, my throat feels like it is bulging and jumping around.

"Say *ah*," Barb says.

"*Aghgh.*" Tears spring from my eyes and I'm sure I'll choke and barf all over the nurses. But somehow I manage to pass the test.

"Good," Felicity says.

I close my mouth, about to suffocate, and point to the bathroom stall—grabbing my crotch like a child, trying to look embarrassed.

Barb nods. "You go ahead and tinkle."

They wait outside, which makes it tricky—but I manage to choke silently and quickly pee a little—and then, while the toilet is flushing, making this huge, industrial, end-of-the-world storm noise, I reached into my throat and gag up the pills. Only two come out, though. The other one must have slipped through.

"Nice work," says Felicity when I emerge. She and Barb whisk me out the door, back to my room, where Albus is drawing with crayons.

"How was Fergatron's?" she asks once they've left. "By the way, this is the best night of my life, like ever. Last time I did something this helpful and cool, it was me and the old cap'n, rescuing ladies from Scottish terrorists." She fans out her drawings. "These are maps. For your escape."

"One sec," I tell her gently. "They gave me something." I'm trying to focus—plan my route into Dr. Ferguson's office before whatever kind of pill I swallowed kicks in all the way and makes me dumb again.

"Was it the blue one? Because if it was purple or yellow or red or orange, you're probably okay," Albus offers.

"Sir Albus, please, I can't think." I get down on my knees beside her and draw my own map to Ferguson's office, just in case things get hazy and I need a reminder.

"If you're planning to go to the Fergatron's office again, you've got to be back in an hour," she says, glancing at my map. "That's when the nurses come around for tuck-in and if you're not here they'll sound the alarm, which sort of explodes all of our big plans."

"Gotcha." I shove the map into my underwear. Mostly I'm distracted by the childlike crayon drawings above my bed of what must be Diane Sawyer—it's a blond woman holding a microphone, with what look like rays of sun coming off her teeth. I must have done them when I was on my drug binge.

"Oof," I say. "I guess I am a little bit obsessed."

Albus cocks her head. "I don't know, I think they're pretty great. Some of the blokes I work with would probably love a calendar of her!"

All of a sudden, one of the drawings kind of shudders

and breathes against the lavender wallpaper. That pill must be kicking in. I look up at the ceiling. There's a vent surrounded by removable panels. There was a vent in Ferguson's office, too. Maybe if I could just get up there . . .

"Albus, I need you to give me a boost."

"That's sir to you, Corporal," she warns, crouching under me like a stool. "And remember: be back in an hour, or else!"

You'd be amazed at how many wrong turns you can take in a ventilation system when you're on drugs. I'm clomping along on my hands and knees, trying to make as little noise as possible, but it's like being in a pie tin. Luckily no one seems to hear; below me, through the vents, I can see other roommates going about their business: two girls on one bed, drawing masks around each other's eyes with a Sharpie marker; another pair making out (Is this the future for me and Albus/Adele?); I even pass the nurses' station, where Barb and Felicity are racing each other in swivel chairs.

Then finally I am looking down at Ferguson's desk, that same pen mug. The lights are on, for some reason, even though he's absent. Do they waste energy simply to make the place look creepier from the outside? There's also the eight-by-ten photo, which I can now see is of a very hideous woman, her face broad and pale, with multiple moles and a snaggletooth protruding over one lip.

I lift the vent and lower myself through. At one point my feet are still way above the table—three feet or thirty, I can't really be sure because there's something wrong with my depth perception—and all of a sudden there's a loud thud and I realize it's me, crashing down against the desk.

"Ow," I mutter. But nothing hurts. My muscles feel like they're laughing, actually. My mind feels fine, I think. I look over the edge of the desk and see shards of mug and glass, that awful woman's picture half-slipped out of its frame against the carpet, pens and pencils everywhere. I hold still and listen for footsteps, expecting Barb and Felicity to barge in at any moment. But it's eerily quiet. So I get up and check to make sure the door is locked, and then crawl under the desk, looking for Ferguson's key, which must have gotten tossed when the mug shattered. The pattern on the carpet—some kind of speckled blue—is starting to shimmer, making me nauseous, so I close my eyes and fan my hands.

"Eureka," I say softly, and grip the key in my fingers.

I open the drawer, thumbing for my file and the plastic bag with Ruth's diary in it. Inside the Ziploc, there's another key, and I stare at it a while before realizing it probably opens one of the other locked drawers. I find the drawer with my initials on the label and open it. My possessions! Inside is my backpack, complete with original contents: bear spray, cell phone, SAT vocab cards, my watch, my utility belt. I can't believe the police station returned the Ursidae gas. I cradle the whole lot happily before stumbling back to the desk for my file.

It's only got a couple of pages in it, and based on the date of today's session and the date I got checked in, I've been here a week. I have to read quickly because I'm starting to realize that if I stare at anything too long, it moves.

I make it through the first couple interviews, and there's nothing really shocking. Staake's still a jerk-for-brains, Dom's a worrywart, yadda yadda. All I can think about, really, is the approved visitors list, and how Dom must have sat there racking his brain for names of my friends. The fact that he put down Davey even after we had all those fights sort of makes me want to cry.

Okay, here we go:

Ralph Johnston *Unsolicited interview. RJ called to speak to nurse one hour after departure of father. Testimony transcribed at time of call and accepted for patient's file on grounds of RJ being family-approved visitor and longtime acquaintance. RJ says, "Yes, I decided to help the police after becoming aware of Kippy's secret delusions. I tailed her in my car to Mrs. Klitch's, the Frieds, and to the high school—and again to Mrs. Klitch's, and I reported her whereabouts to the police. Why did I report her? Well, I was worried about her state of mind. Don't get me wrong, Kippy's the kind of girl you want to trust. Between her easy smile and Aryan features, she has an angelic quality—she looks very much like her mother. But there is something darker there. I have known her for her entire life, and while it's easy for her father to forget all the trouble she's caused, I have a bit more of an objective view. Even when her mother was alive, Kippy exhibited symptoms of hysteria and paranoia. I remember her mother often coming to me asking for parenting advice, because Kippy would have tantrums and break things. The death of her mother only worsened Kippy's mental health. The death of my own parents, who were like grandparents to Kippy, issued another blow. This most recent tragedy could be viewed as the veritable 'last straw.' Kippy's issues are so deeply seated that I foresee a lifetime of therapy and medication being necessary for her reintegration into society. Currently, she thinks she is the TV personality Diane Sawyer. I only hope that her time at Cloudy Meadows helps her and her father to better understand and treat her illness."

I drop the file on my crossed legs and lean against the desk, struggling for balance. First of all, when my mom was alive, Ralph was barely a teenager. There's no way that she would have asked him for parenting advice. She was the type of person who told my teachers to take a leap when they said I needed to get more effectively "socialized." And I never had tantrums. I was just hugging people all the time! Yeah, I eventually had to go to NVCG because of the Code Stranger thing, and because Dom didn't know what else to do with me, but that was Dom's problem—he's even apologized for it since.

In the margins by Ralph's interview is the note that Ferguson must have made during our meeting:

Patient's personable yet nervous nature corroborates
RJ's phone comments that KB is "sweet" yet "scattered."
What lurks beneath KB's surface?

I reread Ralph's comments and feel my ears burn. What does he mean he started to help the police with finding me? I mean, he did say that he was worried about me, but why would he tell me to go ahead and follow my heart and investigate the loose ends if he was just going to get me in trouble? And why does he sound so poised? The Ralph I know is always apologizing out loud after every sentence. There's something not right about it. I grab Ruth's journal from the Ziploc and turn to the inside cover:

Potential suspect types
1. Racist-ish
2. Can justify what they've done
3. Homicidal lesbian?
4. Doesn't like interruptions.
   Wants to be in charge.
5. Likes calling people names
6. Likable

I shove the journal back into the backpack. Ralph is racist . . . ish. All of his Thor dolls and Norse mythology—that's Nazi stuff, isn't it? I mean he did say "Aryan" on the phone with the nurse. And I didn't think of it before—probably because he's always taken care of me, always been there—but Ralph also doesn't like interruptions, and he does want to run everything. And while he's not a homicidal lesbian, he did kind of have a thing for Ruth. I hated her for thinking he was creepy. But now I remember how she was the only one he paused his video games for. Ruth even told me once that he was always staring at her, and that it made her uncomfortable. Only back then I figured she was just being full of herself.

And yes. He's likable. It's why this never occurred to me before. Because I love Ralph. Because he's someone I've known a really long time, one of the only survivors in my life.

I go back to the records and turn the page. There's more.

Ralph Johnston *Unsolicited interview, cont.: "I can't even tell you how many nights Kippy sat here on my carpet, telling me that there was some kind of huge conspiracy at play. She admitted to me that she was carrying bear spray—and no matter how I tried to reason with her, she would not relinquish it to me. Honestly, I started to fear she might be a threat to herself or others. I don't even recognize the person she's become. I only hope you can cure her."

Okay, what? Ralph was the one who gave me the bear spray—unless he was just giving it to me to set me up. How else would Sheriff Staake have gotten the tip about "some girl with white-blond hair" wandering around with Ursidae gas?

I reach into my backpack for my cell phone and turn it on, then smooth out the phone tree from Mildred. I'd call Miss Rosa, but even though I'm pretty sure she cares about me, she's also superprofessional, and might just encourage me to take advantage of the therapy here, or something. I've just got to trust that the one other person I can think of meant what she said in that parking lot.

Mildred answers after the first ring. "Hello?" It sounds like I woke her up.

"Uh yes, hello? I know according to this doctor's calendar it's a school night, and you have to serve lunch tomorrow, but this is Kippy Bushman calling with an emergency."

I can hear blankets rustling. "What is it?" she asks grumpily.

"I—"

"Is Davey in trouble?" she adds, sounding more alert.

"Kind of," I answer. It's true, I realize, in a way. Davey's parents are still out of town, and he's there in his house all alone. Dom could have told Ralph that Davey's been helping me, and Ralph could easily find him. Then again, Davey's a trained killer. "Mostly I need a ride," I say. "I'm at Cloudy Meadows."

"Regular ride or getaway car?" Mildred asks. Her voice sounds cheerful now. "I fucking hate that place."

I didn't think about the fact that Mildred could get in a lot of trouble for this, maybe even get sent back here. So I decide to be honest about what my intentions are, just in case she wants to bail. "I need to get dropped off at a house that isn't mine, where I plan to break in and look for evidence connected to Ruth Fried's murder."

For a second I think she's hung up.

"That dead girl was Davey's sister," she says, sounding accusatory. I guess she's figured out some stuff about us since the last meeting. "He's probably really sad about it, I bet, huh? Like, I bet he loved her. I could see him being really nice to a sister he had. He's just that kind of guy, which is sexy, in my opinion."

"Yes . . ."

"I'll be at the back gates at midnight. Next to the cow pasture. That gives you two and some hours to find a way outta that ward."

I think of the series of big glass doors they buzzed me through when Dom and I arrived. There were codes and keys involved. "Any tips?"

"Honey, I always just wake up on the outside. Who knows what shit I pull." She laughs to herself.

I'm pretty sure I see a shadow pass on the other side of the door, but it might just be my eyes playing tricks.

"I'll tell you one thing, though, they do lights out in, like, ten minutes," she says. "If you're not in your bed by then, they'll sound the alarm."

There're definitely footsteps in the hall. I guess Barb

and Felicity are making their rounds? "Thanks, Mildred, see you at twelve," I whisper quickly.

"I'll leave if you aren't there," she warns.

"So how was—by George, you're covered in dirt!" Albus says when she sees me. She's brushing off my shoulders with her tiny hands. I look down at my pajamas and see my knees and shins and socked feet are all gray from crawling in the vents. "You really need to work on your incognito, you know that? Hey, you didn't happen to grab my file while you were in there, did you?" She snatches the backpack from my grasp and slides it underneath her bed, then starts stacking up the crayon maps.

I shake my head. "I had to run back. The nurses' station was empty when I passed it, thank God. I need to leave tonight, Sir Albus. I left it a mess in there. The minute they go in they'll know it was me, based on what's missing. . . . I got some information. I need to be outside by twelve."

"Changing plans on me, eh?" Albus scowls at me. "Who exactly are you working for, Private?" My rank keeps dropping. Suddenly her ears perk up. "Hurry, get under your covers!" she says, scrambling under hers. "They're incoming!"

I dive into my bed just as Barb knocks open the door

with her hip. She and Felicity enter the room, holding trays of milk and cookies. My stomach yanks from side to side in jubilee. "Thank you," I blurt, wiggling my fingers at them. I've got a niggling suspicion about drugs in the food, but these cookies look straight out of the box and I'm starving. Except for that one pill, I haven't eaten all day. I pound the milk in one go and shove the cookie in my mouth. Albus eyes me, looking disappointed. As soon as the nurses look away she dumps the milk on her lap.

"Oopsies!" she squeals, and while the nurses are distracted, clucking around her with tissues from their apron pockets, she crushes up the cookies in her hair, making a loud *nom nom nom* sound, as if chewing.

"Oh, Adele! What a healthy appetite!" croons Barb, patting Albus on the head absentmindedly.

"Let's get this off then," says Felicity, unbuttoning the milk-splattered pajama top. Barb swoops in quickly with an identical replacement shirt, but not before I get a glimpse of Albus's pale, flat chest.

"Seriously, how old are you?" I ask when they've gone.

"Forty-five, pretty near my pension," she says, shaking crumbs out of her hair. She turns to me, all slanty-eyed again. "I can't believe you ate the cookies, after all that effort. The milk, too."

"What?"

"That stuff's to help us sleep, you nincompoop. One last dose to keep us prostrate till breakfast." She shakes her head. "I thought you wanted to get out of here." She sighs. "I thought you were a soldier."

"You could have told me!" I sit up quickly and sort of rotate my shoulders, blinking, trying to stay alert and limber. "You mean the last thing they do is give you cookies? You don't even brush your teeth before bed?"

Albus beams at me, exposing two perfectly straight rows of bluish teeth. "British men don't care about teeth. Plus, this is like a spa for big old Albus. Spending money on this place is the nicest thing my troops have ever done for me."

I fight the urge to tell her that Cloudy Meadows is state funded, that the hippo pajamas she's wearing were probably donated from the nearby department store.

My mind drifts toward Davey, who's not pretend like Albus's companions, but was my actual wingman. I guess all I can say in my defense is that I didn't know how he felt. I mean, yeah, looking back, he wanted to spend all this time with me, and he never hung out with people from high school—even though a lot of his friends are still in the area—and he came over to my house and sat with my dad, who is weird, and who offers mental-health packets to strangers. And he kissed me.

But I was waiting for him to say it, I guess. Partly because it felt rude or immodest or presumptuous to assume. I guess I let myself think that being around him too much might make me transparent, that he'd see the hope I had inside and would get scared of me. And then I'd have all this love to give, again, and nowhere to put it.

"Albus, what do I do about Davey?" I murmur.

"Think less and act," she snaps, reaching under her bed for the maps.

She's right. I've got to stop self-psychologizing. The point is, I made a mistake, and there's something awful about needing to apologize and feeling like everything is permanent because the person you hurt won't talk to you. If I could, I'd tell Davey how the happy weight of secret love is just as heavy as sadness. It is jagged and diamond shaped, swells in your chest to the point of pain. And when there is no hope left, when you've ruined everything, this chunk of rock explodes, and there is shrapnel.

Unicorns are cool.

"Private?"

I jerk at the sound of her voice. My eyelids feel heavy. "Yeah?"

"Those drugs are kicking in, huh? Wake up! Time's a-wasting, hop hop." I hear her riffle through the maps.

"Five minutes." I yawn and snuggle into the covers, moving my feet back and forth across the sheets for cold spots. There is the feeling of sinking, and then suddenly my face stings. I look up to see Albus leaning over me. She slaps me again, harder this time.

"Wake up, I said," she snaps. "Now you listen to me— you've been moaning in your sleep all week about this girl, Ruth, and if she really mattered to you, then by George you show it! Friends stick together, and ladies need saving, even dead ones. Are you a man or a coward?"

"Uh . . ."

She raises a hand as if to slap me.

"Okay fine, I'm a man!" I say. "I'm a man, like you." I sit up straight and shake her off my lap, then crawl across the floor looking for the crayon maps, which I spread across the linoleum. "Now tell me how all this works." I sincerely hope these floor plans aren't just another part of her fantasy.

"Easy," she says. "All you gotta do is get to the basement. Barb let me help her with the laundry once and I found out it's the only place where they don't have alarms on the windows. So you get into the laundry slot and bam!" She runs her finger over a green square with some kind of zigzag across it. "There, it's around the corner from the nurses' station."

"Is the laundry chute a vertical drop?"

"Don't be such a pansy."

"And what if they catch me?"

Albus groans as if I'm wasting time. "Act confused, say you're looking for the bathroom. Pee on yourself if you have to! If they don't believe you, they'll take you for electroshock, so make it count." Fear flashes across her face. "Electroshock hurts, Kippy. They say it doesn't, but they're wrong."

I stare at her a second—just a weird little girl with big fantasies. She shouldn't be here. She should be at a Montessori school, or something—sitting in homeroom with the kind of kids who have big vocabularies and wear fairy wings to class. "Why don't you come with, Sir Albus?"

She shakes her head firmly, like she's convincing herself. "I leave once my troops show up—and remember they prowl around like lions, those two, so the minute you find the hatch, throw your body in. Oh, and that cookie, it'll probably make you hallucinate." She tosses me my backpack from under the bed. "Good luck, soldier," she adds, saluting me. I want to hug her—she's just this little girl—but it would ruin her whole facade.

"Aye aye, sir." I salute her back. Knowing that you might never see someone again makes you want to say better good-byes. If I could, I would hug the whole world, and even the rainbows would be my friends!

. . . I guess those cookies really are taking effect.

The door to the laundry chute makes a loud, screeching, metallic sound when I open it. At least I hope this is the laundry chute. Sir Albus didn't say anything about an incinerator. There's a steep, downward slide, leading into shadows, and the opening is big enough for a large suitcase. I crawl in quickly before I can change my mind. The door slaps shut behind me, and I'm tumbling into blackness, my knees thumping each other and my shins cracking against metal walls. Despite being buckled in the front, my backpack swings around and the flashlight inside hits me right above the eye. I see stars and taste blood just in time to land in a knot on bags and bags of laundry. Lightning flashes through the slits of ground-level windows, illuminating the basement's concrete pillars.

I scoot onto the wet floor, and my leg gets zapped all the way to the tailbone. The whole place is flooded. I throw myself back on the laundry bags and reach up to touch my hair, which feels frizzy and tangled, and vaguely warm. One of the industrial washers sparks and trembles, then makes a collapsing noise and smokes. I grab a dirty rag off one of the bags and wipe blood from my eye. The cut on my forehead is dripping, and my legs are convulsing. Thunder cracks outside and I crawl across the laundry bags toward a table, pulling myself up on top of it to look out the window.

There's no latch so I reach into my backpack for the flashlight and bang that against the glass. It doesn't even crack. I look around for something to break the window with and there's a shovel leaning against the wall, its tip in the water. I grab it by the wooden handle so I won't get zapped. It's heavy, and I'm starting to feel caged, and my legs feel weak. But then I'm reminded of those stories of minivans crashing into water and children using their own tiny fists to break through car windows and save their parents. I think of Davey and swing the shovel like a baseball bat. Glass flies everywhere, and I use the rag to wipe it off the sill. I toss my backpack through then crawl out after it, pulling myself forward through the rain on handfuls of muddy grass.

Lightning zags across the sky again, illuminating the forest and the cow pasture just beyond it. It's pouring so hard the droplets actually sting. My pajamas are filthy with sludge, and my fingers are curled into these involuntary fists against my chest, probably from getting electrocuted. I feel like that dude from *The Shawshank Redemption*—covered in crap, free at last, ready to get back at everyone who ever wronged me—except my digital watch says it's

11:45 p.m. and I'm running through the trees like some kind of hunchback zombie, and who even knows if I'll get to the meeting point before Mildred leaves without me.

The fence around the pasture is eight feet high, with barbed wire strung in parallel lines between two wooden posts. The lowest rung of wire is less than a foot off the ground, so I dig a depression in the mud underneath it to give myself some wiggle room—crawling through on my belly only to snag my backpack on the tines. *Leave it behind*, a voice inside me says—and I start to tug it off my shoulders—but I can't abandon my bag, not with my phone and the bear spray and Ruth's diary in there. So I untangle the fabric and tear it loose, then drag my one still-buzzing leg across the remainder of the field.

The cows are lowing in their pen. Knowing how cows get during storms, their eyes are probably white and rolling, terrified. The wire fence on this side of the pasture is only about four and a half feet high, and without any barbs, I guess because it's just for keeping the regular kind of livestock in. I'm thinking I could probably jump over it if I had to. I mean, if I had some sort of springboard, maybe.

That's when I see what looks like a company truck speeding up the wooded lane. I crouch low behind one of the trees, thinking it's someone who works at Cloudy

Meadows. It slows to a halt and I see it's actually a FedEx truck. Lightning illuminates the windows: Marion's at the wheel and Mildred's in the passenger seat. I wave my claws at them. Familiar faces. I'm smiling so wide my cheeks hurt, and without thinking I run toward the fence, eager to climb over it.

Mildred's shouting, "No, no, no!" as I reach for the wire, but it's too late and I'm thrown backward and everything goes black.

Ruth here again. Ralph Johnston is some kind of freak, but his googly eyes and weird clothes kind of make you wonder about his dick. I'm just saying. Someone like that, they could have a really big dick and not even know it. He's probably a virgin. I'm not interested in investigating, obviously. The guy dresses like some 1990s mom decked out to go rollerblading. Still, it is kind of fun to say things that might give him a boner and then look for evidence of greatness underneath his track pants. I bat my eyes at him and he turns around and buys me the most awkward stuff. Like those cans of gefilte fish. I'm like, "Oh thanks, Ralph, it's really sweet of you to research my culture and what have you. I'll totally give this to my mom to use in our next Passover meal!" And then I run the cans over in Kippy's car, just to feel them explode.

LOOSE

"Are you still mad at me?" I'm asking Davey. The sun is shining and I am lying on my back in the grass, and he is pressed against me, his hair tickling my forehead. I'm trying to move, to pet his hands, to grip the back of his neck and pull him toward me. But I can't move and he's being too gentle. "More," I blurt, startling us both.

Suddenly he's gone and so is the sun. It's chilly and there's something wedged beneath my spine. My cheeks inflate, and I bite down, tasting blood. Someone squawks. Davey? My eyes flutter open and at first I think the white vibrating walls are those of an ambulance—only I'm on a bunch of scattered cardboard boxes in the back of the FedEx truck, the floor rattling under my butt, bouncing my heels in all sorts of directions. Marion's crouching over me, holding his lip and looking perplexed.

"That CPR working yet?" Mildred calls from the driver's seat. "I'm getting dagnabbed jealous."

"Oh no," I murmur, feeling sick.

Marion leans down and whispers, "Did you just try and smooch me one?"

"No!"

"Your mouth was moving." He raises his eyebrows, and uses the corner of his Harley-Davidson sweatshirt to dab his bleeding lip. "Romantically, too—it was moving romantically."

"I was trying to talk!" I roll over and spit, trying to get the taste of his blood out of my mouth. "You know, like, 'Get off me, I'm alive'?" Can I really not be close to someone's face without biting? I claw at my eyes, digging out sleep. There are blisters on my palms from grabbing the electric fence. My fingers are shaking. "How long was I out for?" I ask. Marion's braided ponytail is hanging near my face and I swat it away to scratch my lips.

"'Bout a minute. Enough for us to get you in the car and get moving."

"Big dreamer," Mildred yells at me from the front seat. "Luckily I don't know shit about mouth-to-mouth so Mar and me swapped seats. Finally got to drive this old girl again." She lets out an evil laugh and smacks the steering wheel. "Later we'll torch this bitch—"

"Torch this what?" I ask.

"This truck, stupid." Mildred grins. "And after that Mar and I'll go home and cuddle."

My brain still feels a little funny—either from the fence or the sleep drugs. "Why didn't you tell me about the cookies and milk?" I ask, but Mildred just laughs.

"Milly used to drive for FedEx." Marion glances proudly at Mildred. "Also, me and her are dating now. Lots in common. She was with FedEx trucks, for instance, and I hauled freight for Harley." He staggers to his feet and hunches slowly toward the passenger seat, swaying to and fro. "Here." He tosses me a sweatshirt. I hold it up and it's about a million times too big. *I AM AN OLYMPIC ATHLETE* is written in block letters across the front.

"He was at my place when you called," Mildred says, turning around to talk to me. "Pretty dreamy, huh?"

"Eyes on the road and such!" Marion barks.

"Oh, shut it, you big lard," she snaps.

I want to ask about the girlfriend Marion mentioned on the bus—the woman he said spoke like a velociraptor—though I guess this means that him and her are over. I suppose if he hit Mildred, at least she'd hit back.

"Congratulations," I mumble, rubbing my neck. It feels like I've got whiplash. "Uh, so, is this your truck,

Mildred? The one you drive?" I crawl toward them to hear better.

"You think I'd work *two* shitty jobs?" Mildred snaps, tossing me a towel to dry off. "No, sir. FedEx fired me for reckless driving, but I still know how to finagle a hot wire! Better than getting spotted breaking you out in my own vehicle, am I right?"

I want to tell her it won't be any better if they catch her in a stolen car, but I'm sort of afraid she'll call me an ungrateful fart muffin. I wring out my socks and try to dry my pajamas with the towel before putting on the sweatshirt. I should be freezing but I'm not. The thing about electrocution is it makes you feel cooked.

"Can't you get in trouble for this?" I ask cautiously.

"Yes," Marion says, nodding feverishly, smiling like a maniac. They both look terribly pumped up to be doing so much wrong.

"Oh no . . . did I get you off the wagon, or whatever it's called?" I know a few alcoholism terms because Dom has those pamphlets—but it didn't occur to me that breaking rules could be an addiction, and that helping me escape might be the top of some slippery slope for an NVCG member. Who knew that stealing things and violence were even related? Maybe they just give the same kind of in-charge feeling? "Miss Rosa will kill me if I, like, messed up her process or whatever."

"Yeah, Miss Rosa's real professional," Mildred says dismissively.

Marion holds up a finger. "No violence committed yet, just some laws hurt," he tells me reassuringly. "Though we do hope you're up to some mischief. You're only seventeen or something, right?"

"Sixteen."

"Good. You wouldn't even get tried as an adult. Your record'll be wiped clean in two years and you'll still have your whole life ahead of you." He smiles. "You should take advantage of that."

"Yeah," Mildred says. "Please tell me you're gonna kick somebody's ass."

"Living vicariously is one of the only thrills we get these days, aside from driving fast," Marion adds.

"Or blowing up dolls," mutters Mildred. She looks at me in the rearview mirror. "Don't pretend not to be like us, honey—just because you're free now doesn't mean you haven't got a screw loose. Hey, Kippy, you're a loose woman, get it?—Ha!"

"Yo." Marion snaps his fingers at her. "My turn to drive, I decided." The two of them begin the complicated process of switching seats while driving.

"Um, but you guys just stole a car," I blurt, because I

want to focus on something other than the fact that they're driving and doing gymnastics simultaneously, and also because I'm hoping they'll tell me that they understand what they've done and it's all part of some well-constructed plan. I can't get caught before I get to Ralph's. "Like, this is a really big deal."

"Oh, can it, you big pussy," Mildred says, struggling across Marion's lap. "We brought you some supplies, too. Wanna cry about it?"

My mind turns to Mildred's penchant for home-made explosives. I'm not sure I want whatever gift she's brought me.

"Kippy, you should really consider having us along. No need to go it alone." Marion squeezes Mildred's shoulder. "Now that we're dating, Milly and me are fun as pie. Couldn't get more carefree."

I look at their excited faces in the rearview mirror and bite my lip. Their expressions are eager and nostalgic all at the same time. The truth is, I could use the company, not to mention some logistical assistance, since I've been electrified and drugged. Still, who knows if they wouldn't just go batshit on me once we get to Ralph's, make a ton of ruckus in the heat of their excitement, and draw a crowd or kill somebody before I find what I need, whatever that is. I'm not even sure what I'm going to do yet—and if I'm going to make it up as I go, I'd better go it alone.

"Guys, I—" They look so excited I'm not sure how to put this. I try again. "I think you should just drop me off and torch . . . this . . . bitch, like you said."

It's quiet, and for a moment I worry I've hurt their feelings. But then Marion starts nodding in that soulful way.

"Go balls out, baby," he says. "Be as tough as nails—as big as all of us put together."

"And tell us about it afterward," Mildred adds.

Marion nods. "Call us right away."

The two of them start bickering about which new WWE personality is the toughest—General Awesome or Babu Eight Ball. Meanwhile, I bounce around on my haunches on the FedEx boxes, wondering if Ruth was right in that one diary entry about me, where she said I was a badass—hoping with my whole heart that I really can do this by myself.

"Oof." I flip open my cell phone, scrolling for Davey's number. I stare at his name on the tiny green screen and listen to rain drum on the metal roof, wondering if I have the guts to call him.

"I need to call Davey. He's mad at me," I announce.

"What, you bite another of his fingers off?" Marion asks.

"Sort of." My heart pounds. I guess I'm worried Davey

might tell me something bad about myself, like that I'm selfish, or mean, or ugly, and that I might believe him. I sort of figured he would leave from the beginning—go back to the war—but then I found out he was home for good, and then we kissed, and it changed things. The leaving part became less obvious and therefore scarier, because now if he left it was a decision and it had to do with me.

And so maybe in a way I did things to make him leave, like, on my own terms. Like, maybe to be in control of it, or something. I self-sabotaged.

Ugh, there goes the Dom in me again.

"Fast food joints don't care. The kids who work there this late, they're illegal Mexicans, you think they'd turn *us* in?"

They're arguing about whether it's a good idea to stop at Wendy's in a stolen truck. I give them my two cents— "No, it is not a good idea, not a good one at all"—but they sort of bat the air with their hands and tell me to fuck myself. So I hunker back down in the corner of the truck and open my phone again.

"Could you at least drop me off first?" I ask, glancing between the windshield wipers for local landmarks. I give them Ralph's address and look at my phone. If I call the police they'll just come and arrest me, treat me like an escapee. If anyone's going to believe me, I'm going to need some solid evidence. "We're only like fifteen minutes away."

"Fine, fine," Mildred snaps.

Part of me would rather call Dom instead of Davey. I mean, he's my dad. Then again, the last time I tried to confide in him he carted me off against my will to an insane asylum.

I sigh and punch in Davey's number before I can change my mind. I'm feeling a lot less light-headed, so I guess the cookie pills are wearing off, but my hands still hurt from that fence. I look at myself again in the rearview mirror. My hair is all frizzy and my chin and cheeks look spotted with soot. I try to rub it off, but Marion tells me to stop.

"Those are bruises," he says. "Don't make it any worse."

The phone rings twice and goes to voice mail—"Hey, this is Davey, leave a short message"—and my stomach sort of drops, because he must have clicked the Ignore button.

"Hi," I say slowly. Marion turns around to look at me, thinking I'm talking to him, and I swat the air, mouthing, "Privacy." He and Mildred start whispering and giggling. Their moods change so quickly. The silence on the phone sounds like rushing wind, and I take a deep breath.

"I'm sorry, Davey. I'm really, really sorry. I did a wrong, stupid thing."

"Oooh," Mildred says, looking at me in the rearview mirror. Marion slaps her arm lightly and laughs.

I shut my eyes for privacy. "I guess all I can say is that I didn't know you liked me? If I had, I never would have kissed Colt. And if anyone else treated you this way I'd hate them, so I don't know why I did it—I mean, why didn't you tell me you liked me? Sorry, it sounds like I'm making it your fault—it's not your fault. It's just I liked you so much I figured that . . . you know . . . when you kissed me"—I can hear Marion giggling again and lower my voice—"I don't know, Davey, I guess I figured it was some kind of mistake on your part, like maybe biological hormones or whatever. I didn't expect you to like me because I liked you so much. Does that make sense?" I kick the wall of the truck and roll my eyes. It isn't coming out right. "Listen, I don't want to bring up Ruth, but it feels impossible, because people can just *go*, you know? They can just disappear. And I should have said good-bye better to all of them, or whatever—and I guess if you really don't want to talk to me anymore, that's fine, but I need you to know that I . . . I don't know." I focus on my feet; Dom once said that if you're nervous, thinking about your feet is a good way to ground yourself. "Davey,

I'm haunted by the way I treated you—and basically the reason I'm calling is because I'm on my way to one last investigation, and I could really use your help." I peer out the windshield. We're turning onto my street. "I'm on my way to Ralph Johnston's house, and I need a wingman, and I'm scared—so maybe you could come, if you don't actually hate me all the way." I hang up.

"That sounded like it went well," says Mildred.

"Stop here," I tell her. We're about four houses down from the Johnstons' place—far enough away that Ralph won't notice the idling car.

Mildred pulls over and cuts the lights. She and Marion jump out into the pouring rain, then yank open the back doors and wrestle me out onto the sidewalk.

"You're ready for this," Marion booms, slapping me on the back.

Before I know it, they're shoving things into my arms—a hammer and nails, and a hunting knife. I don't know what exactly they're implying with the hammer—or the nails, for that matter. Even if it turns out Ralph is 100 percent guilty, the idea of plunging a knife into him still makes me want to barf.

I push it all back at them. "It's too heavy," I say, wiping the rain from my eyes. "I gotta travel light."

"Well, at least take this," Mildred insists, and gives me

a package wrapped in black tape. A naked baby doll with eyes that open and shut when you rock it is strapped to the top. "Careful." She digs around in her pocket and pulls out a clear plastic box, the kind of thing you put soap inside for traveling. She opens it carefully, holding it out to me as if it's an engagement ring, shielding it from the rain with one hand. Inside is a tiny remote, with wires sticking out all over, tied in knots. "The detonator's homemade, so it's a little bit finicky," she says sheepishly. Marion nudges her with his elbow as if this is all modesty. "But it'll create a pretty big boom, I'll tell you what." She snaps the soapbox shut. "Put that somewhere safe," she adds, and watches while I slide it into the front pocket of my backpack.

They salute me, turn on their heels, and drive off without looking back. Thunder rumbles in the distance.

I nod frantically. "Okay, yeah, bye guys, thank you," I say to no one, then slink down the street to Ralph's lawn and ditch the weird baby-doll package in his mailbox. Not to be ungrateful—I'm all about being a ruthless investigator and taking things to the max. But if there's anyone on the planet who shouldn't keep a finicky bomb (made by a crazy person) inside her backpack, it's probably me.

TROPHIES

I'm hunched behind Ralph's bushes, just under his front window, trying to keep my phone from getting wet while I grapple with the buttons. My fingers are shaking, my pajamas are sopping, and I can see lightning snapping above me.

"Focus," I whisper. I press my back against the house and dial Ralph's number. I can hear his cell phone ringing on the other side of the wall. It's loud, some kind of blaring, complicated ringtone that he once told me was a Norwegian war anthem. He'd gotten it off one of his Thor websites. Ralph keeps his cell with him at all times, so based on how well I can hear the anthem, he must be sleeping on the floor in the front room again. Sometimes he gets out a sleeping bag and hunkers down there so he can play video games whenever he wakes up. Knowing he's just on the other side of the wall makes me feel sick.

"Pick up," I whisper, but he doesn't answer, so I call again, squeezing underneath the porch to stay dry.

The phone stops ringing and on the other end I can hear the rustling of shiny fabric—sleeping bag against lady's tracksuit.

"Kippy?" he mutters. "Jesus, do you know what time it is? I thought they took away your cellular phone at Cloudy Meadows."

"Hi, Ralph." I'm trying to pretend I don't know him, that the familiarity of his voice is a ruse. He already thinks I'm crazy—nothing's going to change that, so I might as well accuse him and wait for him to tell me he's wrong. "I know what you did," I say. The lights go on in his front room. I duck out from under the porch into the rain and peek in the front window. Inside, Ralph is staggering around in his tracksuit, picking up his home phone off the floor.

I duck back under the porch. "I know about you and Ruth." I've got to keep him from calling the cops on his other line. "You're not even going to deny it, are you? Well, you don't need to; I've got evidence, and I've broken into a Kinko's"—where did that come from?—"I'll fax the police what I have the second I hear sirens. I'll fax the papers, too. They'll listen." Who faxes?

I hear him set down the other phone. "That's impossible," he says. His voice is cold and hollow, controlled.

I pinch the space between my eyes and swallow. "So you do know what I'm talking about?"

"Where are you, Kippy?" he asks. Through the spaces in the boards, I can see him pressed against the window, staring out at the front yard.

I duck even farther into the shadows. "I told you, Kinko's. Come meet me and we can talk about it." I'm telling myself there's still a chance that this could all be wrong, that maybe the only reason he's acting weird and wants to know where I am is because he's worried.

Still, I need him out of the house so I can look around.

"The Kinko's in Friendship?"

"Yup," I say, and immediately regret it. If I'd said Nekoosa, it would have given me almost two hours—forty minutes each way—lots of time to snoop. Now I've probably got less than twenty.

Ralph is breathing heavily. I can hear the squeak of cardboard boxes and things crashing in the background. He must be going through his collectibles. Maybe he's looking for something to bring me, maybe like a present or something—a peace offering—like old times?

"Call me when you get here and wait outside. I'll come find you," I say.

"Sounds just fine." The front door bangs shut, and the porch creaks above me underneath his weight. Rain is pounding on the driveway. He's dragging something heavy. He stomps down the steps with whatever he's got clunking after him—and then there's metal scraping on the front walk. I crawl to the edge of the porch and lie on my belly in the mud, watching his feet through the slats— trying to see what's going on. There's still a chance, I am thinking again, there's still a chance that Ralph is good— that he is getting into his minivan to come and reassure me. It's dark and I can barely see what he's carrying. But then the moonlight catches the blade of the two-handed machete right before he chucks it in the car.

It's better to just say, "Don't come," than to wait around in your heart for someone to bail, I think. Davey hasn't called me back. He hates me, probably. So as I push open Ralph's front door, I text him: "Never mind, I got it."

Ralph just left to kill me with a giant machete and I've only got fifteen minutes so don't bother would be too hard to explain in less than forty characters.

What happened with Ralph, anyway? Was it the way his parents died or the way he was raised? Violent deaths can make you violent, right? Or was it the video games? And the Johnstons weren't ever very demonstrative people. I mean, they gave us food and cared for our lawn—and they never pressured Ralph to have a job—but they weren't big huggers, or anything. Still, they were good people. Kind people. So was he always bad and I just never noticed?

"Anytime you need anything, we're here," Mrs. Johnston told me.

"Us and Ralph will always take care of you," Mr. Johnston said.

I set the alarm on my watch to give myself a sense of time—but right away it's clear that there's too much to go through in fifteen minutes. All those boxes I passed on my way to and from the bathroom are stacked in towers all the way to the ceiling. I see one at the top that's labeled *Artifacts* and try to grab at it, but I'm too short, and end up knocking over the whole stack. Ceramic, pink-cheeked figurines of children wearing lederhosen break at my feet.

Just then, headlights hit the front windows and Ralph's minivan lurches up the driveway. I look at my watch: eleven minutes left. He couldn't have gone to Kinko's. Did he even drive off? I stumble over the mess I've made and claw my way up the stairs to his bedroom, then sprint past his bed and straight into his closet, slamming the door. It's pitch-black in here and smells like a gym bag. Above me, rain pounds on the roof.

He could have just driven down the road, I realize, suspected something, sat and waited, then rolled back with his lights off and watched through the window for movement in the house. I wasn't careful enough. All the lights were on in the front room; he could have seen me walking around from a block away.

I hear the front door opening.

"Kippy?" Ralph calls. His voice is cold again—loud and empty. I imagine him below me, turning off lights, tightening his grip on the machete. "Kippy, I know you're in here, so perhaps you should please stop being such a little bitch, okay? I'm not going to hurt you as long as you're a nice girl."

My knees feel weak and I crouch lower in the closet, leaning back against what feels like a bookcase. There's something tickling my cheek and I use my phone as a flashlight to look around. At first I think it's some kind of costume—a Halloween beard, or something, with tinsel stuck between the hairs. But then I realize it's human hair. More than a foot of brown curls tied with a bow and nailed to the bookshelf. Ruth's hair, I know just by looking at it. I'm pretty sure I can even smell her shampoo, that peppermint-scented stuff she loved. What looks like tinsel is actually her necklace, the one I gave her for her birthday, the other half of our friendship heart. The one I thought she'd thrown away because they didn't find it on her corpse.

I touch the hair and choke a little bit, scanning the rest of the closet with the light from my phone. I definitely don't have enough sandwich bags for all this evidence. Ruth's yearbook picture, photos from her Facebook page printed out in color, her face taped over all the heroines in comic books. I'm pressing End again and again to keep the phone screen lit, choking back sobs. There're shriveled bits of bloody skin still clinging to her hair. Why didn't I know he was creepy? Why didn't I believe her when she said he was a freak?

Downstairs, I hear boxes rustling, the clinking of ceramic pieces being kicked across carpet.

"Kippy!" he roars. I feel warmth streaming down my thighs and realize I'm wetting my pants.

"Shit," I whisper, skimming tears off my cheeks. I start clicking through the contacts on my phone. Even if I called Dom now, he wouldn't answer—he never picks up the freaking house line—I remember when hospice called us about Mom at night it was always me who rustled awake for the call. Nine-one-one would probably just put me through to whatever doofus is working at the police station. I stumble upon Sheriff Staake's private number and press talk, drumming my fingers on my teeth. *Pick up, pick up, pick up.* The only thing I've got left is a man whose main goal in life is to catch me—well, catch me then.

"Who is this?" Staake demands. I can hear TV in the background.

"You're awake," I whisper. "Sheriff Staake, please, it's me, Kippy."

"Gosh darn it all, Bushman! I thought they'd fixed you up over there. How the hell'd you get a phone?"

"Sheriff, please." I'm hiccupping softly, trying to stop crying so I can be understood. "I'm trapped in Ralph Johnston's closet. He's got all this stuff of Ruth's. Tons of her hair, even. . . . He's going to kill me, he's looking for me."

"My foot," Staake says. "What they got you on, some kind of quaaludes? I'm hanging up."

"Listen to me," I hiss, and I can feel the tears drying on my face. "I know about Colt and Lisa. I know that's what you're mad about. Now you can keep on being mad about that, or you can come and frigging save me. Because if you're wrong, I'm going to die, and then the whole town is going to hate you for letting two pretty girls with bright futures die."

He doesn't answer. The storm outside is getting louder.

"Come and arrest me then! I escaped Cloudy Meadows. I'm at Ralph Johnston's."

There's creaking on the stairs. "He's coming," I whisper, and hang up, stuffing the phone in my back pocket. For the first time since Mom died and our pastor said that it was the thing we should do, I pray. *Please God let this not happen, and if it does happen let it not be with the machete—*

Beep!

Beep!

Beep!

It's the alarm on my watch. Before I can silence it, footsteps are turning in the hallway, coming closer.

I am brave, I remind myself, remembering Ruth's entry. One of the last things my best friend in the world ever thought about me was how brave I am.

I reach into my backpack for the bear spray Ralph gave me, and make sure the nozzle's pointed in the right direction. Then I swing open the closet door.

Ralph is standing six feet away, holding the machete, and as he raises it above his head, I empty the entire contents of the can, covering his face with swirling, orange designs.

"Farggh!" Ralph screams. He grabs his face and staggers back against the bedroom door, dropping the machete. I grab the soap case from my backpack. If Staake isn't

coming, then maybe an exploding mailbox will get someone's attention. I wince and squeeze the detonator.

Shrapnel hits the windows downstairs, shattering the glass—but you can barely hear it above the thunder outside. I look out the bedroom window and Ralph's mailbox is opened up like the petals of a flower. Only none of the lights are going on in neighbors' houses. The storm is too loud. Nobody's waking up.

Ralph's sprawled out blocking the bedroom door, still choking like crazy from the bear spray. He's also in the way of my exit. I yank open one of the windows, knot my backpack straps in front of me, and swing my legs over the ledge. Two stories is a lot higher than I thought, but then I look over my shoulder and see Ralph grimace and rise to his feet, and it doesn't look so far. He's opened one of his eyes just a sliver, and it's his lazy eye, rolling this way and that inside his head. The animal inside me bucks and I pitch myself over the ledge.

There's a crack that sounds like a tree branch breaking, then pain like a firecracker from my foot to my pelvis, ricocheting up my bones. My leg is splayed out at a funny angle, and as I shift on my butt, I can hear the pieces of my phone crunching in my pocket. Rain slaps my face. I look across the street at my house.

"Dommy!" I yell.

Leaves are whipping through the dark across the grass. I scream his name louder but am drowned out by the weather. I start to drag myself to the edge of the yard, but I have to stop every few minutes because the pain in my leg is making me dizzy. I'm almost to the road when something grabs me by the hair and tugs. Before I can call out, there's a hand clapped over my mouth, burning my lips with bear-spray residue. I bite the fingers, screaming as hard as I can, but the wind is too loud.

"You ruined my mailbox," Ralph says into my ear, curling his fingers into my mouth until I gag. "I didn't want to hurt you, Kippy." He laughs—a horrible, high-pitched sound—and starts dragging me back inside. I swing around wildly, trying to scream, but hear only croaking noises.

"Davey!" I cry. Then Ralph is tearing wet grass from the lawn and stuffing grass into my mouth, choking me.

"You girls never know when to shut up. Always saying other people's names when I'm the one right here." He takes me by the wrists and drags me up the steps, jostling my broken leg. "What were you doing with the bear spray, Kippy, hmm?" He gives me one final yank through the door and I vomit grass onto my sweatshirt. "Those cops were supposed to take it from you." He makes a *tsk* noise. "You're too much like Ruth. She was a liar. She took the stuff I gave her and that's supposed to mean you like somebody. But then I found her in the dark and all she said was no no no." He slams the door.

I hear myself choking.

"Davey is dead," he says softly, petting my hair as I spit up grass and bile onto his carpet. My throat is on fire. I look down at my leg. Shattered bone has pierced through my pajama pants and blood is soaking the fabric. I vomit again. "There are so many things I've had to do." He sighs, kneeling down beside me. "You will be the first real friend I've ever killed." I try to crawl to the door, but he throws me back against the wall. "Your dead soldier boyfriend probably already informed you that it gets easier. How after a while it's like putting something out of its misery. You remember that deer, don't you? The one we hit on the highway after Mom and Dad passed?" Anger flashes in his eyes. "And then that horrible, lonely woman—that alcoholic witch—she was a disgrace to this town. Killing her stuck with me, certainly. When I accepted her offer for a beer, she behaved as if she had found a lifelong friend. How immature. I can still see her face when she asked me to stop." He looks at my leg and gasps, squeezing just below my knee. I scream, sounding like an animal. "Oh Kippy, does it hurt?"

I know that this is not the Ralph I know, and still I

nod—*yes it hurts, yes it does, please stop*—because his voice is so familiar and I think that maybe he will decide I've endured enough.

He squeezes harder and I screech.

"Oh Kippy, you really are such a specimen. A Nordic princess," he says, looking deep into my eyes. He lets go of my leg and takes my chin gently in his hand. "Am I correct in thinking that nobody knows where you are right now?"

I think of Mildred and Marion and begin to cry—and that's when I hear sirens, somewhere far off in the storm. In one swift moment I both love and hate Sheriff Staake— that sweet and terrible man—because you would never turn on your sirens to come rescue someone from a killer, so he must just be coming to arrest me again.

Ralph doesn't seem to hear them. His eyes look vacant. "With Ruth it was different," he says. "With Ruth I had to pretend she was a witch, like in Total Escape Three. And she was, you know. It took me too long to realize how heartless she was. I gave her sweet food and she told me sweet things, and made me believe sweet things. But in the end I made her eat her words."

I close my eyes. "What did she say?" I ask, trying to keep him talking.

"The same thing everyone says before they die. 'No.' 'Please.' 'Stop.'" He scoffs. "It's all so disappointing and boring—before that, though . . . before that, she lied. Once I started dragging her, she told me she liked me. But then she tried to run."

I pretend he isn't talking about Ruth. "It sounds like she had it coming, Ralph." I remind myself that the excruciating pain in my leg is evidence that I'm alive. "I get it."

"Yeah." He nods. "I was polite—I asked, you know—I wanted permission. Weeks earlier I'd said, 'Ruth, let's hang out maybe,' and Ruth goes, 'Sure, Ralph, sure. Whatever.' So instead of making plans, which is so formal in my opinion, I meet her halfway the night I know she's coming to your house, right?"

"Right, of course."

"And I just want her to talk to me, you know? But even though she'd already promised me, once I'm actually standing there she changes her mind—looks at me like I'm special needs. Tells me to back off. And that's when I realized she was just a scarecrow—a fake person. A fucking cunt." If they don't get here soon, there won't be any evidence that I was ever here. "Can you believe that, Kippy? I'd had it, you know, just had it. So I grabbed her and shook her and finally she started listening."

"That's smart," I whisper. I have to buy time. "I mean, you had to punish her, right?"

His lazy eye rolls. "I wasn't even planning to cut her

open, you know. It was only when she was hanging there that I thought, *Maybe I should see what she looks like on the inside.*" His eyes change. He's heard the sirens. He looks toward the window and looks back at me, silent.

I give him my most pleading look, and even try to smile. "Remember when your parents brushed my hair?" I whisper. Outside the windows, the sky goes yellow with lightning. "Ralph, please. I want to stay." For a second he searches my face, his eyes bright with what I think is love. Then he grabs me by the hair, and slams my head against the wall, over and over, mimicking the way I just said, "Please."

The ringing in my ears is a welcome distraction from my leg, and I am thinking about how much Dom will suffer if I am gone, and how he will never be all right again, and isn't that the saddest part about this? It seems strange to be thinking so clearly while someone is trying to murder you—to not be able to fight back even though you thought you were the kind of person who would. Ruth and I both held stock-still before we died. She wouldn't move, and I couldn't.

"You stupid girl," Ralph mutters. "You know for a brief moment I wanted you to catch me. It seemed such a pity for someone else to be taking credit." There's blood in my eyes, but I can hear him opening the door to the basement, and I know this is it, that no one will find me—that Ralph will find a way to make excuses. And as the world around me gets fuzzy, fading to a bluish black that is speckled with stars, I am pretty sure I hear the sound of breaking glass and Davey's voice, calling for me through the dark.

BIG GAME

The images come in bursts, like flashes from a strobe light.

I am on my side, on the floor, prying open one bruised eye with tired fingers, and there is Ralph, swinging at Davey's head with a large frame yanked from the wall. (Is it a family photo? One of the staged glamour shots the Johnstons did every spring?) Glass from the frame shatters on the carpet, but instead of falling, Davey kicks Ralph in the stomach, sending him tumbling back on top of me.

"Get the fuck off her!" Davey shouts, grabbing Ralph by the hair and dragging him away. "Hold on, Kippy, I'm coming—stay awake—force yourself to stay awake."

"You're alive," I whisper. I hear Ralph screaming. *Keep him alive, too,* I am thinking, *we need them to arrest him.* My fingers are falling asleep and so am I, but then I can feel myself being lifted and Davey whispering in my ear, "Be okay. Hold on."

The sirens are right outside and I manage to put my arms around his neck. "Your leg," he says. I look over his shoulder and see Ralph hanging upside down in his sleeping bag from one of the ceiling beams, shouting at us. Davey puts his lips against my forehead and explains to me that it's some kind of special-ops maneuver.

"You're so cool," I keep murmuring, and I am waking up to the pain of my leg—I am always waking up lately. And even though I am covered in blood, and mud, and vomit, and urine, Davey holds me. Even when the cops come storming through the broken front door and Dom is running toward us across the yard, screaming my name, he doesn't put me down.

HUNTING PARTY

Apparently Ralph confessed loudly and proudly from his upside-down position, his face deep orange from a combination of gravity and bear spray, admitting to the cops what he'd done and how he'd planted straw and stuff in Colt's truck. How Ruth teased him and deserved it. How Mrs. Klitch was dispensable. All of it.

Davey didn't even know that I was really conscious during any of this, because he's got his head on my belly now, retelling me everything in low tones.

"It was so hard not to kill him," he says over and over. "I knew exactly how to do it. And I'd been trained to do it. And nobody would have faulted me for it." The machines around my metal bed are beeping sleepily. "But I didn't."

Dom will be back from the cafeteria soon with ginger ale and candy. "Before I knew what he did to Ruth—when I saw him hurting you—I wanted to kill him." Davey squeezes my waist.

"I'm proud of you," I say. He's not fishing for compliments or saying explicitly that he managed to control himself—and he's not saying he trusts his brain again—but that's because he's Davey, and I guess also because he trusts me to read him, which I can now, I think.

I stroke his hair. "I told you you're not crazy." It hurts my head to smile. "I'm so glad you're okay."

Davey sits up and searches my face, and I'm suddenly self-conscious about the bandage on my head. "Just so you know, I wasn't ever mad at you," he says. "Unfortunately I don't think you could ever do anything to change my feelings about you." He puts his thumb on my lips.

Forgiveness feels like hope and like a challenge. "I won't push it," I say.

Davey had to leave for a little bit and clean up his house. His parents are coming home early now that Ralph has been arrested. He printed off the latest email for me:

Davey, honey,
Optimism and closure feel delicate but have

arrived. How do you feel? Your father is crying, obviously. I am cracking jokes. FART has been good for both of us.

We want you to know we are certainly real jerks for up and leaving you. . . . All I can say is it seemed like the right thing at the time. Please forgive us. Everything is so fluid and tenuous. All I mean to say is we will grapple with the future as a family. We love you.

Kippy deserves a medal. We cannot bring ourselves to call her for various reasons. She became over the last decade a member of the family, but even more than you, she is a reminder of what we lost. We would like to thank her but it feels too much. . . . Please find a way to convey this for us.

~~And Davey, we are proud of you. No matter what you did to leave that horrible place, we love you. (We are supposed to say that more, if you can't tell. Our leader says so.) We never wanted you over in that desert, and were always puzzled by your need to do such a thing. If we seemed depressed or disappointed by your self-mutilation, it was a separate reaction. Fear for your mental state, not a wounded sense of patriotism, which~~

has ~~never been our bag.~~ It's good you're home, and your father and I will support you and help you to find your footing in this new life . . . just as soon as he stops crying—JK! (As the kids say: LOL, as well.)

Your mother

I asked him why the cross-outs, and he said he didn't want me to not believe what he'd said about how his parents had disparaged his severed finger, but he changed his mind. He explained what the sentences said. "They were pissed at first," he insisted. "And it wasn't about Ruth, it was about the fact that I'd fucked up." I told him that maybe the point of being close like this was just to believe each other, period.

"I guess it's also gonna be tough, them wanting to talk about feelings and work shit out constantly," he added.

"Yeah, but if it wasn't hard, it'd be boring," I said, and he seemed to like that.

Now he's gone and it's just me and Dom. It's a little awkward, to tell you the truth. My leg is throbbing inside the cast, but instead of convincing the doctors to give me more painkillers, like I told him to, Dom keeps bustling around getting things: balloons from the gift shop, way too much candy from the cafeteria. I know he's feeling guilty, or whatever, because his eyes are all red like he's been crying, but I'd rather he just sit still and apologize instead of feeling sorry for himself. Not to be a jerk, or anything.

"Quit spending all Mom's insurance money on crapola," I snap, when he comes in with an armful of miniature teddy bears. "Just sit with me, please?"

"Okay," he says, too cheerfully. He positions each of the bears carefully on my windowsill, then lowers himself into the chair beside my bed. "Lots of people are calling the hospital about you, Pickle. The doctor can't tell them anything, obviously, but I made a list of names in case you wanna call somebody back." He digs in his back pocket, pulling out a crumpled sheet of paper.

"My phone's busted," I mutter.

"We can get you a new one of those, you betcha." His voice is too loud. "And for now I can scamper on down to the desk and get a phone book, and you can use my phone, if that helps." He scrunches his lips to the side and rubs his knees. "Should I go do that?"

"Dom . . ."

"Oh, honey, I'm so sorry," he gushes, reaching for my hand, then changing his mind. "They say they can't give you any more pain stuff for an hour and I know it must hurt. I feel all messed up over this. Not to say it's about me, not at all, I know that's selfish. Looking back it's just—" He runs his fingers through his hair. "Did you know he confessed to killing that Klitch woman, too? I'm your father and I should have protected you, and I should have seen the signs. I should have known before anyone that something was the matter with Ralph Johnston. For goodness' sake, I'm a . . . I'm a trained professional." He shakes his head. "You know, your mother never liked him. She said he was weird."

I reach out and wiggle my fingers for his hand.

Dom squeezes my wrist. "It won't happen again."

"I'm not going to tell you it's okay because I really need you to be my dad right now," I moan.

He nods, and when I start to cry—because my leg hurts, mostly—he plucks some tissues from the box beside my bed and wipes my face so gently that it barely hurts my swollen cheeks.

I went through the list of names Dom had and circled the people I wanted to see. The rest of them I didn't even know. Colt was one of those names I circled, but he called instead of coming by.

"This is awesome, Kippy—I mean, seriously, like, really," he said, "it was totally worth you getting fucked up for."

"Thanks?"

His parents got on the phone after that and said they might stop by, so I added them to Dom's list. Who knows, maybe I'll get some kind of reward out of it. I'm not supposed to have too many visitors, apparently, but I'm sort of a local celebrity now, and the hospital is bending the rules.

"Is that really her?" one of the nurses asked.

I vaguely remember signing an autograph for a doctor—though I'm not totally sure because I finally got more pain pills and keep falling asleep. I'm pretty sure I just saw Jim Steele trying to shake Miss Rosa's hand and her throwing up her arms, aghast, and explaining to him the importance of distance. It seems like every time I open up my eyes there're more NVCG members in the room. They seem to be having a good time talking among themselves and to Dom, but I'd really like to participate.

"Dommy," I murmur, and he leans over the safety rail to hear me better. "Could you please get me some caffeine?" I ask.

"Sure, Pimple, sure," he says, and excuses himself. Jim Steele clears his throat and stands, and Miss Rosa scuttles toward me.

"Oh, Banzai!" she exclaims. "Marion and Mildred are confessing just now their relapse in Federal Express vehicle."

"Hi, Kippy," Mildred and Marion sing in unison from the foot of my bed, sounding forlorn, like maybe Miss Rosa has already reprimanded them. Behind them, Luther and Big Jason are leaning against the wall, playing with balloons. Jim Steele is standing off to the side, looking uncomfortable.

"She can't see you, dummies," Luther snaps, bopping Big Jason in the head with a balloon covered in flowers that says *Feeling Better Is Like Sunshine!* Big Jason wrestles the balloon from Luther's hands. Miss Rosa doesn't reproach either of them; she's too busy staring at me.

"I'm just saying, look at her eyes, they're barely open," Luther adds. "This is Luther by the way, Kippy, in case you can't see shit."

"I know," I croak.

"And Mildred and Marion and Big Jason," Mildred adds. "And this attorney dude."

"Hi, guys."

"Why you did not call Miss Rosa, hm?" Miss Rosa tucks her chin over the safety bar, her eyes magnified behind her glasses. "Mildred tells me that at this Cloudy Meadows they give only pills, no therapy!" She makes a spitting noise. "Despicable! Miss Rosa would get you from this horrible place in, as they say, 'jiffy.'" She nods and pets my arm roughly, cooing like an amorous pigeon.

"There, touching is okay currently. I have already now written to this Cloudy Meadows doctor my displeasure at his antics."

"How are you feeling?" Jim Steele asks, making his way to the other side of my bed.

"I feel very old," I mutter. I put my hand on Miss Rosa's, mostly out of affection, but also to stop her from petting me so violently. She recoils, yelping.

"You don't age until you age, and then you *age*," Jim Steele says, staring at Miss Rosa and looking confused. "Enjoy your youth while you can. Even if it hurts."

"This man here with his gray hair"—Miss Rosa tentatively makes her way back to the side of my bed and points at Jim Steele—"he has alerted all newspapers about your victories. The evil policeman—Steak person—he will not comment."

I squint at Miss Rosa. "Sometimes I wish your English were better."

"She means you're all over the news, Kippy," Luther says. "None of us even knew about all those charges against you till they'd been dropped."

"You're getting credit everywhere for solving the whole thing because of this guy," Mildred grumbles, nodding to Jim Steele.

I look up at Jim Steele, who seems embarrassed.

"You were bragging about it just a second ago, Lawyer Man," Marion booms.

"Yes, stop pretending this modesty," Miss Rosa adds, wagging her finger at Jim Steele.

"What are they talking about?" I ask.

Jim Steele sighs. "Your father got in touch with me." He explains that Dom told him about the mistake with Cloudy Meadows, Ralph's shrine to Ruth, my broken bones. "If there hadn't been anyone representing your legal interests, you would have had to go back to Cloudy Meadows and finish out your stay. You were contractually bound."

"But you hate me," I say.

"I don't hate anybody," Jim Steele snaps. "People around here continually misunderstand my affect." He shrugs. "You'd bothered the hell out of me with your little investigation, but the more I heard about what had really gone on, the more firmly I believed that Staake had been negligent in his duties." He chuckles. "Now you can't just go suing sheriffs—it'll take the rest of your life, for starters, and nothing will happen—especially not in Bumbafuck, Wisconsin, where everyone has a hard-on for law enforcement." He clears his throat. "Excuse me. Anyhow, I decided that the only way to approach it was to leak the story, get you famous, turn public sentiment, and let Staake stew in his embarrassment for a while. Simple."

"Tell her about how they got Diane Sawyer to comment on it," Mildred says, playing with Marion's hair.

"You're kidding," I blurt.

"That young-looking old woman? Oh, for sure, I saw it with my own eyes," Luther says. "She called you an inspiration. YouTube that shit."

"Staake's not man enough to fight public sentiment," Jim Steele adds. "He dropped the charges this morning. Though he still won't talk to the press."

"But he's got the gall to show up at this hospital," Dom adds, standing in the doorway. Everyone turns to stare at him. Two cups of coffee are steaming in his hands, and he looks furious. "It's true. The asshole's here right now— you want me to turn him away, Cactus?"

I roll my eyes. "No, Dom."

"Would you rather one of these guys did it, so it's less embarrassing?" Dom gestures at Luther and Big Jason, who are once again preoccupied with the balloons. Their muscled forearms are flexing as they turn the balloons over in their hands—reveling in the notion, I guess, that they could easily pop these things and won't.

I shake my head. "No, that's why I circled his name on the list. I want to see him."

"Honey—"

"Hmmph." Miss Rosa clicks her heels together. "NVCG will retreat to hallway for self-control purposes."

"Yeah, because otherwise that guy's ground meat," Marion says, and Mildred rolls her eyes.

"Us all breaking the law together has bonded him to you or something," she says.

Jim Steele puts up his hands. "I don't want to hear any more about that. As of now, all I know is that everyone in this room is a law-abiding citizen, and if anyone asks me about it later, that's what I want to say."

"I don't want to hear about it, either," Dom says, crossing the room to hand me my coffee. "As far as I'm concerned, anyone who encouraged that escape from Cloudy Meadows put my daughter in harm's way. Honey, why don't you let me at least sit here while you talk to him?"

"No! He's not going to kill me, okay?"

Miss Rosa reaches up to pat Dom's arm, then puts her hands behind her back. "Perhaps you will come with us to do the trust falls, Mr. Banzai," she says. "It is very important for to choose meditative strategies over confrontation."

Dom smiles down at her. "I totally agree." He looks at me.

"Go!" I tell him. "Have fun!"

Sheriff Staake's usually pink face is pale, his eyes ringed purple. He glances at me and looks instantly afraid.

"Sit," I tell him, feeling like a queen.

He drops a card on my lap before lowering himself into the chair. "Got tons of these at the station. I brought the one that seemed most important—given how that Quinn girl was the only one whose allegations I couldn't drop myself."

I open the card. Glitter and confetti fall out on my lap.

Under the circumstances,
I've dropped my charges against you.
Xoxo, Libby
PS: Gah bless . . .

Less than two more years of school, I tell myself.

"So," I say, flicking the glitter off my lap in Staake's direction. "Tell me: When you were coming last night, was it to arrest me or rescue me?" I wasn't planning to torture him like this, but now that I've got him here it's kind of hard not to. He looks miserable. "Because that'd be an interesting thing to add to whatever apology you were planning for the press."

"Oh, Bushman," he says, burying his face in his fingers. He folds his hands in his lap and his mouth quivers as he looks up at my leg. "I can't believe how hurt you got."

I can tell he's thinking about how he'd feel if I were his daughter, Lisa, and he looks so much like a dad all of a sudden that I get uncomfortable.

"Um—well, you know, it can't be helped, or whatever." I push a strip of loose gauze out of my eyes, and gesticulate as if this situation is not a big deal.

He looks at his feet, sighing through his nose, and I get frantic.

"Don't cry, please."

"I want you to know I'm gonna give a press conference," he says, swallowing. "I'm gonna own up to what happened, but I'm gonna tell it my way. I got swindled by that freak, I did."

"I know you did," I say. "But you were also a jerk."

"Well, sure, fine, but that's how I am." He looks at me sort of helplessly. "But I sure wish I could be that kind of person other people thought was nice."

"Okay, Mr. Staake."

"You can call me Bob." He wipes his eyes, then holds out his hand.

I shake it. "Hi, Bob," I say.

I'm going to give Ruth's diary to Davey when he comes back. It's all crumpled from being in my backpack while

I was getting dragged around and pummeled. But I can't look at it anymore. And I figure I've struggled through enough of it now to say you're never really ready to read a dead person's thoughts, not if you loved them and cared what they thought to begin with. If I held on to that journal, I might never be able to put it down. I'd reread the hurtful stuff and cling to the few positive passages, and try to analyze how real things were between us, even though I know people probably only talk about the bad things in their diaries, because what's the use of recording what you don't have to work through? And I'd rather give it up while I feel like I know that things between Ruth and I were good, basically, solid—and that ultimately she'd appreciate me sticking it to the bad guy, and for being even momentarily badass in her honor.

On the inside cover, below all the phone numbers and psychopathic traits, I left a message for Mrs. Fried:

Mrs. F—
Proceed with caution because I couldn't
get rid of all the sex parts.

I'd like to tell her I'm sorry about the eulogy, and that I understand why she can't see me, though I still wish she would. But I know it's not worth worrying about because right now I've got more company than I can deal with. Dom, Miss Rosa, and the rest of NVCG are filing into the room, Davey will be back soon, and the hospital phone by my bed has started ringing off the hook—newspaper reporters and third cousins I've never heard of, Principal Hannycack and some Wisconsin senator. Even Diane Sawyer's office calls, asking about an interview. Mildred thinks the phone number got posted online, or something, and Marion is screening all the calls for me, telling people to call back, jotting messages, telling crazies to feck off. But at one point he holds out the receiver and says, "This one's funny, just a kid or something, listen," and it's Albus.

"Good job, soldier," she chirps. "I taught you well—oh, shoot, gotta go—it's the Barb and Felicity brigade—over and out—*aggh!* Unhand me, nurse warriors!"

It still hurts to smile, but really it's kind of hard not to, because I thought that I only had one friend in the whole world, and look at all these people.

ACKNOWLEDGMENTS

First, I'd like to thank Jessica Almon, who guided me through the process of writing a novel both in the technical and spiritual sense, mostly over the telephone. I will always associate this book with the sound of her beautiful voice in my ear, telling me to "just keep going" and "no, it's not boring" and " yes, I promise, Hale." She is so creative and brilliant and kind. I feel very lucky to have gotten to work with her, and even luckier that she and I became friends in the process.

I offer up my endless gratitude to Erica Sussman and Chris Hernandez (aka Best Editors Ever), both of whom saw potential in the story from the beginning, and offered thoughtful, brilliant feedback—and generally just helped me make it so much better. I couldn't have done it without them.

Additionally, I'd like to thank Michelle Taormina, Jon Howard, Gweneth Morton, Christina Colangelo, Ali Lisnow, and Alison Donalty at HarperCollins.

Thanks also to James Frey, Judy Goldschmidt, Matt Hudson, Bennett Madison, and the other good people at Full Fathom Five.

Thank you to everyone who ever tried to teach me how to write, including my friend and veritable coach, Pinckney Benedict; my former instructors and gurus, Bret Anthony Johnston and Elizabeth McCracken; and the professors at Southern Illinois University–Carbondale's MFA program. Most of all thanks to Ben and Susan Zarwell, my beloved high school teachers, mentors, surrogate parentages, and guardian angels.

This seems as good a spot as any to tell my father thank you. THANKS, DAD! But seriously, a huge thank-you to my dad, Chris Hale. He is a captivating person and a wonderful father. No matter what kind of weird stuff I've dabbled in (and it's gotten bleak at times), he has always been on my side.

Obviously, I am eternally grateful to those who read my book before it was ready. Lauren Kunze labored tirelessly to help me get the first chapter in working order, and it wasn't easy, and she is amazing. Also: Louis Begley, Jesse Barron, Marissa Lee, Jenni Kuk, Shelly Hale, Ellie Harbeck, Mara Hale, Kermit Moore, Hannah Hughes, Sarah McKetta, and Nicole White. Their loving notes were incredibly helpful.

Another person who read this book, over and over, at multiple stages of development, happens to be my partner, Simon Rich. He is compassionate and dazzlingly smart. I feel exceedingly fortunate every day to be in love with such a wonderful man.

I'm also grateful to my grandparents, Margie and Russ Hale, who not only read this whole thing, but also wrote up a thoughtful critique of it! They have always supported me and been there to instigate crucial tête-à-têtes.

Side note: sorry if this is starting to sound like I'm accepting an Academy Award or something, but it's my first book! (I'm almost done.)

There were also a lot of special people who kept me company/sane during the often dramatic writing process—which pretty much includes everyone I've already mentioned, but also: Tom Schulz, Amy Heberle, Justin Becker, Nikhil Srivastava, Margaret Ross, Dan Paul, Andy Harnish, and Jessica Easto. Thank you. I don't know what I would have done without you.

And, of course, while we're listing people who keep me sane, thanks to my wonderful, awesome, magical siblings: Carly, Michael, Mara, Ellie, and Drew.

Finally, most of all, this book is for my mom, Patti Schulz, the best mom/real estate agent in the world, who has been reading my stuff since I could (sort of) spell. Thank you, Mom, for believing in me, even when I did not believe in myself, and for always doing everything you could to help me take the next step (even when that meant listening to me read aloud fifty pages at, like, 10 p.m. because I needed "immediate feedback"). You are the funniest and most loving person I have ever met, and I couldn't have done it without your support. I love you.